Toulouse For Death

TOULOUSE
FOR
DEATH

Gregory C. Randall

This book is dedicated to my mother, Mary L. Randall. She taught me how glorious art can be.

ACKNOWLEDGEMENTS

Historical thrillers are based on a real event. This book is no different, all the events surrounding the Merkers' gold are true and as factual as the published books present. I am indebted to Robert M. Edsel and Bret Witter for their excellent book on the small and underfunded group of archeologists, cultural experts, artists, and museum curators who saved European cities, art, monuments, and culture as best they could during World War II. Their book *The Monuments Men* is an excellent source for those of us who want to understand that there was more to war than destruction and death.

I also now understand the World War II footsoldier. Since before Roman legions crossed the European continent, the foot soldier fought and died for their respective countries. In Michael C. Bilder's and James G. Bilder's *A Footsoldier for Patton*, I gained an intimate understanding of the day after day life and death battles the men on the ground as they fought from the beaches of Normandy to the gates of Berlin. Both of these books helped to more fully flesh out my characters.

The Internet is now ubiquitous. Through Wikipedia, the free encyclopedia, I was able to quickly research artists, people and locations for this novel. In fact, using Google Earth, I located an apartment in Paris for one of my characters and the locations of the final scenes. I recommend Street View for an affordable European vacation. All the major characters in this book are fictitious except for Otto Skorzeny who was one of the most dangerous professional soldier and anti-Semitic Nazis I have researched. His entry in Wikipedia presents an unrepented Nazi who, for the last thirty years of his life, continued fighting World War Two. He died in 1975.

I also must thank and acknowledge my editor, Dennis DeRose for his painstaking efforts to help make this book more precise and readable. And lastly, a thank you and a kiss for my publisher and companion of the last forty years Bonnie Randall for her insightful questions and ideas for the story, the book is better for it. She is the other redhead in my life.

Winter, 2011

Chapter 1

1a

"The village was dead," Alain Dumont said, as he breathed through the plastic oxygen nasal prongs that hung, like a painting, from his ears. "Mind you, this was not the first village we fought through and destroyed. But, it was the first one in Germany. All the frustrations, anger and need for revenge that had built up during our advances through eastern France and Luxembourg were now focused on this first German town. It did not escape our pent-up rage."

He heaved again, as if trying to shake the horrific sixty-year-old memories off his shoulders.

"The village was utterly and completely flattened. Me and my boys walked single file in a track no more than a foot wide—barely room for a dog. The rubble, blasted from the buildings, filled the street. The buildings themselves still smoldered, and bodies lay half in and half out of the wreckage. God, those Germans loved their brick"—he slowly took another breath—"now they were buried under it."

Dumont took another short pause, mustering the strength to continue.

"There were fucking snipers in the church towers," he went on. "We'd advance a block and take fire from everywhere. Some of my men pushed through the interior walls of the buildings; they dug and blasted their way from house to house. We lost fewer men that way, and sometimes it was faster than waltzing down the center of the street with a sniper's bullet for a dance partner. If we were lucky, we had a tank following us; they rolled over everything. If a sniper fired, we leveled everything over a foot tall ahead of us; it was an advance by attrition. We left nothing alive. But these villages were full of cellars, some interconnected, many filled with old people who wouldn't leave. Funny thing was that we didn't see a lot of younger women and kids—they were gone. We found them hiding in the tunnels later; those damn tunnels were under all of this section of Germany. And to be honest, I was glad. Never did like killing women."

Sharon O'Mara sat in a huge green leather wingback chair, her back to the church-like leaded-glass windows. The sun cast a panel of light across the oriental carpet to the base of a library wall that held thousands of books. Dark wood filled the spaces between the shelves and the artwork. Caught in the full wash of the sunlight, wrapped in a multicolored cloak, sat the wizened old man to whom she had been listening for nearly an hour. Oxygen tubes and paraphernalia coiled over the back of his chair, like attacking snakes. A man dressed in dark gray stood a discreet two paces behind. Sharon had been introduced earlier; Remy Adler was Dumont's nurse and assistant.

"Don't fret, Sharon. Remy here doesn't understand English well, but he's a great help," Dumont said. "So, where was I? Oh yes, yes, yes. What I'm telling you now, no one alive, other than myself, knows."

It had started with the usual hello . . .

"Sharon dear, Evelyn Lucca here. How are you?"

Evelyn Lucca, of the STIA leather goods company, had been a close friend since Sharon O'Mara had cleaned out the nest of Chinese gangs that had used Lucca's company to mask a deadly operation drop-shipping guns, sex slaves and forged handbags.

"Evelyn, what can I help you with?" O'Mara said, with a curt tone to her voice.

"Always straight and to the point. And, Sharon, dear, work on your friendly demeanor once in a while."

"Sorry, Evelyn, just been a tough day since sun up. Basil"— that was Sharon's dog—"threw up on the carpet; the power went out for an hour so the clocks and the computer are screwed up; and now they say my new car won't be ready until Friday. Just annoyed, that's all. What's up? And, again, I'm sorry."

"I may have another job for you," Lucca said.

O'Mara's interest shot up. She was getting a little tired of chasing down inflammatory YouTube videos sent around by a guy who didn't like the barbecue sauce at her favorite rib joint. She needed a real gig.

"Tell me more. Momma might be interested, right Basil?"

"How is the old mutt? I miss him."

"He misses you too, but thankfully he's lost the ten pounds he gained when you shared our house, and he's getting more exercise. That bullet in his hip may have slowed him down, but he, like the rest of us, is finally over it."

"Sharon, this isn't just a job; it's also a personal favor to my family. Do you know who Alain Dumont is?"

"Yes, the high-tech investor and billionaire. I thought he died a few years ago?"

"Yes, one in the same, and even though he has his challenges, he's still alive and, thank God, has all of his senses."

Alain was an old wartime friend of her father's, Evelyn went on to explain. The two men had met in Paris, both survivors of the Nazis and the war. Alain immigrated to the United States five years after the war ended, settled in San Francisco and, through his investments, became very, very rich.

"He never forgot his friends and has helped my father and our family with investment capital for almost fifty years. "His advice is even more beneficial," Evelyn said.

"You do have the nicest friends, Evelyn. What can I do?"

"Alain is ninety-three years old, still sharp, but his body is wearing out. There are some things, he says, that need to be done before he dies. This isn't some sad affair but something he's happy to do and is looking forward to it. He asked if we knew someone we trusted to help him with some delicate issues. He assures me that it's all legal, but the person must be a woman. He's always been a ladies' man, so debonair, so casually elegant; in fact, he's my godfather. I can only attest to his honesty and our family's close relationship. I don't know what the job is, what's involved, or even what it's worth. That's between the two of you. He would like to meet you, a casual interview, just you and him."

For a long moment, Sharon thought about the late summer and what she had on her schedule. A scribbled note on the pad at her desk read 'tomatoes.'

"Just checking a few things," she said to Evelyn. "My usual arrangement, like the one with you and your family, would that work?"

"I think you need to find out what the job is first. Alain never does anything small."

And that is exactly what Sharon O'Mara found out, two days later, when she met with Alain Dumont at his mansion on upper Broadway in San Francisco. He asked very pointed questions about her experience, her sense of privacy, her skills as both an investigator and as a soldier. When she told him about her experiences in Iraq, he grew irritated and excited. He asked questions about tactics and weapons, the enemy's defensive actions and logistics. He had spent the summer and fall of 1944 and all of '45 in parts of France and Germany, he told her.

After two hours, he offered her a scotch and a job.

She smiled and said, "Yes."

"Good. I really don't give a damn what the doctors say, a good drink is an excellent way to seal a deal and feel better. I'm happy to have you as a part of my small family. I would like to have a follow-up meeting tomorrow. Evelyn says that you work with contracts, so do I. This is my contract," Dumont said, extending his hand. "I'll pay you one hundred thousand dollars and cover all your expenses. You'll be given a credit card that you can use however you see fit. Evelyn said you were having some problems with a car; use the card to get it fixed. I need you working with me, not worrying about transportation. Have all the bills sent directly to me. I want no worries."

A stunned O'Mara pushed aside the tubes and kissed the gentleman on his cheek. He smiled and kissed her back, as best he could.

"Sharon, I mean this in the most lascivious way. If I were only fifty years younger, you, my dear, would be in big trouble."

She blushed, and kissed his cheek again.

"Mr. Dumont, I mean this in the most welcoming manner. So would you."

1b

The next day, Sharon sat in the green chair in the elegant room dressed in a soft yellow blouse and white slacks. Enthralled and gobsmacked, she listened as Alain Dumont told her the most remarkable, intriguing story she had ever heard in her life.

"I was drafted and put in an infantry regiment that was part of Patton's Third Army. After the Normandy landing, yes, yes, I was there, Sharon, I crawled up the beach in the late afternoon," Dumont said, a touch of sadness entered his eyes. "We pushed through the hedgerows, where I lost a lot of friends and watched stupid stunts get men killed. The Germans were experienced; many had fought on the Russian front, and they were grateful to be in France. We tried hard to make sure they died there in those hedgerows. To be dead in Russia or France, who gives a damn, but being captured was a different matter, the good German soldier would kill himself before being captured by the Russians."

"Did you free Paris?" Sharon asked.

"I thought our division would take the city, but we were then positioned to the south, near Fontainebleau; I wouldn't see Paris until after the war. We pushed beyond Paris in the late summer and then toward Verdun and Metz; we called Metz the "Meat Grinder." That city ate us up. Patton pushed us hard to attack, but we couldn't move fast enough; we were exhausted and running out of gas. Metz was a city of forts and Fort Driant was the worst; we should have just gone around it, thousands died trying to take it. Patton still pushed us forward; it gave the Germans time. They resupplied their men and then they killed us. There were so many dead that our men were stacked into trucks like they were nothing, remains to be gotten out of the way, it was so wrong." Dumont inhaled slowly, a shiver passed through his body. "After Metz was taken, we kept pushing east, past the Maginot Line. The last Germans in the area surrendered in early December. We thought the rest was going to be easy, then Christmas and . . ."

"The Battle of the Bulge," Sharon interrupted.

"Yes, it's not what we called it, that's something the press corps or somebody else cooked up from a map or plan of the region, the Germans pushed a westward bulge into our advance. We were a hundred miles to the south, on the other side of Lux-emburg, and that son-of-a-bitch Patton pushed us through the coldest fucking winter I'll never forget; lost two toes, they froze off. I remember being stuck in a hole in the ground blasted out by a German 88, or some other gun; there was a foot of frozen water at the bottom of that hole. I hid there for two days, praying to a God that I knew in my heart had turned his back on us. For two days, I stared at the head of a German soldier, his helmet still strapped under his chin. It sat on the edge of the crater, his eyes frozen open. I tried to push it away but I took fire from someone; hell, it could have been an American thinking the guy was still alive. My coat froze to the ice; if I had to get out I'd have had to take my coat off. That's when I met Gillis and Graham."

"Who?"

"Jimmy Gillis and Danny Graham, they joined my outfit as green replacements a month before; I saw them around but didn't know them. We were taking tree bursts and all hell was exploding and these two guys jumped into my hole. For two days we talked and got to know each other, covered each other when we had to take a crap or a piss, or crawl out to get ammu-nition and food. You tell yourself, never get close to anybody, the guy could be dead in a second, but somehow we managed to hang together. One way or another, we saved each other's lives, more than once."

"There were stories that the German's were killing prison-ers?" Sharon asked.

"Yes, it was true. It pissed our boys off so much that there were rumors that there weren't a lot of German prisoners for a long time. War is war, write all the rules you want but, in the cold of a fucking winter it's simple, kill or die; protect your buddy, kill the enemy. I took a grenade fragment about this time, cut a small piece out of my shoulder; it got me out of the war for two weeks, then right back into hell. We pushed east then north, one time we had to double back, we got too far ahead of our supplies. Learned a lot about trucks and logistics then; always keep the supply lines open."

"You need to rest," Sharon said, refilling his water glass.

"Sharon, in a few weeks or months, or, God forbid, years, I'll be getting all the rest I need, and I'm not even to the best part yet."

"Best part?" O'Mara asked.

"Oh yes, my dear, the best part. The frozen woods of January became the sodden fields of late winter; I'm not sure what's worse, frozen ground or mud so thick it sucks your boots off. This was the stuff that made trench foot popular. If your toes didn't freeze off, they rotted off. By March we were well within Germany, the German's were fighting for their homes; the killing became even more brutal. Children carried guns and killed my men; the only thing you could believe in was your buddies."

"Iraq was the same, but different. Hot and cold, dry and wet. The heat could set off our munitions, or freeze fingers in winter. Children also carried guns and blew themselves up. My war was also a battle of surprises, anxious road trips and exploding drainage ditches," O'Mara said refilling her coffee cup.

"All wars are the same, yet different," Dumont said. "Then April came and for a few weeks the weather warmed and the sun turned the mud to solid ground. Flecks of green started to appear in the gray landscape. I remember walking through the wreck of a village and seeing tulips and daffodils pushing their way up through the debris. Outside a burned-out farmhouse was a dead German soldier, had been there a while, a red tulip had grown through his swollen, rotting hand. Other flowers pushed their way up around his carcass; I still think about that, it was something to see. Then came April 10th and my world changed." He stopped and slyly looked at her. "How about lunch?"

"Lunch, you've got to be kidding," Sharon said. "Lunch?"

"Yes, lunch, I'm hungry and I know you are too. I'll ring for Remy and we'll have a civil lunch with a delicious French wine from my own vineyard and then I will tell you the rest of the story."

1c

Sharon helped Dumont to his feet and they walked into the small alcove off to the side of the library; the glassed-in porch overlooked San Francisco Bay. The Golden Gate Bridge framed the left side and Alcatraz captured the center of the view. The Bay was calm, hundreds of sailboats scurried about; two ferries passed each other on their way to and from Sausalito and Fisherman's Wharf.

A small salad with Dungeness crab was served on porcelain plates, real silverware graced the table, elegant crystal goblets held a crisp French Sancerre, crunchy sourdough bread sat in a large basket.

"To our new partnership," Dumont said as he lifted his glass.

O'Mara returned the toast. "Wonderful salad, and the wine, lovely."

"From my vineyard along the Loire. It was one of the first things I purchased when I began my "evil empire," as I call it. That was long before the Star Wars movies and other such things. Calling it that always helped me to remember its roots; roots that only I knew."

"You're the most curious person I've ever met, Mr. Dumont, and beguiling. Could you go on?"

"Easily, my dear, easily," Dumont said as his eyes strayed to the Bay, a red container ship was passing in front of Alcatraz, 'PCL' in huge white letters marked on its side. "That March we pushed toward Frankfurt, then northeast to Fulda, by April 2 we were near Bad Hersfeld. The Germans were surrendering in huge numbers, took several men to guard them, it pulled good men off the line. But some of their outfits did not give up; most of those bastards were SS. This part of Germany was a contorted terrain of rolling hills and valleys and was riddled with mine-shafts. Every village had towers that ran elevators deep under the countryside into hundreds of miles of salt and potassium tunnels. The tops of the hills were carved out with open mines, their slopes were covered in thick forests; and the flatter open valleys were farmlands. Actually, apart from the fact that every-thing and everyone wanted to kill you, it was very pleasant." Dumont took another sip of wine. "Then my world changed."

Alain Dumont stood and slowly walked to the window and braced his hands on the dark wood sill, fog had started to push its way under the Bridge; its long tongue licked the western rocks of Alcatraz. He almost vibrated from the strain of the effort.

"Gillis, Graham and I, along with the rest of our squad, were ordered to take a hilltop that held a commanding view of our advance," he continued. "No Germans were seen until we reached the top; then all hell broke out. Two of my guys were taken out immediately. We quickly pulled back down the hill and regrouped. I split the rest of our squad to keep them occu-pied and I took Gillis and Graham to flank the crest and come at them from the rear. We found the road they used to reach the top; two light trucks with SS insignia were parked a hundred yards below their location. We took out the drivers and worked our way up and, in less than five minutes, killed them all, or at least that's what we thought. The rest of our squad came up and secured the command post. One German was on his last breath; he was bleeding out and our medic couldn't stop it, he kept say-ing over and over, "Goldbarren, Goldmynzens," over and over. Gillis wanted to know what he was saying and I said gold bars and gold coins. Where, I asked. Merkers was the German's re-ply. He held on for another ten minutes, then he died."

"My German was pretty good, my real parents emigrated from the Alsace region around the turn of the last century, they were killed in a train accident when I was about one and I was raised in the German-settled area of Pennsylvania. My step parents taught me French and German; it's been a big help all my life."

Dumont poured more Sancerre in Sharon's glass. She could not take her eyes off the man.

"Nothing like a little treasure and loot to get a soldier's blood pumping," Dumont said, as he poured a small amount into his own glass and saluted Sharon. "My boys held the top and patched up our two injured from the first assault. Gillis, Graham, and I decided to scout ahead, and see where the road led, it wasn't on our maps, didn't want any surprises. The three of us went back to the road and worked our way down the hill. We stumbled onto an abandoned side road that dead-ended at a tunnel cut in the face of the hill; twin iron doors secured the entry. Vines and debris had hidden the road and the doors for a long time. We hiked back to the main road and then down into Merkers. As German villages go, it was small; a huge elevator tower stood in its center, and we weren't the first GIs to reach the village. It looked like the staging area for the next advance. We found out quickly that it really was the biggest legitimate looting job in history. We had walked into a robbery."

Dumont escorted Sharon back to the library, Remy cleared the plates and silverware; Sharon noticed that he would take furtive glances in their direction from time to time. She was fairly certain Adler knew more English than Dumont let on or maybe even knew about.

"Hidden in the salt tunnels and mines under Merkers, for miles in almost every direction, was the entire wealth of Germany in gold, German marks, English pounds, and U.S. currency. The art collections from its museums were stored here as well as thousands of pieces of stolen and plundered art. Hitler wanted to keep this treasure from the Allies and only in the late months of the war did he allow his nation's wealth to be moved from Berlin and hidden there. As fate would have it, questions to some displaced French women by American military policemen and some good follow-up led to the discovery of the horde.

By today's gold standards, the mass of gold was worth tens of billions; even then it was worth hundreds of millions of dollars. Chaos reigned. Even Eisenhower and Patton were given a tour of the tunnels. Our regiment, along with a couple of others, was ordered to guard the tunnels and help with the transfer. At one time there were a thousand men coming and going, they even lowered jeeps into the tunnels to help move the stuff; they brought up the gold in small munitions trailers and whatever else they could find. It was all so bizarre, men were dying by the thousands, not more than ten miles away, and we were focused on moving a hundred tons of gold and art. Bizarre."

"What did you do?" Sharon asked.

"What all good soldiers do, follow orders. They had some of us in the tunnels, in fact we all rotated, but it was so oppressive and corrosive down there that our guys couldn't last more than a few hours at a time. They would leave and then others would be sent down to relieve them, I think the three of us went up and down maybe ten times, it was almost a half mile down. It was like Danté's hell had been decorated with Renoirs and Titans. As I said, it was bizarre."

"Must've been hard to resist putting a few baubles in your pocket?" Sharon asked, with a smile.

"Way beyond that," he said, returning her smile. "Soldiering and war just bring out the best in men. Some of history's finest art is memorialized in paintings like the *Sack of Rome* and the *Rape of the Sabine Women*. Sad, but that's the way of it. It was like that then. As the three of us were coming up out of the tunnel, we came up with a brilliant idea to help ourselves to some of the loot. Hell, we were tired and rationalized that we'd earned it fighting across Europe. We were all in our early twenties, and if there is one thing a soldier wants more than a piece of ass, it's loot, treasure, booty. So we hatched a plan. We were involved in moving the small trailers loaded with gold up from the tunnels and getting them to the next area where they were staged above ground before going on to Frankfurt. Every once in a while, a bar would disappear and end up in a large manure pile situated against one of the barns, we lost count of how many we buried there. But when you're moving thousands of bars and boxes and bags of gold, some just naturally get lost."

"Naturally," she said. "We found treasure in one of Saddam's palaces, a safe with two hundred and fifty million U.S. dollars in new one hundred-dollar bills, still in their original Federal Reserve wrappers. War is big business. There were rumors that some of that money just disappeared before the Treasury boys could get there. Looking back, it sure would have been nice. As you can see, I'm not that kind of girl."

"There's a larcenist in everyone's soul at one time or another, all-out war knocks down all the moral walls and teachings you've learned and then opportunity becomes the governor of your life."

"Sad, but true."

"Well, Graham and Gillis went back to retrieve one of the SS trucks still up on the hill. The Allies were using German trucks whenever we could; they took some paint to cover the SS insignias and the other markings. Gillis painted a big US on the door and roof. Looked strange but they wanted to make sure that some P-38 didn't take a shot at them. Graham tied a U.S. flag to the panel on the side. They drove the truck to the back of the staging area, pulled the keys, disabled the distributor and went back to work. The next morning, the gold convoy left for Frankfurt. It was strange, military police front and back, planes flying cover, hell, it looked like a battalion was acting as security. Then they started to bring up art, boxes, crates, bundles of paintings, sculpture, everything was chaos again, but at least the stuff was lighter. Not to be left out, we took two bundles of canvases."

"Bundles?"

"Yes, bundles. Someone had removed the paintings from their frames and just rolled them up, like a bedroll. Must have been twenty paintings in the rolls; one said 'Goldfarb' on the outside paper wrapper, there were four paintings in that one. Gillis thought it was funny that, after all the gold, someone would wrap the paintings and label them 'Goldfarb'. Silently

I disagreed, I thought to myself that someone named Goldfarb probably owned these before the war, someone who was now very dead."

"Stolen by the Nazis?" Sharon asked.

"Most probably, we hid those bundles in the barn, under some straw. I also took the most delightful small statuette of a dancer. Then the three of us waited."

Sharon looked past Dumont to the small alcove centrally placed within the shelves of books; even she could tell that the small bronze statue of a ballerina was a Degas. She looked back at the old soldier.

"Yes, strong yet delicate; forceful yet so feminine. Yes, that's the one." Dumont turned his head toward the statue, Sharon saw a slight shiver pass his cheek, "But back to the end of the story; the art left the next day, not as much hub-bub as when the gold left. That evening, we pulled out the bars, and stacked the rolls of paintings in the truck. In all the scrounging around for boxes to put the bars in, we also found a rough box that had been stacked with some others; it was sitting next to the elevator doors, like it had been placed there quickly. The name 'Trittenheim Winery' was stenciled on its side, most of the other boxes had German labels and swastikas or the formal imprint of the German army on them, only this one said winery; we took it to celebrate. We loaded our bars, they weighed about twenty-five pounds each, in the boxes. We ended up with forty bars, or about a half ton. I never thought we took that many. But busy hands, and six of 'em to boot, are happy hands, and, well there we were. We loaded everything in the truck, slid out that night; I remember that it was during a rain shower, or something. We wrapped the paintings in green army canvas, and headed back to the tunnel in the side of the hill."

"No one saw you, it was that easy?"

"Can't say that for sure, but everyone was exhausted from working in the tunnels, so the camp was quiet, most of the security had left with the caravan. In fact, I don't even remember sentries being posted, the war was almost over and the front was fifty miles away, we were lax. We managed to open the iron doors and clear away some old machinery. We drove the truck inside. We couldn't resist looking at the paintings, the largest was rolled out and I took Gillis' and Graham's photo standing in front of the painting, like the trophy it was; I was struck by its colors. Gillis took the camera, a little Kodak Brownie that he carried through the war, getting film when he could; I never did see the photos. We shut the door, raked out our tracks, and hiked back to camp. We agreed to meet after the war so we set a date and location, and hoped the loot would still be there; we would figure out how to get it home at that time. As I said, we were three war-weary twenty-year olds, our future was getting better and every day the war's end was nearer."

"The next morning, we were getting ready to move and catch up with the war. I said there were prisoners everywhere, we forced many to help with the removal of the gold, kept an eye on them, but used them. These prisoners were now being marched to the rear. A small group of SS officers were held to one side, separate from the regular army. I've never seen a more professional dangerous group of men; they looked at us with disdain and at their own people with disgust, as though surrender was not an option. But there they stood, as prisoners. I couldn't let it pass. Me, I had to get in their faces, stupid, but you know me by now. One SS officer stood six inches taller than the others, blond, his uniform dirty, but by the cut it wasn't standard issue, he had a swagger and couldn't have been more than a year or two older than me, and he was an SS Obersturmführer, like a 1st lieutenant, but I knew different. I had seen a lot of Germans by then, this guy was more than what his uniform said he was."

"He was disguised as a lower grade? Strange, thought their egos wouldn't let that happen."

"Yes, but I'd seen it before. So I got in his face and started yelling at him in German, shocked the hell out him. He thought we were all inferiors, till I ripped him a new one."

"What's your name, Adolf?" I screamed in German. "Why the hell are you dressed like a prick Obersturmführer, Kraut?

Wie ist Ihr Name? Jetzt, sofort!"

"The others in his little group moved away from the man, like they thought he would explode and take them with him. I'll never forget that man, he didn't blink, ignored me the whole time, his sharp blue eyes stared directly over my head, like I didn't exist."

"Mein Name ist SS-Obersturmführer Otto Speyer, Schwein!" was all he said, I laughed in his face; he had the audacity to call *me* a pig. I'll remember him till the day I die; he had a large dueling scar on his left cheek. I always wondered what happened to the poor cadet who gave him that scar."

"What happened to him?"

"Don't know, we moved on, they were moved to the rear. Never saw them again and, for that matter, I never really cared."

"Obviously you survived, what happened to Gillis and Graham?" Sharon asked.

"A week later, we were crossing an open cornfield, keeping low. We were taking some small arms fire from the woods, we were told that this was one of the last die-hard divisions left in the area, and they did die hard. We were only expecting rifle and machine gun fire, when the sky opened up with mortars; the German mortars were better than ours and more powerful, I hit the ground and felt the concussions for fifteen minutes, it seemed like hours. They must have fired every mortar left in this part of Germany; hundreds fell. I crawled through the debris and found Graham; he was dead. Cut in two. I looked for Gillis, found his left arm, knew it was him from the high school ring he wore. Still remember it to this day, 'Roosevelt High School' it said. I pulled it off; eventually I sent it to his mother anonymously. Never found his body. I started to pull back and, just as I reached the tree line, another barrage hit. I woke up a week later in a hospital in Luxemburg."

Out of habit Sharon reached for her cigarettes, and then caught herself.

"That's all right, if it weren't for this contraption wrapping my head, I'd join you. It was those damn things put me here, but hell, I'm ninety-three, light 'em if you got 'em.

Sharon smiled and put the pack back in her STIA handbag.

"Where was I? Oh yes, Luxemburg. I took a bit of shrapnel in the back of my head; nothing serious, just banged me around. In a month I was good, real good. The war was over, we were going home, and all I could think of was Merkers. Now that Gillis and Graham were dead, it was mine, all mine. Got a two-week pass to Paris and spent the time taking care of a few things. Found an apartment that had a garage under it, it was in the 7th Arrondissement. I stocked up on some canned goods and bought civilian clothing. The apartment was furnished; the original tenant was killed during the war. The landlord didn't ask any questions, American dollars were better than gold, and I spoke only French, the owner never knew who I was. While civil on the outside, Paris seethed with the need for vengeance and retribution. Bodies were found most mornings in alleys and parks, Parisians held little respect for collaborators and scores had to be settled."

"Baghdad wasn't any different. Waves of terror washed back and forth across the Tigris, first one side, the Shiites, and then the Sunni. And when the Al Qaida pushed themselves into the country with their suicide vests, everyone suffered. I lost good men in those days."

"That's why I need you on this operation, Sharon. You understand me more than most," Dumont said, he pursed his lips in a sad smile. "Well, I made it back to Luxemburg and rejoined my outfit, hung around waiting for whatever would come and a fortunate accident happened. I was working with a squad clearing munitions from a bunker back near Metz, a fuse caught and we scattered and waited for the explosion, when it happened, the whole side of the hill opened up, must'a been tunnels full of explosives. I was thrown into a wall and covered with debris, out like a light. When I woke up, it was night. The concussion knocked me out but that was all. I took the opportunity, slid down the hill, worked my way from the carnage, and disappeared. Three days later, I was driving the SS truck through Germany toward France; I loaded a lot of worthless stuff in the back, covering the thirteen boxes and the paintings. I looked like every other refugee, but I had money, and it made getting fuel and food easier. No one stopped me for more than a moment and then only for a cursory check. I had the look of a refugee and the papers I acquired in Paris were as authentic as I could buy, my French heritage helped. It was here, Sharon my dear, as I crossed into France, that Robert Alan Dupont died and Alain Dumont was born."

"What?" Sharon cried. "What did you say?"

"More wine?"

Chapter 2

Sharon stared into the sad eyes of billionaire Alain Dumont, not believing what she had just heard.

"Believe it, Sharon. Dupont died in the explosion at Metz, look it up, I did. MIA, I was, they never found so much as a fingernail, mostly because I kept them all. I was lucky; I planned on leaving the Army before being shipped back to the states. The explosion gave me the cover I needed. I had no one back home; my stepparents died a few years before the start of the war. I was alone and free. I drove the truck across the wreck of Germany, fought off thieves and gypsies; I didn't sleep for three days, and, finally, I made it through the streets of Paris to my apartment. I hid the boxes under the brick pavers of the garage floor, sold a lot of the furniture that I used for my cover, actually made a few bucks, and met a very nice young lady. The paintings were stacked in the closet, looking to the entire world like nothing much of value. I settled in and started to develop a reputation as a trader and finder of things, import and export. I also began to study the banking system and learned how to convert a half-ton of gold into real money. Not as easy as you think, gold bars always grab someone's attention. I went to Zurich; now those guys are shady! They would make a deal with the devil and, by dealing with the Nazis, they did."

A sharp knock on the door interrupted their conversation.

"Oui, Remy," Dumont said in French.

"Monsieur, je pars," Remy answered through the door.

"Merci, á demain," Dumont answered; even Sharon could tell his French was elegant, like him. He put his finger up, signaling Sharon to wait. He turned the computer screen on his desk so they could see, hit a couple of keys and a view of the front entry

hall appeared. In fifteen seconds, Remy passed through the door and exited onto Broadway.

"I think he understands English," O'Mara offered.

"I know he does, keeps it hidden well, but there're reasons why I keep him around. He's efficient and manages my health very well. But in my life, I have learned never to trust anyone completely. That's probably why I was only married once, for a few wonderful years; she died from tuberculosis a few years after the war. Dominique was her sweet name, that's her photo." Dumont pointed to a gold-framed photo.

"She's very beautiful, striking, in fact," Sharon said.

"And incredibly smart and street wise, six years of Nazi occupation will do that. Belonged to the Resistance, but she seldom talked about it. She died before I could learn her whole story. But that was sixty years ago, so long ago yet . . ." He paused for a moment; Sharon watched as his face relived memories.

"Anyway, where was I, oh yes, it's getting harder to keep track of my thoughts. They run away like small children and hide. But now I remember. I asked around and met a couple of Swiss bankers, and, after a few years, developed a reputation; I would only deal in gold for my trades. I made deposits in Switzerland four times a year, two bars at a time; I came and went by train. Very businesslike, no questions asked, and in five years all the bricks were nicely settled in my vault. In 1950 they were worth over a half million dollars."

"Wealthy man," Sharon said, still amazed by the change in Dumont from soldier to citizen and now, to lover, wealthy lover.

"By post-war standards, I was very wealthy. But as I said, I was a trader and mover of goods and, when required, services. My businesses in Paris were making money, a lot of money, but I kept a low profile and paid off whomever I needed to. Paris was a nest of vipers then, of all stripes. I still have that apartment in Paris and that old Mercedes truck still sits in the garage; quite a relic now, but it still runs. But now I'm tired, this took much longer than I thought, so I'm going to ask you to join me in one more little adventure, do you mind?"

"No, but we can do that tomorrow, or when convenient," O'Mara said. But Dumont insisted.

"The day can't get any stranger and shocking than what you've told me," she added.

"I think it can, and besides, I've not told you why I hired you. You have taken me on by faith and lovely Evelyn's recommendation, but you don't know why. Don't you want to know what's worth a hundred thousand dollars of your time to me?" She could only nod. "Then follow me."

Alain stood and uncoupled the oxygen hose and removed the prongs. "I'll be alright for a while; it's just a few steps. And I have another setup where we're going."

Dumont walked to the paneled wall and slid away a rectangular piece of walnut, a hand-sized pane of frosted glass appeared. He placed his palm on the glass; the panel glowed for a moment, then a soft voice said, *"Entrez, Monsieur Dumont."*

A large panel slid open and an elevator door materialized, then opened. He waved his hand toward the small room and followed her in. He placed his hand on another panel and the door closed.

"This elevator is programed to go to the upper floors only; it would take destroying this part of the house to find out that it also goes down. Only my left hand will allow it to go down, with my right hand, it goes up."

After ten seconds, the door reopened, an ornate iron grill stood across the hallway, barring entry to another chamber beyond. The room, like the house above, was well detailed in warm walnut and rich fabrics, art paneled the walls, an elegant room. Dumont placed his palm on another panel and the gate slid open.

"Sharon, we are in what's now called a panic room, very unromantic, don't you think? I have called this room my study, my *sous-sol*, my retreat for almost forty years. You, my dear, are the first person, aside from a very small select family, to see this room in thirty years."

Sharon walked into the room slowly; a vaulted ceiling,

painted in delightful frescoes, reminded her of an Italian church she visited in Florence on one of her brief leaves from Iraq. The carpets felt so soft that she wanted to take her shoes off. The walls took her breath away.

"This is my live-in vault. The walls are made of three-foot thick concrete and designed to withstand whatever God wants to throw at this city and me. There's food for a month behind that door; a self-contained bathroom there; ventilation is provided by a battery system I helped to design and build through my investments. This room uses less electricity than three one hundred watt light bulbs. I spend a lot of evenings here. That panel accesses all the cameras and security devices in the house; the cameras can pan for a block up and down the street and the neighborhood. Don't tell anyone, especially that cute thing that lives in the apartment behind me." Dumont smiled, as only a ninety-three year old lecher could. Sharon frowned.

"Be careful, Mr. Dumont, you might get caught."

"Actually it might be fun, but I digress. Sharon," he said, taking her hand, "I'm hiring you to return these paintings to their rightful owners." Dumont waved his hand and, as he did so, the long wall of art started to glow from the overhead lights.

Sharon, always a student of art, stood in awe. First, on the left, was a Renoir of a beautiful young girl, next a Picasso from his blue period, two stacked Gauguin's led to a tall Degas dancer; on the right were two Pissarro waterfronts, another Renoir portrait, an incredible Van Gogh farm scene, and a Monet study of his Giverny home. But commanding the room, centrally hung, among all the other masters, was an impressively large panel of the Moulin Rouge by Toulouse Lautrec; it was so large that she felt like she could walk into the party. The wall behind her held smaller, lesser artists from the Impressionist period, but each was worth millions. The wall she faced was the most spectacular collection of privately held paintings she had ever heard of, she also realized that she had never seen these paintings in any book or art class she had taken.

"Takes your breath away, doesn't it?" Dumont said. "Still

takes mine away, even after sixty-five years."

"You're returning these to whom?"

"Time and taste are strange things, Sharon. At one time, these painters were vilified and scourged by the art world. Pissarro there, he almost starved to death; Van Gogh, well you know what happened to him, only Monet and Renoir went on to lauded old age and died wealthy. And my favorite, Henri Marie Raymond de Toulouse-Lautrec-Monfa, died at thirty-six, an alcoholic syphilis-infected wreck of a young man. Genius and brilliance fills this room," Sharon smiled at Alain. "No, not me Sharon, it is *they* that express what man can do when unstopped by convention and order. Without a doubt, they were shit-disturbers of the first order; I'm two or three steps down," Dumont said with adoration, not ridicule. He put the oxygen prongs on his nose and steadied himself with the back of a chair.

"Were these the rolled up paintings in the barn?"

"Hard to believe, but many of these were in the bundle. I have purchased the others, like the Picassos and the Degas and a few of the Cassatt's, always loved her paintings, especially the children, but these others were in one bundle, four brilliant paintings. Amazing, is it not? These four were appropriated by the Nazis from a French Jewish family from Haguenau, the Goldfarbs; they were forced to flee to Limoges by gunpoint, then they fled to Switzerland with the few things they could carry. They were lucky; all their neighbors were gassed. Since there were no owners after they left, the Nazis, all quite legally, found the paperwork in fact, declared the paintings unwanted and claimed them. Lev Goldfarb's father, Saul, when he was a young student in Paris in the 1880s, bought these paintings, and, in fact, he knew Lautrec in his final years. The Goldfarbs were a very wealthy family; they lost much when they fled, but picked things up in Zurich. Lev Goldfarb, the son, survived the war and lived until he was seventy-two, he died in 1977. After his death, his family left Zurich and now they live in Los Angeles. The youngest, Saul, is a Hollywood producer; he was named after his great-grandfather. There are ten direct descendants of

Saul David Goldfarb, the elder, alive today."

"Do they know you have these paintings? Have you contacted them? I don't remember anything in the news, and this would have been big news," Sharon said.

"Yes, it would have made every news channel in the world. But no, I have not. I have been very selfish and, for a long time, I didn't want to know where these paintings came from, but I'll die soon and they must go back to the family. I have been investigating the origins of these paintings quietly and, by a strange event, I discovered their owners. I was paging through a book in a Tel Aviv bookstore, during a week of meetings with my Israeli partners, when I noticed two black and white photos of an elegant Jewish Haguenau home. Those three paintings were hung on the wall." He pointed at the Lautrec and the Pissarros. I had a clue and a lead and my investigators found the rest of the family, but even the investigators don't know why I was looking for the Goldfarbs. It's your job to meet with the family, discuss the paintings' return, come to a reasonable settlement, and handle all the necessary security. They rightfully belong to the Goldfarb family. Even after all this time, they need to be returned and I want you to run the operation."

2b

After a morning of surprises and revelations, this was the topper. *"Negotiate the return of a quarter of a billion dollars' worth of paintings to an unsuspecting family. Maybe they don't want them; maybe the publicity will be intolerable, maybe they're a bunch of schmucks and don't deserve these paintings any more than I do."* O'Mara's head spun with disconnected thoughts.

"Excuse me?" was all she could say.

Alain Dumont smiled. "Yes, Sharon dear, I want you to do all the negotiating and return these paintings. I have no predeterminations. If they want to hang them on their bathroom walls, donate them to a museum, or sell them; I don't care. But I do know that they'll be back in the public eye after seventy years. From the reports I've received, the Goldfarbs have not strayed from their aristocratic roots. They are all professionals: two doctors, a lawyer, a college professor, the movie producer, and a passel of children. The producer seems to be the most public and outgoing of the family, and the most controversial. He has made two feature films that include the atrocities of the Nazis during the war."

"Great! For some reason, I don't think I'm in the minors anymore," Sharon said.

Dumont laughed, "Are you having second thoughts?"

"On the contrary, I'm excited as all hell. And I get to hang around some really good art," she said, smiling, looking at the walls. "How secret is this?"

"Use your discretion, this will require more than just your efforts; back-up, as you say, may be needed. I'll program you into the palm scanners for the elevator and the front door."

"Thank you, there may be one or two people I'll need to talk to and work with, you will know who and why. I'll pay them out of my fee."

"Excellent, but send me their bills, I'll cover them," Dumont said. He took a series of breaths from the clear nose cone oxygen mask he had put on as they walked in; he started to cough, in hard, body-wracking, spasms. O'Mara moved to help, he put his hand up. "I'll be fine," he spat, "it passes, a moment."

The BART ride back to Walnut Creek seemed a fitting way to bring her back to Earth; she looked at the platinum credit card that Alain Dumont handed her as she left. It would have taken her a month to get the card, even if she could have qualified; he had it in one day. *"Figures,"* she thought, as she looked at the card, *"only he would use a Swiss bank."*

After a brief thank you call to Evelyn Luca and the promise of a dinner date, she sat at her computer and started to plan the operation, such as it was. Basil, coiled on his bed, watched intently as she began to develop a list of "To Do's."

Until she knew otherwise, everything would be done in secrecy, if the Goldfarbs blow it, so be it. That's something she couldn't control. Dumont wanted this done quietly, if possible. He also realized that the family would do whatever they chose to do. For the next two days, she worked through detailed scenarios, schedules, and timelines that would achieve the best results. The paintings would stay in the vault on Broadway until all the transfer issues were resolved, that was one of Dumont's stipulations. If the family requested additional funds, Dumont required that these be directly used for the art, either for transportation or security. He believed the value of the paintings was more than enough to compensate the family for their disappearance. By early Sunday morning, she had an operation schedule as good as anything she had put together in Iraq.

"Kevin, how about an early dinner?" O'Mara asked Kevin Bryan when he picked up his cell phone.

"Wonderful warm afternoon, nothing to do, Giants on tonight, and a good- looking redhead calls for an early dinner, sounds absolutely great, where?"

"How about Va-Di-Vi, an outside table, a little more privacy and fewer ears close by," she answered.

"Sounds more like a business dinner."

"Both, pleasure and business, besides, I'm buying," she added.

"I'm stunned; you must have a new job," Bryan said.

"Yes, and I need your help."

Sharon and Kevin Bryan, a detective with the Lafayette police department, had a strange, wobbly history. He came out of the Oakland PD, after the grind became too much. He landed the job on the other side of the Oakland hills and never looked back. There were still crimes but they were different, as crimes in a wealthy community are. No gang killings, but murder for hire, death by suicide brought on by failure, and the occasional embezzlement and other white collar crimes kept his calendar filled. He had worked closely with O'Mara on two recent cases. One involved a weird transsexual and a BART murder, and the other dealt with the smuggling of sex slaves, Mexican Cartels, and Chinese Tongs. They never dated, were never intimate, yet they

depended on each other more than two very healthy, very available people could reasonably do. Their mutual friends thought
they were crazy. A quiet dinner would be just the thing.

O'Mara spent an hour at the pistol range, scored well with
her Beretta 92F, six tight rapid shots at fifty feet in a pattern the
width of her hand. As always, she got serious glances from the
men in the lounge and envious flashes from some of the wom-
en. She knew that all it took was a healthy body and a pistol
strapped on your hip to encourage the male species.

She dressed in her usual jeans and green silk top; she believed in silk over cotton, not the other way around. Her Luc-
chese boots had a western style about them, but weren't boots,
they were cut open at the back. A black belt matched the shoes.
She pulled her hair back in a ponytail; the outside table would
be on the warmish side.

"As always, stunning," Kevin said as Sharon turned into the
alley on one side of the restaurant. He sat at the first table; a refreshing breeze turned the corner with her.

"Been waiting long?"

"Five minutes," he said.

She noticed the ice in his Jameson had melted a bit, he'd been
there more than ten minutes; she liked that about him, punctual,
especially when there was a gunfight.

Settled in, she ordered a glass of Australian cabernet and
small plates of lumpias and tuna tempura. They shared.

"Well, I'm curious, what's the story? And what's up that allows you to pick up the tab?" he asked, taking a sip.

"Have I got a story? Let me see." Through the next hour
and numerous small plates of tasty treats from the Pacific Rim,
Sharon told Kevin about the Second World War and the stolen
art and gold. "How's that for one of the biggest thefts you could
imagine?"

"War does strange things, as you well know. Not sure there's
a prosecutor anywhere who would chase down a ninety-three
year old war hero. Not after what he's done with his life. Hell,
the foundation we use to help our troubled kids is almost fully

financed by his foundation. The man is a pillar, seems he's trying to do the right thing; most of us never get a chance to fix our mistakes." He raised his glass to the sky.

"Agreed, so here's what I need to do," Sharon said, and through servings of two desserts and two glasses of port, she outlined her schedule and laid out the timelines.

"Need help?"

"Wondered when you would ask. I will at these points, security, the transfer, crowds at the news conference. I'm sure that, with a movie producer in the mix, publicity will be paramount, so we need to anticipate everything, including the venue here and probably in LA. We can work a lot of that out later, once I've met with the Goldfarbs."

"When's that going to happen?"

"The first call will be tomorrow; I'm going to start with the oldest daughter, Zoe. She is a cardiologist at Cedars-Sinai in Los Angeles and then we'll see how the family reacts. I'll head down later in the week and meet with her and the family. Then I'll know what I've gotten myself into." She took another sip of port and thought about the coming week.

2c

The short sixty minute Southwest flight into LAX was hardly relaxing. Bryan dropped her at the terminal, then there was the usual long early morning line at security, an hour wait for the plane, and finally she walked aboard in B group, at least she still got a window seat. The previous week was a blur.

She reached Dr. Zoe Goldfarb-Binder through her answering service; they missed each other twice, but it gave the impression that O'Mara had something important to talk about.

"Dr. Binder," Zoe Goldfarb-Binder said.

"Thank you for taking my call, Doctor, obviously you don't know me. My name is Sharon O'Mara and I represent an individual who has something that your family lost many years ago. He, quite simply, would like to return these items to you and your family."

"Excuse me, something that our family lost?" Zoe asked. "You represent someone, who?"

"Yes, I do. This gentleman acquired these items shortly after the war in Europe. I have been employed to meet with you and whomever you designate to discuss the best manner for their return," O'Mara said avoiding the 'who' part of her question. "I'm not at liberty to offer more information over the phone, but I would like to set up a time, hopefully later this week, to meet with you personally and discuss the process for the return of the items. I'll be in Los Angeles on Thursday and Friday, the location for this meeting is at your discretion."

"May I ask who this gentleman is?"

"Unfortunately, not at this time, but everything will be laid out for you when we meet. Is it possible to meet later this week? I realize that you'll have to coordinate this with the other members of your family; are you interested?"

A long pause followed Sharon's question.

"Let me discuss this with my brothers and sisters, they are all in Los Angeles, but we all have hectic schedules, so I'll need a day or so to discuss it with them. Are you sure that we're the people you're supposed to meet with?" Doctor Binder asked.

"Yes, we're quite sure you're the owners of these items," Sharon answered.

"I see, as I said, let me make some calls, where can I reach you?"

"I'll call you back. Would tomorrow evening be acceptable?"

"I'm not sure, but yes, please call after seven, I'll be home." Zoe gave Sharon her phone number. "That number is unlisted, but I will take your call even though this is one of the strangest calls I've ever received."

"Dr. Binder, you haven't heard anything yet. Strange is not the word for it."

"Excuse me?"

"I'll call you tomorrow."

Sharon's call was immediately taken by Dr. Binder that next evening.

"Ms. O'Mara, I have one of my brothers and one of my sisters here, we're not quite sure how to take this. May I put you on speaker?"

"I fully understand. Yes, which brother is there?"

"The youngest, Saul Goldfarb," Zoe answered.

"I believe he's the movie producer?" Sharon asked.

"Yes and my sister, Sarah, an attorney. Both of them are very skeptical, and Saul suggested that we should make other inquires before the meeting."

"I understand, but unfortunately I can offer no more information. Can we meet somewhere?"

"The Beverly Hills Hilton, it's close to most of us and should suit your stipulation; is that acceptable?"

"Yes, I'll meet you at 5:00 on Thursday."

The call ended with more side questions and conversations; Sharon could hear comments from the others but couldn't hear what was said clearly.

"Thursday at 5:00, we'll see you then, Ms. O'Mara."

She met with Alain Dumont the next day and explained the arrangements; he was pleased.

"It will be a relief, I think, I'll miss these wonderful paintings, but things like this are only held for a period of time before they're passed on to others, not unlike fine antiques or antiquities. We think we own them, when, in reality, they own us and tease us with the pleasure they give. Then we grow bored with them, sell them, or sometimes they outlive us. At least I'll be able to pass them on while I'm still alive, but like delightful children, I'll miss them," Alain said; his eyes passed over the paintings wistfully.

"These four, I'm sure, were stolen from the Goldfarb's, many of the others I acquired through, as they say, more scrupulous dealers. But I can't say where they came from, but the Renoir, the two Pissarros and the Lautrec came from their home. I've put together a package for your use during the meeting; there're other bits of literature inside with additional pages supporting their providence. Two of the pages are copies of the Nazi orders legally seizing the paintings, they're the only paintings listed. There was furniture and silver listed also but they were lost to the war and time. I also have a copy of the book I saw in Tel Aviv; I suggest you use this as your means of entry."

The flight left on time and arrived five minutes early, the driver she ordered met her as she exited the terminal. In the back of the limousine, she opened her briefcase and paged through the book, a tag had been left at the appropriate page. The book was the work of a Strasbourg photographer who had saved thousands of photos and negatives when he fled to Israel after the war; in fact, he had sneaked into Palestine during the English occupation. After the formation of the Israeli state, he fashioned the book, more in a manner of celebration of the Jewish culture in the Strasbourg and Haguenau region, than some form of a memorial. Only by the happenstance of Dumont's lunch stop was any of the four paintings' history known.

After checking in at the Hilton, she asked about the meeting room, it would be available at 4:00. She asked the desk to call her on her cell when the Goldfarbs asked about her. She told the desk to please escort the family to the room after the call; she would be waiting for them. She asked that wine, sparkling water and some small plates of treats be set up in the room, at least it would be a civil meeting, and besides, she was thirsty and hungry.

At 5:05, the door to the small conference room opened and five well-dressed, quite obviously successful people walked into the room. O'Mara, dressed in crisp black pants slacks, a white silk shirt, and just enough bling to allay fears of a less than well-off woman, stood to one side, talking with the staff who delivered the wine. To some, she looked like an attorney.

"Thank you, I think we can manage without your help, the setup is great." Without missing a beat, she walked directly to Zoe Goldfarb-Binder, graciously extended her hand, and said, "Thank you, I see that you have brought your whole family, excellent. I am Sharon O'Mara; I hope that all the intrigue hasn't lessened your curiosity?"

"Only heightened it, and all of us are more than intrigued, especially Saul." Zoe turned to her brother.

"Sharon, these are my brothers and my sister. Saul, David, Eli and Sarah," Zoe said.

"Yes, I recognize all of you, and your children, I believe there are five?"

"How do you know that, Ms. O'Mara?" Saul Goldfarb demanded.

"I think we need some refreshments, wine?" Sharon asked.

"I think we need answers, Ms. O'Mara," David said.

"Shortly, but please don't worry, what I will present will more than repay your inconvenience. Shall we sit, it'll be more comfortable." Sharon poured glasses of wine.

"I'm on-call, so sparkling water will be fine," Zoe said.

They moved to the table, a soft green tablecloth covered the cheap folding table; at least the chairs were comfortable.

"Well," O'Mara said, "I suggest we get started, is that okay?"

"It's your party," Saul said.

"Hardly, the party is actually my employer's, but first a few preliminaries. I have a few papers which must be signed before we begin, you are all professionals and Sarah, as a corporate attorney, you are well aware of confidentiality agreements and non-disclosures, these need to be signed before I begin. Refuse to sign and I will leave the room, immediately. You must all sign," Sharon said.

"I need to know more," Saul said.

"You will not learn anything more other than my employer has something that was taken from your family, all he wishes is to return it, nothing more. There is no cost to you or your families, nothing. Please sign." O'Mara placed the two-page documents in front of each of the Goldfarbs; Sarah scanned the document.

"This is very general and binds us to nothing except our silence for the next thirty days, nothing else. Is that adequate for your purposes?" Sarah Goldfarb asked.

"Spoken as an attorney; yes, it's only for a short defined period. After that, you will be free to tell whomever you wish, but my work will be completed long before then. Please sign."

She waited while each sibling looked at the document and then watched as they each signed. As they were handed back, she counter-signed the documents.

"I will forward copies to you tomorrow, by messenger, before I leave. And thank you."

"And?" Saul asked.

"Please be patient, Saul," Zoe said. "Ms. O'Mara, I apologize."

"No need, hell, I would be more than concerned and a little put-off by this process, but this is how it must be done, and from now on please call me Sharon, we are going to get to know each very well over the next two hours and I will try to keep your interest up. Now, do any of you recognize this home and this room?" Sharon asked as she opened the book to the marked pages; she turned the book toward the family.

"That's grandfather's home in Haguenau, we have all seen it and, when I was a child, years after the war, I ran through that room," Zoe Goldfarb-Binder said.

"Well, I need to tell you a story," Sharon said to the stunned family, most shocked was Saul, who, upon seeing the room, started to cry.

For the next hour, Sharon took the five Goldfarbs back to post World War Two and the events that led up to the acquisition of the paintings. She was careful to develop a script that, while still the truth, also revealed very little about Dumont and the actual finding of the paintings. The family had little information other than what their grandfather, Lev Goldfarb, had told them about those days and the family's escape to Switzerland. Their Haguenau home and wealth was important, but his family's lives were more important to Lev. They were forced by the Nazis to abandon all of their property when they fled.

"My grandfather said that, as they crossed the border, past the guards and the gates into Switzerland, they were spit on and screamed at by Germans who were there to taunt escaping Jews," David said. "Everyone was reduced to the simplest of families, no money, little clothing, there were no options. Our grandfather, always an astute businessman, had secreted money into accounts in Switzerland, as a way of dealing with the massive inflation of the 1930s and as a hedge against the Nazis. It helped, at least he could put a roof over his family when they arrived in Zurich, but they were just one family in an exodus of thousands."

"I understand, the war changed and destroyed much of Europe. Much has been lost and much has been found. My client acquired these after the war," Sharon said as she removed an envelope from her case. "He believes that these paintings belong to your family."

She laid out the four eight-by-ten glossy photos of the paintings; the Lautrec was in the center. For a moment, the five Goldfarbs just stared and then Zoe traced her finger around the face of the young woman in the Renoir.

"My father told me stories about this painting when I was young; he said, as he grew up, that she was the prettiest girl he had ever seen; he lived in the house for ten years before they escaped. That painting was his favorite. She is even more beautiful than I imagined. There were no photos; they left in such a hurry."

"Grandfather often talked about the Toulouse-Lautrec and the party that went on in the painting; he said that when his father, our great-grandfather, bought the painting, Lautrec was ill and afraid that he would not be able to paint anymore, this may have been his last great work," Sarah said.

Saul stood and paced across the back of the room, lost in nervous thought.

"May I ask a question?" Eli said. "What's in it for your client? These are very valuable, extremely valuable, giving these up would be more than what a normal person would do. I don't understand."

"I assume that this person is very wealthy and the return of these paintings will not cause him much financial hardship. Isn't that correct, Ms. O'Mara?" Saul said, stopping his pacing.

"Correct."

"We are under an agreement not to discuss this outside of this room, except among ourselves, is that correct?"

"Yes," Sharon said.

"Then we want to know who this benefactor is. I think that it's critical for us to understand why we are being given such a gift. As Jews, we are skeptical of many things, and gifts such as these seem to come with strings; what are these conditions?"

"None, other than he would prefer that the paintings be placed where they would serve the most good," O'Mara said. "But that's his wish, what you do with them is your business when this is concluded. He is not a private man; he has not shunned the public, but has kept a low profile in his personal interests and activities. And yes, he's an extremely wealthy man; he is ninety-three and will die soon. He is, as he put it, cleaning house. He has enjoyed the company of these works of art, and now that he is aware of their rightful home, he wants to return them. He is also offering assistance, if you wish, to place them in a museum; there are many options at your disposal.

The brothers and sisters looked at each other, and like most tight families, seemed to understand one another.

"We wish to know his name, it will not leave this room," Zoe said.

"I cannot give it, that's his wish and my requirement," Sharon said.

"Then why the hell would he care about us? We're nobodies to him. What's in it for him?" Saul demanded.

"Not everything requires a self-serving purpose, Mr. Goldfarb," Sharon said, interrupting. "In this case he believes it's the right thing to do. You will not have the opportunity to meet him or ask him those questions; I am your only source of access. May I go over the other stipulations and the schedule?"

Sharon reviewed the schedule, the timing for the transfer, the request to keep it a simple affair and to keep the information amongst the family. After the Goldfarbs left, she returned to her room, cracked open the mini-bar, poured two Black Labels on ice, called Alain Dumont and reported what had happened.

"Excellent work, my dear, excellent, I'm glad that it went well. I think we are on schedule, can I expect to see you on Saturday?" Dumont asked.

"Yes, I'll be there. Nine o'clock?"

"Yes, that'll be fine, and then we can deal with all the press that may be hounding us, like a hunt when they can't find the fox; it'll be fun."

"Press, what do you mean?"

"I suggest you wait until the Los Angeles *Times* comes out in the morning, you will know then."

"Alain, what do mean?"

"Patience my dear, patience."

Chapter 3

"Millionaire to Return Stolen Nazi Art to Family" was the lead in an article above the fold on the front page of the Friday morning edition of the Los Angeles *Times*.

"Shit!" was all O'Mara could say when she opened the paper. "Patience, my ass," she added as she read the article. Almost everything was there, but the thread seemed to lean more toward the family and Saul Goldfarb especially.

Her cell phone started to buzz, the screen said Zoe Goldfarb.

"I'm sorry Sharon; he went behind our backs, directly to the paper. He has a lot of contacts, always looking for a story. This one was too big for them to pass-up; at least he left your name out."

"A small favor, but we anticipated this. Our options are few and Saul knows it, I could act on the non-disclosure and cancel the whole deal, but that would only make the press hungrier. I suggest that we accomplish the transfer as quickly as possible. I'm going home today. I'll follow-up with an email and information; it'll take place in San Francisco. The benefactor doesn't want this to drag on; it'll be done quickly and cleanly."

"I understand. I'll look for your email."

O'Mara continued to steam, but she now understood what Dumont had meant about patience; he knew all along this would happen. He was prepared for it, but it would have been nice if he had let her know, then again, she knew that this would probably happen. The damage was minimal, now to finish the game.

At mid-afternoon, Kevin Bryan picked Sharon up at the gate by Southwest Airlines; she threw her one bag into the cramped backseat, pulled out her cell phone, saw there were no messages, and settled back into the seat.

"It was in the *Chronicle* this morning, too," Kevin said. Sharon had told him about the *Times* article from the Los Angeles tarmac before she took off. "The son-of-a-bitch couldn't keep his mouth shut."

"It's too big a deal for him, especially with him being a movie producer big-shot. Puts him in an interesting position; everyone wants to know who the mystery person is. Surprised that I wasn't chased by the press, just lucky or they hadn't moved fast enough. Even though I wasn't in the article, he would have told someone."

"Lucky for you, not sure your neighborhood could handle the press; they have a less than favorable impression of you."

"No kidding, that's all I would need; they'd ride me out of Walnut Creek on a rail. Basil?"

"Misses you, but I dropped him off, so he knows you're on your way. And how are you?"

"Good. And you?"

"Very good, things are quiet, just the way I like them. No murders, no kidnappings, just a couple of very quiet days in bucolic Lafayette. The chief allowed me to sit at my desk and finish paperwork, now that's a luxury."

"You owe me a dollar for using the word 'bucolic'," Sharon said. She had charged him for every word she considered highend; he now owed her five bucks. "I picked out the car, and Mr. Dumont has given me the means to make it happen. I can deal with it later in the week and then I won't have to keep bugging you for a ride to the airport."

"There's always BART," Kevin said with a grin. "Where and what did you buy?"

"Believe it or not, I found a 2004 Jaguar XJR, black, not green, but I can live with that. It's at the dealer on Mt Diablo, excellent condition with only 65,000 miles, and new tires. He's holding it. And the price isn't too bad at $20,000. Ten years newer than the one I lost in the shooting, but very comfortable."

"You and your Jags, what's that about? They're fussy, leak oil and are British. With our Irish heritage, I'm shocked you'd go for them."

"Name me one Irish car company, Kevin. Besides, it's a great car, and it makes the boys' heads turn."

"What boys?"

"Boys, Kevin. You know those fellows who are young and exciting and like to look at girls in fancy cars, not old and codger-like, sitting, watching TV sports all night."

"Who are you talking about?" Kevin said as he checked the rear view mirror.

Basil met them at the door, and scooted his way up and down the hall, banged into her twice before she could let him out into his backyard kingdom. After a short pause in the corner, he returned to the door, pushed his way past them, sat, and stared at his jar of bones.

"Two seconds, Baze. Wine?"

"Something stronger, I'm off-duty till morning."

O'Mara poured herself a Red Label on the rocks and a Jameson for Bryan. He'd already sat in the more comfortable chair on the patio.

"Out, that's mine," she ordered when she brought out the drinks. He moved to the lounge, as ordered. Kevin extended his tall frame and stretched out in the less desirable perch.

"Always the forceful wench, cheers." He tipped his glass to her. "Here's to a more successful transfer."

"I sure-as-hell hope so. For the most part, they're all just fine people, successful, all have money, so it was a windfall, not like it would be to someone else."

"Yeah, like little ol' me, I could use a little windfall like that," Kevin said taking a sip. "Like they say, the rich get richer."

"Whiner! You're just a dark Irishman. I don't think this group would cash them in. I think there's a long tradition in their family; selling these paintings would not honor their ancestors. I think it helps to flesh-out their family, gives it more substance and standing in Los Angeles. I guess they will look for a museum or some other way of displaying the paintings to the public. Saul, the movie producer, is already trying to find a movie script from all this. Zoe is the traditionalist; sees the connection to the past. The others are still in shock."

"How's Mr. Dumont?"

"He knew they couldn't keep a secret; that's why he didn't want his name revealed. I find it hard to believe that Saul found a copy of that book so fast, within hours and in time to get the photo in the newspaper. He does have resources. No pictures of the paintings, I kept those. I showed them the documents and the copies of the Nazi letters; they were shocked that the paintings were found."

"Still makes my skin crawl every time I watch a World War Two special. I'm amazed that the world let that man do what he did for so long before they did anything to try and stop him, and it took all-out war, killing forty million people. Then the coward put a bullet in his head. So many died and for what, the master-race, hell, it's still scary seventy years later." Kevin went back to the kitchen and refreshed his drink. "Another?"

"No, I'm fine. Don't worry about the Jaguar, I'll walk over in the morning and pick it up. I need to get into the city to make the final arrangements at the Fairmont, and then meet with Alain. A lot to do; don't want to wrap you up in all this anyway. After the transfer and the relocation of the paintings to Los Angeles, I'll see what other things I can pick up. After all this excitement, there won't be much on my calendar."

"I can help you fill it out, maybe a road trip in your fancy car? Who knows? Dinner in Monterey and a drive down the coast? Dinner? I'm famished. What's for dinner tonight?" Kevin asked.

"You're always hungry. I have the fixings for risotto, will that work?"

"...With smoked chicken?"

"Of course, find a wine in the closet."

3b

"Gramps, I wish you could see this, someone is giving a bunch of French paintings to a Jewish family in Los Angeles.

The article says they were found after the war and the owner says that he found out they were stolen from this family's grandfather by the Nazi's, pretty damn strange," Bob Gillis said to his grandfather. The older Gillis sat in a large chair, his medicines arrayed on the low table next to him like soldiers in formation; his right hand held a glass of bourbon on ice, the sleeve of his left arm was neatly pinned back.

"Lot of stuff still coming out about the war, even after all these years; remember they sent that damn concentration Kraut back to Germany to be tried just a few years ago? Son-of-a-bitch fought it for years, damn Nazis should get all they can throw at them for what they did," Jimmy Gillis said to his grandson.

"There's a photo of an old house, says it's in France. The picture shows the paintings hung on the walls of the living room, before the Krauts stole them; you should see 'em. Quite a house, too, must have been a real mansion. Says the Goldfarbs were thrown out of Germany by the Nazis and then skedaddled to Switzerland, they lost everything. The paintings were stolen and this guy; doesn't say who, has had them since after the war and only found the Goldfarbs in the last few years. Can you believe the son-of-a-bitch just wants to give them back to the family, either the guy is real rich or just plain stupid, I vote for rich. You okay, Gramps? You okay?"

"The glycerin, Bobby, give me one. Heart's doing some flip-flops."

Bobby Gillis found the right bottle and took a gelatin capsule out and put it in his grandfather's hand; the old man washed it down with a swallow of bourbon.

"Get me that box of war pictures would you? It should be on the shelf over there." Jimmy Gillis pointed over his left shoulder.

"Why, you can't see 'em."

"But you can; please get the box."

Bobby found the shoebox; 'WWII' was marked on the end, maybe another twenty other boxes sat on the shelf, all well labeled. The younger Gillis had looked at these photos a thousand times since he was old enough to walk; as a boy he remembered looking at the bodies of the dead soldiers and he liked the pictures of the tanks. When he was in his twenties, he spent eight years in the army, left honorably as a sergeant after spending two tours in Iraq; he saw more than enough bodies and the tanks saved his ass more than once. He had not looked at the photos in years.

"Somewhere in there are snaps of some guys on a truck with a painting in the background, you remember it."

"Yeah, kind of," Bobby said as he started sorting through the black and white pictures.

"I should be sitting next to a guy on the bed of a truck; a large painting is unrolled behind me."

A few minutes passed and Bobby stared at the photo and said, "Got it, kind of a big painting. Just a minute." He picked up the article and compared the photos. "Shit."

"They both the same?"

"Son-of-a-bitch, they are. It's the same goddamn painting. How did you know that?"

"Pour me some more bourbon, and a little water to stretch it. I got another war story to tell you. This one's about the Goldfarbs and a half ton of gold."

Bobby dropped a couple of ice cubes in the glass and topped it off. He placed it in his grandfather's hand.

"Well, that's a picture of me and Danny Graham and that painting behind us we had just stolen from the Germans. A corporal, his name was Robert Dupont, a good guy, is taking the picture. I remember, after all the months we spent fighting across France into Germany, he was the one guy who kept our asses out of trouble and kept us from getting killed. All of us new guys had a life expectancy measured in hours after we arrived at the front; we were lucky. We called him *Frenchy*. He talked French and German, almost pure like. But now Bobby boy," Jimmy Gillis said, swirling the ice in his glass of bourbon, "let me tell you about the time I was the richest God damn private in all of Germany."

James Gillis told his grandson the story of the caves and the gold, the paintings and their loot and how they hid it. "No one but us knew about the truck and the gold, must have been half a ton of the stuff, couldn't hide it in your pack, so there it sat, all of us hoping it would still be there when we got back. But we weren't so lucky. Crossing a field, just a week before the end of the war, we were ripped apart by a mortar barrage, that's where I lost this arm. They told me they put Graham on a litter in two pieces, I think he's buried in a cemetery in Belgium, but they may have moved him home later, just don't know."

"What about Dupont?"

"I was told he survived the barrage but was hit heading back into the woods. One of the guys said he was in a hospital for a while, but said he was killed after the war cleaning out an ammo dump. Shit, he was a good man; owed him my life a bunch of times. My records got all screwed up; in fact, I found out ten years later that I was listed as dead when I went back for some help with the arm. There were two of me, two James A. Gillis's, one dead and it sure weren't me. But probably to this day, if you look me up, I'm still dead, the army and their paperwork. I still miss Dupont; still think of him. In fact, someone sent my high school ring back to your grandmother 'cause I was dead, never knew who."

"The gold?"

"Took me almost nine months to recover and finally get some time off before being shipped home. Took a jeep and toured east out of the Luxemburg hospital I was in, toward Germany, shit, the countryside was still torn up, people was starving, even in the country. It was early winter and it was all I could do to stay on the road. Found Merkers and backtracked to where the tunnel was, the doors were still there, no tracks. It took me an hour to open the frozen doors enough to shine my flashlight inside. Empty, it was, as empty as a banker's heart, nothing there."

"No kidding, not even the truck?"

"Not even the truck. Someone had beat me to it, not that I was surprised but I sure as hell was disappointed, was making plans all the way there. How I was gonna get married to your grandmother by the way, buy a big house, maybe buy a gas station, and be successful. But all I got was a cold ride back to the hospital. I left for home on a cruise ship two weeks later; some cruise, me and three thousand other guys. But Bobby, in fact, I had your dad name you after Robert Dupont; you didn't know that, I'll bet. Well, that's my story about being rich at least for nine months, but hell, I wonder where those paintings came from? They were on the truck with the gold, someone must have stolen them and then maybe sold them after the war, maybe this benefactor's had them all along, who knows?"

Bobby Gillis sat with his grandfather for another hour until the man fell asleep.

"Hell," he thought to himself, *"San Francisco's only four hours from Bakersfield. Think I'll just go up there and see what this fuss is all about, get a good dinner, hang out for a while, and check out the show."*

3c

After reporting the events of the meeting with the Goldfarbs to Alain Dumont, Sharon O'Mara spent the rest of the weekend scheduling the return of the paintings. She called the Fairmont in San Francisco and scheduled a meeting with the hotel manager. This would not be your usual business meeting; Saul Goldfarb's release had decided that. She assumed that there would be a lot of reporters at the presentation; Los Angeles and San Francisco press would be well represented, that she was sure of.

"Mr. Blanco, are you aware of the newspaper article about the return of the paintings to the family in Los Angeles? I would like to reserve a room to make that happen."

"We are excited to be of any help," Mr. Blanco said, realizing the potential public relations coupe. "We have had many meetings here, as I'm sure you're aware, and we can set up the Pavilion Room for your use; it can hold up to 200 people. I suspect you believe there will be a number of people from the press?"

"You pay attention to the news, Mr. Blanco. Yes, I fully ex-

pect the press to attend, The Pavilion Room? Excellent choice!"
Sharon said, thinking of the paintings.

"It's on the main floor which will make it more accessible.
We'll need a deposit to secure the room. Refreshments?"

"It'll be easier if we meet, are you available on Monday? This
is short notice but I would like to know if next Friday is available?"

"Next week, I'll check." He knew that he would move the
devil out of the upstairs Diplomat Suite if he had to, to make
sure the date was free. "Yes, it is."

"Good, 10:00 Friday morning. I'll see you Monday at 9:00 to
go over the schedule, and thank you."

"Thank you, Ms. O'Mara, I'll see you then. And, if I may ask,
are you the same Sharon O'Mara that helped to bring down the
handbag forgery and the slave ring?"

This was the first time she had been recognized for her professional work; she was flattered, but concerned. "Mr. Blanco,
I'm the same person. But if you value this event, I would caution
you about telling anyone, for now. I will move it if necessary."

"I understand," Blanco said, chastened. "My question was
never asked, and thank you for thinking of us, see you Monday
morning at 9:00."

It was her goal to keep it below the radar, which was Alain's
hope. Saul Goldfarb and his family would do what they had to
do, but she would be prepared this time.

The meeting with Mr. Blanco went well; a large raised dais
would be set along one wall, chairs arranged like a theater,
proper microphones and power as needed, no refreshments, just
ice water; the presentation would be quick and efficient. If there
were drinks and food, the crowd would just hang around hoping for a scoop. He suggested that hotel security be present.

"For your hotel and your guests, that will be fine. I will have
my own security; please don't worry about the art, that's our
concern. We'll also assist the family after the presentation," Sharon said. "I'll call with the specifics on Thursday."

"And we have reserved rooms for your guests as requested,

five suites, again, thank you. It will be an excellent event. Thank you and I understand about the security."

She gave Blanco the Swiss card number and signed the necessary documents.

"I will see you on Friday morning at 6:30, as arranged."

The week hardly dragged, every minute was taken up by some aspect of the presentation. The paintings were removed from the vault and properly secured in crates; she did this herself, under the watchful eyes of Dumont. He continued to chatter away about the paintings and other businesses he had been involved with over the years. Remy came and went. He never made a comment about the artwork; he attended to Dumont's needs and medication. To O'Mara, Dumont seemed to grow younger, like a burden was being lifted from him. He even stood taller when out of his wheelchair.

"Are you sure you don't want to attend?" O'Mara asked, for the fourth time.

"No, my dear. This body could not stand the strain or the excitement. It's an activity for the young, all this hub-bub and most especially the questions. No, no. I'll watch it from here. You will have the camera set up?"

"Yes, closed circuit, but my guess is there will be TV crews as well. But to see it live, I'll route it through the Internet; you can watch on your computer."

"Ah, the wonders of this age. I was the initial investor and I'm still a major stockholder of the company that owns that technology. Starting to turn a nice profit, even though private; I shouldn't tell you but one of the really big boys is sniffing around. If that happens, I am going to make a bunch of young geeks very wealthy," he laughed. "Very, very, wealthy, and it won't hurt my bottom line either."

O'Mara arranged for an armored truck to arrive quietly in the middle of the night and transfer the crates to an intermediary well-secured warehouse. As the paintings left, she watched as Alain Dumont caressed the four boxes, as they were carried to the truck, and heard him say goodbye, like they were his children.

"I held them for a while and it was my privilege. I'll miss them, but they will never leave me."

At the warehouse, she placed the smaller crates in non-descript cardboard boxes, labeled as canned fruit. The large Lautrec was covered with a cardboard sleeve that said, "display materials – convention." At five o'clock a.m., Kevin Bryan entered the warehouse; the high windows were still dark.

"Ready?" he asked.

"As I will ever be, been a long week. A drink at the end of the day will be my reward."

"The armored trucks are due at 6:00, good call on another company. Helps to buffer Dumont, I hope. I wonder if they'll question why fruit boxes are going to the hotel and the need for security."

"I told them, when I reserved the trucks that it was for a new release of a special fruit product, very hush-hush; lots of concern about what's being announced. I got the idea from the hotel's meeting schedule; Central Valley Fruit Packers is having a meeting at the hotel. I'm hoping to lose the delivery under the ruse of their conference."

"I'm with the truck?" Bryan asked, confirming her directions.

"That's your job, ride shotgun. I know your taste in art tends toward velvet buxomed babes, so I know they'll be safe."

"I'm hurt. I know Art, I really do, and he's a primo bartender at Pier 23."

"Don't let Gina know you're seeing other bartenders, she wouldn't be happy."

"After this's over, we'll reconvene at her place. That work?"

"Works for me."

At five minutes to six the armored car arrived at the warehouse, the loading took less than two minutes; they waited until 6:15. Five minutes later they were heading across San Francisco. The early sun had risen before the commuters; the streets were wide open and the trip took twelve minutes. O'Mara had timed it earlier; they beat her earlier time by three minutes. They pulled up to the loading dock at the rear of the hotel; Mr. Blanco was already there, waiting for the delivery. O'Mara pulled in behind the armored truck in her new Jaguar.

"Very nice car, Ms. O'Mara, I'll have my valet park it. Is the fruit ready?"

"Yes it is; and it's very ripe," she said. He laughed at her joke.

The driver left the cab and walked to the double rear doors. Bryan came around the corner of the truck and waved at Sharon; as she started to wave back, Bryan turned his head and looked down Sacramento Street, squinting into the early sun.

The noise of motorbikes filled the air over the grinding of the cable car cables on Hyde Street. Sunrise threw a shaft of light up the canyon of buildings from downtown; it illuminated Bryan's arms as he raised them. Before O'Mara could pull her own pistol, four men drove into the loading dock, each carried a 9mm automatic pistol, all wore full helmets and no one left their motorbikes.

"Open up," the tallest ordered. The motorbike roared between his legs, grey smoke began to fill the dock from the four motorbikes; a slight German accent covered his English. "Now! Everyone else, down on the floor."

Mr. Blanco fell to the floor, O'Mara, Bryan and the driver dropped slowly to one knee, then the other. O'Mara took in everything, their clothing, pistols, shoes, everything. The leader wore a gold ring with a red center; it looked like a cross of some kind, the rider's hands were large, yet feminine.

"On the floor, now," she bellowed. O'Mara lay flat on the cold concrete. The stains on her black blouse would never come out.

The double doors of the armored truck swung open, the interior guard, not seeing the four riders, jumped down from the rear of the truck. The closest thief pistol-whipped the guard to the floor. He never saw it coming.

Just outside, on the street, a van screeched to a stop; its rear door flew open, two hooded men bailed out and immediately headed to the armored truck. One climbed in and slid the boxes out; they were quickly loaded in the van. It sped away as fast as it arrived.

"Do not move," the only one who spoke ordered. "The first face I see will be shot."

The motorbikes roared out of the dock and onto the street, two went up Sacramento and two went down, against the traffic; they swerved and just missed a Muni transit bus grinding up the hill. O'Mara ran to the sidewalk and watched each cycle turn a different direction on Hyde Street; she could still hear their engines roaring up the canyon walls of the buildings.

"Shit," was all she could say, as Bryan ran to her side.

"How the hell did that happen?" Bryan yelled. "No one knew; no one had any idea where they were coming from, when we'd get here, no one."

"Well someone did, this was a team, well disciplined, precise. What did it take, less than a minute? Then they were gone, goddamnit, goddamn it to hell." Her phone buzzed, and started to ring, the caller ID said 'Dumont'.

"Alain?"

"Sharon," she could barely hear his voice, it was garbled. "Come fast, they broke in, I'm in the vault elevator, just escaped but I have a slug in my back, and it ain't pretty."

"Kevin, my car now, Dumont's been shot. Mr. Blanco, give the Goldfarbs as much information as you can, tell them I'll be back, hopefully later this morning."

She pulled out onto Sacramento and headed west, she flew through Van Ness, turned onto Divisadero and then left on Broadway, Kevin was on his phone to the San Francisco police as they made the twenty-four blocks in minutes. Her phone rang. No ID.

"What?" she yelled.

"Ms. O'Mara, it is unfortunate about Monsieur Dumont, but he has something I want. I will trade you the paintings for the case, I will call you later, remember, I want the case, and Monsieur Dumont knows where that case is." The accent was again German, and female.

"What the hell? Kevin, now there's a ransom involved, some broad wants to trade the paintings for a case; I have no idea what she's talking about."

"She?"

"Yes, seems our art bandit's a woman."

They pulled up to the Dumont house; the door was wide open. Weapons drawn, they quickly searched the main floor. One body was found in the hallway leading to the library.

"For an old man, he can still shoot," Kevin said, as they worked their way deeper into the house. In the library, she found blood on the carpet, and splatter on the wall near the panel. She put her hand on the glass, the scan flashed and the door opened immediately. Dumont was slumped in the corner of the elevator, a small pool of blood had started to form on the marble floor, his hand held a Luger; he was still breathing hard through the nose prongs.

"Alain, Alain," Sharon said softly, her lips close to his ear, "Alain?" Sharon held Dumont's head and caressed his cheek tenderly; sirens roared outside through the wooded confines of upper Broadway.

"I'm here my dear, just barely, but still here; there's something you must do for me, it's very important." He inhaled and exhaled slowly, blood appeared in the corner of his mouth. "I may die, or not, I don't know. I may only have a few minutes left rather than the few days we talked about. There is something you must find in Paris; it's hidden but you need to find it and keep it away from the Nazis. Sharon, my dear, warn the world, they're back."

3d

"Are you all right, Mr. Blanco? Not exactly the way I was expecting the day to go, is it?" O'Mara said as she walked back into the hotel late that afternoon; the press vans had left, only one blond beach boy looking reporter was holding the fort in the lobby. She saw Saul Goldfarb's bald head. If the event was anywhere else but the Fairmont, the reporter would have left hours ago.

"I'm fine, but the Goldfarbs are not exactly happy; as you might imagine."

"I can *only* imagine, Mr. Blanco. Where are they?"

"I believe Saul Goldfarb is talking the ear off that reporter, and the others, after the press and the police questioned them, returned to their rooms."

"Thank you." Sharon caught Saul's eye and he quickly separated himself from the reporter and crossed the lobby; he was obviously not amused by the events.

"What the fuck happened? I thought you had everything under control, you said everything would be taken care of, you said…"

"Saul," she wiggled her finger for him to step closer, and she whispered quite distinctly, *"Shut-the-fuck-up!"*

"What did you say?"

"I said, and I will repeat it slowly so even you can understand me, *shut-the-fuck-up*. I may lose a very good friend this evening, and since that gentleman owns those paintings, you had better pray to God, or whatever you hold high, that he doesn't die. Those paintings, if recovered, are still his. If he dies, the complications of ownership, probate, donations, and a hundred other things, may keep those paintings off the wall of your home and away from your family for a decade. And if you continue to scream and make a scene, I will make every effort to make sure that happens. Now, Mr. Goldfarb, do we understand each other?"

"Well, I've never been treated so coarsely," Saul Goldfarb said.

"Yes, you have; you've treated others worse," Zoe Goldfarb-Binder said, as she walked up to the pair.

"Zoe, are you okay?" Sharon asked.

"Me, you're the one who was robbed by a gang of thugs. We were all having breakfast, telling each other how fortunate we were, while you could have been killed. And what's this about another man being shot?"

"The owner of the paintings was at his house. Thirty minutes before we were robbed, he was being terrorized in his home and was shot. It happened just minutes after we left his house with the artwork. He's at the hospital, in a coma, and he may not live. I was just telling Saul the facts; he has difficulty understanding things."

"I understand, do you Saul?" Zoe asked, turning on Saul. "Do you understand? Again, it's not just about you and your reputation; there are other things, bigger things, than all that stuff."

Saul, rage starting to build, spun away from the two women, and walked away; he waved off the blond headed man from the press and headed to the bar.

"The time he's spent with a shrink is working; five years ago he would have gone ballistic; he's better now," Zoe said.

"Better? Thought he was going to have a stroke," O'Mara said.

"Already had a small heart attack, life style choices and genetics are a tough road for him. But are you alright?"

"Yes, I'm fine and I've been through far worse. I'm sorry about the paintings, we're doing everything we can to find them, and I have a friend and colleague still at the gentleman's home, trying to piece together what happen. As I said, Alain is now in a coma."

"Alain?"

"I forgot that I never told you the benefactor's name, I'm sure he wouldn't mind now. And now that the police are involved, it will be in tomorrow's paper. I think even your brother could figure it out. The owner of the paintings is Alain Dumont."

"The billionaire, that Alain Dumont?"

"Yes."

"Incredible, his foundation gave our hospital over a hundred million dollars to expand the children's care facility; I even met him once maybe ten years ago. Unbelievable!"

"Yes, he's a phenomenal man and has lived an amazing life, let's hope that you can say thank you to him," O'Mara said. "Alain emphasized that the paintings belong to the Goldfarb family, and it's still my job to see that it happens. But it's more complicated now." She scanned the sparse crowd in the lobby, the press beach boy was motioning to her, and he wanted a story. But, in the shadow of one of the great lobby pillars, a man stood, sharp and angular, with a shock of black hair; broad farm boy shoulders supported a face she knew, but couldn't place. *"Who the hell is he and where do I know him from? Damn he's familiar."* Then it changed to: *"Why the hell is he here?"*

Bobby Gillis stood off to one side, stunned by who he saw in the lobby. A wave of hot dry air gusting over burnt sand blew through his nose; not real, but only too real. *"The lieutenant, shit, why the hell is she here?"* He reached for his pistol, but it wasn't there; it hadn't been there for five years. But seeing her made him want his pistol; he remembered that day… every day. It would be embedded in his mind deeply for the rest of his life.

Chapter 4

Otto Speyer stood near the window of his ranch, overlooking the dormant vineyards that rolled up the Argentine slopes toward the extinct volcano; Tupungato, the town by the same name, lay to the right in the valley. He sat the glass of Malbec on the window sill, and waited for the call, *"She's late, she should have called by now, the morning is getting on. There's only a four hour difference, it's almost lunch; she should have the paintings or the box, I've waited sixty years, but she's late!"*

The cell phone, clenched in his hand, started to buzz.

"Ja, gut, ja, er wurde erschossen, hast du die Kiste? . . . Nein, es finden." Speyer hung up and took another sip of the blood red wine, *"I hope the kid didn't screw it up, our future depends on that box. I've always been hard on my granddaughter, but she's a good girl, a true believer. She'll become a good leader. She can lead this family back to what is its blood right, 'Blut Recht, unsere Heimat,' our homeland, our new homeland."* A tear coursed down the hard tanned cheek, and hung for a moment on the scar that cut from below his right ear to the tip of his chin. *"Blut Recht, unsere Heimat,"* SS Oberstgruppenführer Otto Speyer said, as he took another sip of wine.

He had waited for this day for over thirty years since Madrid, hundreds of false leads had been followed; men were lost trying to find the box, good men, true men. But this lead, this one man, a German, changed everything, all through a chance meeting three years before by his granddaughter when she was in San Francisco at a wine conference. It was an introduction at a party by a friend; the man was Franco-German and very good-looking. He was shocked to hear someone speaking German.

He smiled. "My name is Remy Adler, from your accent you maybe don't live in Germany?"

"Margrite Speyer, my family owns vineyards around Mendoza, Argentina. I'm here for the conference and meetings with our publicity people. It's a pleasure to meet you."

The wine turned to dinner and conversations about Argentina and California. "Strange how we ended up here," Speyer said. "You from the Alsace, me from Argentina, and we meet in San Francisco, yet our families are German. My grandfather moved to Argentina before the war, he didn't like the direction Germany was going in the 1930s, so he left and started his vineyards; he was one of the first. It's a good life and allows us to travel the world. He named the winery after his family's winery in Germany, Trittenheim. That's why you see the large Old German script 'T' on the label, strong don't you think?"

"Very strong, does catch your eye," Remy said, continuing to smile, struck by his luck; the woman was striking, and lacking a wedding ring, maybe single. The only jewelry she wore was a large gold ring with an inlaid cross on its crest, and a Rolex. *"And she has money,"* he thought.

"My full time job is private nurse and assistant. I met the gentleman in Paris. I worked in Germany and Paris, easy with the EU structure, and I was placed with this very elderly man, he liked me, and asked if I would like to work with him full time, so here I am, and so are you. Tell me more, is there a Mr. Speyer?"

"No, only my grandfather, I've been much too busy to settle down, get married, and have children; my family is our company."

Over the next year, they saw each other every time Speyer was in California; Remy even went to Los Angeles to spend a weekend with Margrite. He believed they were getting close; he even hoped there might be a future with her. But Alain Dumont was an ongoing challenge; he kept him busy. Then Dumont started to change, he became more secretive, would disappear into his private study for days, then emerge tired and drawn. Then he collapsed.

"Remy, please call for the doctor," Dumont said over the house intercom, "I need you. The elevator is open, please come down."

He found him shaking on the leather couch in the most glorious room he had ever been in. He attended to his needs and was able to get him up the elevator; Dumont told him the backup code and he punched it in, his doctor arrived and they left for a private hospital Dumont had funded. He walked back into the elevator and returned to the study.

"He has the most wonderful collection of art," Remy said, trying to impress Margrite Speyer.

"Who?" Speyer asked.

"My employer, Alain Dumont. He has Renoirs', and Pissaros', and this huge Toulouse-Lautrec, all hidden in a private room that's impossible to break into. He's very old, he was originally from France but has lived in California since the early 1950s, he is the nicest man, but I shouldn't be telling you this; your wine has just made me quite talkative."

"Toulouse-Lautrec has always been one of my favorites," Margrite Speyer said. "Now there's a man that knew how to party, we aren't like that in Argentina, we're more serious." She raised the glass of her family's wine and toasted Remy.

"I've never been there, is it nice?"

"Very beautiful, simple, quiet, the mountains are like a wall to the west, and the sunsets are spectacular. Someday you'll be my guest and I'll show you my vineyards," Speyer said, taking Remy's hand, his blue eyes never left the beautiful Argentine's face.

"They may be the ones, Grandfather. The Lautrec might be the one in the lost bundle, and if so, there may be a connection. If I can get him to take a picture, then we'll know."

For the next few weeks, Margrite Speyer continued to woo Remy; she could see he was smitten; she used it to her advantage. She bought him a book on Toulouse-Lautrec; she discussed his style and his paintings, especially the Moulin Rouge.

"I saw the Lautrec painting of the Moulin Rouge in Chicago a few months ago during a wine buyer's meeting, it's wonderful," Speyer said.

"You saw it! I've only seen pictures. Did the woman really have a blue face?" Remy asked.

"As blue as the sky over Mendoza, but with pink lipstick," Speyer said, laughing.

"As much as I like that painting, it's not as nice as the one Mr. Dumont has. It's maybe four feet by six feet, you feel like you can walk into it. And it's so colorful, just like a party, a photo frozen forever."

"It would be something to see," Speyer said.

"Well, I know that Mr. Dumont would never let that happen and I've only seen it once."

"More's the pity. Wine?" Speyer asked, changing the subject. "This is a vintage Malbec, it's rich, yet soft." She poured Remy a glass.

"Wonderful, and the color, superb; maybe I can sneak in and take a picture; he'll be away for some tests at Stanford next week, so maybe I'll try."

"Please don't, you'll get in trouble if he finds out. It's a trivial thing, please don't bother."

"I'll see. I know you would love to see a picture of the painting, let's see what I can do."

Alain Dumont was away for two days for his tests, age had taken its toll. He had neglected to change the complicated numbering sequence he had temporarily given Remy. Remy remembered it from his emergency visit and took another tour of the study. The paintings still took his breath away, especially the young girl in the Mary Cassatt painting. He took a series of photos and quickly returned to the main floor. He had to wait two weeks before Margrite Speyer returned.

"Isn't it everything that I told you?" Remy asked, setting the photos on the small table at Perry's.

Speyer was briefly stunned and then recovered, "It's beautiful, you were right, it's one of the best I've ever seen. And these others were with it?"

"Oh, yes. These Renoirs' and Pissarros' are hung next to it, like they belonged together. Mr. Dumont was away and I quickly took the photos. If he were to find out, I would lose my job."

"I'm sure you'll be fine, now what else did you do while I was away; I missed you."

That evening, Margrite Speyer talked to her grandfather; she had to wake the elderly man.

"Grandfather, it is the painting and the Renoirs' and the Pissarros' are also with it. Unbelievable luck, they're all together. Do you think the case is also with them?"

"Very possible," Otto Speyer said. "None of the artifacts or the materials in the case ever surfaced, just as these paintings were never found. Let's hope that the case is with them. His employer, as you know, is an incredibly rich man and would have the resources to protect their privacy as well as his. See what else you can find out."

What Margrite Speyer found out from Remy and the Los Angeles Times was that Dumont was going to return the paintings to a family in Los Angeles, a Jewish family. Remy told Margrite everything he had overheard during O'Mara's meetings with Dumont. The conversation was extremely painful for Remy.

4b

March, 1945

SS Sturmbannführer Otto Speyer stood patiently outside the Führer's office waiting to be summoned, his Prussian heritage obvious to the staff that quickly walked up and down the corridor. For the past eight years, of his twenty-six, he had been a devoted member of the party and a true believer in the man behind the door and the cause of his nation. Speyer's family, for ten generations, had loyally served the regents and leaders of Prussia and Germany, and he was honored to be alive to serve the greatest of all Germany's leaders. Why he was summoned, he didn't know, but whatever was wanted of him, he would perform his duties to the fullest, or die trying.

The door opened and SS Obersturmbannführer Otto Skorzeny quickly stepped into the hall, "Come Otto, I have something important for you to do."

Speyer looked through the door expectantly, "No, my boy, not today. The Führer has left, and you're lucky; today he's not in a good mood; you would not want to attend to his needs. Things are difficult these days, he has left for meetings. Come, my boy," Skorzeny said, he stopped and looked hard into the young man's face and smiled at the long welt on his right cheek. "I have always liked your name and especially your scar. We have much in common, don't we? Your *Schmiss* was by a left-handed swordsman, mine by a right-handed one, there's much, I think, between us."

Speyer, noticeably stiffened by the unsolicited praise, clicked his heels and followed Skorzeny into a small office directly behind the Führer's. A long table spanned the room, an elegant carved oak case sat in the middle, a swastika carved into its face, polished handles were mounted on each side, and a bright clasp held the lid in place, there was no lock.

"You are to deliver this case to the Führer's home in Berchtesgaden as fast as possible. You will travel alone, you will be given papers guaranteeing your passage, and you will dress as a simple Obersturmführer so as not to attract notice. You know the German roads and you know how to travel under the present conditions. The skies are not Germany's anymore, so you must be careful. This would have been transported by plane a year ago, but not anymore."

As Skorzeny finished, two soldiers walked into the room with a drab wooden box, 'Trittenheim' was written on its side, the oak case fit neatly inside.

"May I ask what's inside, sir?" Speyer asked, smiling at the case that once held wine from his own family's vineyard.

"I will tell you this much, my friend, what is in here," Skorzeny said, as he placed his hand on the case, "will control how we return to power and how the world will again fear the

Reich. There are mementos of the Führer, personal items, and a small box that must not fall into the hands of the enemy. There are also two rolls of paintings that belong to Reichsmarschall Goering; they are to go with the case. There are other safeguards in place, but there is no need to allow the enemy to think there is more. The box contains only half the information, I have the other half, at some point, God willing, I will find you and we will put them back together."

"I understand, sir," Speyer said.

"Take the best route you can to the south, travel only when it's safe," Skorzeny said. "I hope that, if aircraft are patrolling, they won't waste ammunition on a small staff car; you will use a Kubelwagen. It's waiting outside near the service entrance; these soldiers will show you where; there's food and extra gas on board. It's my hope that you don't stop for more than a moment to take a piss. They're expecting you at Berchtesgaden; they will inform me when you arrive. Good luck Otto, make us proud. Heil Hitler!"

With a click of his heels, SS Sturmbannführer Otto Speyer saluted Skorzeny, nodded to the soldiers who hefted the box and left the room.

That was two days ago; Otto Speyer now sat in a barn watching the rain bounce off the hood of the Kubelwagen, smoking a cigarette. It was his first break since he left Berlin; he needed at least three hours of sleep before he could go on. The map showed him the route, he was allowed freedom to deviate, but he hadn't counted on a deviation of over fifty miles. The P-38s and English Spitfires forced him to use smaller roads and the thin, early spring tree cover gave little protection. He also ran into the opposing problems of advancing troops and retreating wounded. The advance already looked as defeated as the retreating men.

Berchtesgaden, during the summer months, was a trip of over four hundred miles; with the war, it would be almost twice as long and a thousand times more dangerous. His map marked the village of Merkers as a safe zone, nothing more, *"Safe from what? Three others are noted further south, if I live long enough to get that far,"* was all he could think in his exhausted condition.

At the last checkpoint he was told the Allies were less than fifty miles away, near Geissen. Even a fool could see that he would be cut off before he could make his next stop. Only highways of death stretched ahead of him.

Crushing his cigarette, he drove to Merkers, hoping the thick foggy weather would keep the Allied planes out of the air. A small group of SS officers stood outside a small building; from the signage, it was a makeshift headquarters.

"Your commanding officer, please," Speyer said, addressing the officers. He could see worry and fear in their eyes, "Now! This is Berlin business, and salute, you dogs."

"To a puke Obersturmführer, fuck you."

Speyer caught himself before he reached for his sidearm, he had forgotten his demotion for the job, but their attitude still pissed him off.

"He's in there," the lieutenant said, pointing to the door.

Hunched over the desk was the Sturmbannführer of the Merkers outpost, a half bottle of schnapps sat to one side; Speyer had never seen a man more exhausted in his life.

"And what the fuck do you want, Obersturmführer? And from the cut of your clothes, you've seen a tailor recently, my guess, Berlin. So, what do you want? It better be nothing more than a chunk of sausage, because that's all I have, and along with this case of schnapps, one or both will be finished before tomorrow morning."

"I don't need food; I'm fine but you're drunk on duty, that's punishable by death," Speyer said.

"We'll all face that either tomorrow or the next day; the Americans are near Bad Hersfeld; they'll be here, my guess, by tomorrow. For us and for you, the war is over and I can forget this fucking hole in the ground," the captain said. "Then maybe I'll get some sleep."

"What hole in the ground?"

"Son, I have the whole goddamned German treasury buried a half mile under our feet, be careful where you step, you might trip over a gold bar." The captain poured another glass of schnapps and offered it to Speyer.

"Nein."

"Nein now, ja tomorrow, we'll see."

The captain told Speyer about the caves, that they were as secure as possible. Maybe the advance would sweep past them. Being a prisoner of the Allies would be a lot better than being a prisoner of the Russians. At least with the Americans, they might have a future. Reports said the roads to the south were now closed; the American advance moved in fifty to one hundred mile jumps each day. Speyer would have to hide the box and the paintings.

"I can only offer my hole in the ground and the hope that the Americans don't find it. But, I assure you, your little box will be lost down there. Come, let me show you," the captain said, grinning. Speyer thought his grin was like that of the cat in *Alice in Wonderland*, years later he would only remember the smile, not the man.

Speyer was shocked, what fool came up with this idea; only a bureaucrat in Berlin would have thought this version of Dante's inferno would protect the accumulated wealth of Germany's treasury, but it was all they had. He left the rough wine box and rolls of canvas near the elevator; if he had a chance he could retrieve them quickly and escape. It never happened.

The next morning, the largest army to cross Europe rolled over the countryside of central Germany on its way to Leipzig and Nuremberg. SS Obersturmführer Otto Speyer found himself held, along with the other SS officers, in a fenced pigpen, his boots sinking mid-calf in shit. The Americans, thousands of them, raced by in jeeps, tanks, and trucks. The soldiers were well-fed, many wore new uniforms. Otto Speyer knew they could not defeat this army; it would have to wait for another time.

Speyer also learned of their arrogance, after the Americans discovered the cache in the mines. As they passed by, they would make rude gestures, pretending to shoot them, even drawing their hands across their necks. One even pissed on them over the fence. At least the men he was with were good soldiers, all strong SS leaders; he was proud of them. Even the Sturmban-nführer, the captain, stood his ground; at least they would die like soldiers.

The chaos of the past three days was punctuated by one of the most bizarre parades Speyer had ever seen. They were placed near a building to be viewed by Patton and Eisenhower before the American generals were given a tour of the tunnels. Patton took one look at the prisoners, and in a strange moment, he saluted them. Two days later, they were marshaled together to be moved out. As they stood in loose formation, an American corporal singled him out, and, in excellent German, harangued and swore at him; he ignored the soldier and looked above him at the hills of Germany; he was just one more American show-ing how tough he was. The next day, they found themselves in a prison camp full of SS officers; even the American knew not to mix the SS with typical German soldiers.

The next six months were a blur for Speyer, but just before Christmas he was released and allowed to return to his home, Trittenheim. He hoped he would make it early enough to trim the grapes before the spring. While waiting for his transit pa-pers, he was re-arrested and charged with war crimes, being an SS officer was all that was needed. He was told the courts would sort it out; he waited for another six months, justice could wait; he could not. The loss of the Führer's case gnawed at him. *"Was it swept up in the caravan to Frankfort, was it taken as some Ameri-can's war booty or was it just lost?"* He never found out.

But Otto Skorzeny found him, the leader saw him at a trans-fer camp while Speyer met with lawyers, his trial would take place six months from their meeting, the time stretched into the summer of 1948. In July, Skorzeny told him to be ready to leave, and, in the custody of US Military police, they left the camp. Three miles outside the barbed wire, Skorzeny started to laugh, the guards started to laugh and, to Speyer's surprise, they spoke German. Their escape was complete. A month later, Otto Speyer found himself on a freighter leaving Genoa on his way to Argentina, a free man.

4c

The Present

Speyer sipped his coffee and looked up toward the Andes, they weren't as formidable as the Alps, but they comforted him. The alluvial soils were perfect for the Malbec grapes that grew in long rows that stretched to the base of the rocky hills. For almost fifty years, he and his family raised grapes on these hills and cattle on the grasslands to the east. He hadn't changed his name like many that spent a night at the ranch as they traveled secretly through South America. He had been an excellent soldier but not a fighter. Wars had to be fought both in the trenches and the offices of the Reich.

The paintings were the clue that set his machinery into operation. For half a century, he hoped that they would surface; he knew if the paintings were found the case would be near. Now, even an old man could hope that the dreams of Skorzeny, and others that had often stopped at his bodega, might come true, a rebirth of the Reich here, in Argentina, a land that had been the new fatherland for his dead son and his more-than-willing granddaughter.

"Margrite, I will tell you a story," Otto Speyer said to his ten-year old granddaughter, as they sat on the porch of the bodega more than twenty years earlier. He told the young girl about Germany, the war, the righteousness of their cause and their belief in the future of a new Reich, the return to power of the new German race.

These stories were told to Margrite Speyer many times; she grew into a vivacious young woman, believing in her race and its inherent strength. Her father and grandfather toured South America, Brazil, Uruguay, Paraguay, and other ranches in Argentina and met quietly, over glasses of wine and schnapps, with others of the same belief. These men and women formed the nucleus of the extended family that held Margrite Speyer to their bosom; they comforted her after her father's accident. They met to discuss strategy after one from their group was captured and returned to Germany, or worse, secreted into Israel. The war left memories that would last long past the final soldier's death. But the Holy Grail, to Margrite, was the case described in a letter left to her when she was just a baby by Otto Skorzeny and the stories her grandfather told of the tunnels under Merkers. The case held relics of the Führer and the box held the keys to the great secret wealth of the Reich. This lost case fired her imagination and stoked embers in another part of her brain, embers that smoldered with the words *unimagined wealth*.

"Yes Grandfather, I have retrieved the paintings, and they're exactly as you said. They're the same ones you described that were on the inventory sheet Herr Skorzeny gave you. And I must say they are wonderful paintings, especially the Lautrec. It is spectacular."

"Was there a fight?" Speyer asked.

"We surprised them at the hotel, our men were in and out in less than a minute; the shock on their faces was something to see. Their leader, a strong looking woman, was stunned, but she quickly recovered; we were gone before it got messy."

"And how did it go at the house?"

"It didn't go as well. Dumont was alone, the key and code I took from Remy got us in, but an alarm or something alerted the man. He was sitting in a large chair in his study when we entered, two team members and myself.

"You are here for the case, I assume?" the old man asked.

"Where is it?" I demanded. "We know you have it, I'm here to take back what's ours."

"Everything in that case was evil and taken by force from those you conquered and murdered."

"No matter, old man, all we want is the case and you will live out what miserable few years you have left. What happens after that will not be a concern of yours."

"Not true, young woman, it has been a great concern to me for over sixty years; I have prepared my whole life to prevent you and your kind from recovering that information. Like you,

I believe in legacies, futures that go on long after we are dead, positive futures. Yours' is one of blood and death."

"Our new Reich will live for a thousand years," I said.

"And how did that Third Reich of your grandfathers' work out?" the old fool answered.

"Grandfather, the arrogance of the man, but he would not stop," Margrite continued.

"If I remember correctly, it lasted barely fifteen years, hardly a thousand, and it had a charismatic leader to boot. Even as beautiful as you are, I hardly think you could lead a takeover of Germany and return it to its past." I watched him carefully as he slowly stood and pulled the oxygen tubes from his nose, then I noticed a luger held close to his side.

"We have designs other than Germany. It's nothing more than a communistic puppet state, sure they say it's a social democracy, but there's no strength, it's lost its way, it acts as a nursemaid to Europe. We will be different."

"That's what every thug government says when they take over, 'We will be different.'"

"Enough! Where is the case?" I demanded.

"Young woman, it's not here, and, in fact, it's not even on this continent. Yes, I have it, and, if you kill me, you will never find it, never."

"At that Grandfather, he quickly went to the wall of the study, placed a hand on a panel and an elevator door opened. He pointed the luger at us and fired, the closest man went down, I returned his fire; I know I hit him before the door of the elevator closed. Please tell Eric's parents that he died for the cause.

"Eric, he was a good boy, I will. Did you get to Dumont?"

"We tried to find a way in for ten minutes, but that fool Remy was right, only one way in and he controls it, for all I know, he's dead in that elevator. I went to the backup plan and we headed to the hotel; we found them at the loading dock. We couldn't take Eric, we were on motorbikes."

"Get the paintings to the safe location. You said there was a woman in charge of the return of the paintings?"

"Yes, Remy was most helpful. He said that her name is Sharon O'Mara. After a little checking, we found out that she's a private detective or something like that. She was in the papers recently, a couple of incidents at the port of Oakland, dealing with gangs. She seems to be competent even if we catch her off-guard."

"I know you, Margrite, stay away from her. She will not be caught off-guard again," the older Speyer said.

"It's my guess that she may know where the case is; Remy said she was meeting with Dumont, preparing for the presentation. He was given the last three days off, it surprised him, Dumont depended on him."

"This O'Mara woman was all the help he needed."

"I called her after we left the house; she was in a car, probably going to Dumont's. I think he called her, so maybe he was alive then. I offered to trade the paintings for the case. She acted like she didn't know what I was talking about; maybe so, but she will find out. Then we can act."

"Excellent Margrite, excellent, and Remy?"

"Sadly, I think Monsieur Dumont will be looking for a new nurse, Monsieur Adler will not be able to return to his employer."

Chapter 5

5a

For two days, Sharon sat at Alain Dumont's bedside. The oxygen prongs were still in place, but instead of the tubes she was familiar with, he was now attached to IV drips of morphine and saline solutions. She was amazed they could find a vein in his withered arms, but she also admired the strength of the man. She had never met anyone with a tougher will to live.

"You need to go home and get some sleep; Basil is wondering where you are. He isn't taking this well, mopes around and barely touches his food," Kevin Bryan said. "We'll get the bastards."

"Damn straight we will, they'll pay for all this crap, one way or another."

"You need to talk with Evelyn, she's going crazy and is on her way back from Italy, wants to see you as soon as she arrives."

"I'm sure she does, seems bad things happen when I get mixed up in someone else's life," Sharon said.

"And good things too, there're a lot people out there that are very happy that you did stick your nose into their business."

"I guess so, hard to be comforted with Alain lying here."

"I know, I talked to the San Francisco detectives handling the break-in and the hotel, they've put them together, considering it one case."

"Makes sense."

"You said there was a nurse, Remy was his name?" Bryan asked.

"Yes, Remy Adler, German-French, Alain hired him in Paris and then brought him here. Why, did you find him, does he know anything about all this?"

"We'll never know; they fished his body off the rocks of Trea-

sure Island. They threw him in the Bay after torturing and killing him. The coroner says it happened sometime before the hotel
and the attack at Dumont's house. Chances are he was the source
of the information; when they didn't need him, they killed him."

Dumont moved his arm slightly, Sharon took his hand. He
opened his eyes, his lips tried to form words, he inhaled slowly.

"Alain?" Sharon said, getting closer.

"Sharon, my dear," his voice barely audible, "are you back
from Paris, did you get it? Please tell me you did, please. They
must not find it."

"No, I haven't gone yet. I've been here with you."

"I don't matter; you must go to Paris and get the case. They
must not find it. Forget about me, get the case." Dumont turned
his head toward Bryan. "I heard what you said, Remy was a dear
friend and he didn't deserve this. Young man, you need to take
Sharon to Paris and get the case, or else the world will suffer the
way Remy did." Dumont inhaled slowly and closed his eyes.
The steady beating of the monitor continued.

"He is a tough son-of-a-bitch, Sharon, a tough soldier."

The nurse came into the room and checked the tubes and the
various devices, she noted a few things on the tablet computer
and left. She had tried to get O'Mara to leave twice before and
didn't try again.

"There is someone in the lounge that wants to see you, Ms.
O'Mara," she said as she left the room.

"Who?"

"Didn't say, but he's good-looking, dearie, very good-looking," she said, glancing at Bryan.

"And I'm what? What?" Bryan said.

"Calm down Kevin, she doesn't know you that well. Let's
go see who's in the lounge. Are you okay Alain? Do you need
anything?"

"Just the case, just the case, it's in my apartment, you'll know
where. The address is in my vault, in a book in the drawer; you'll
figure it out. I'll be better when you get back," he offered with a
smile, and closed his eyes.

Bobby Gillis paced around the lounge; he had put off this meeting for two days since he saw O'Mara in the hotel, the time for a reckoning had come. He watched her step out of the elevator, another fellow, very tall and lanky, dark head of black hair, followed her. He watched her scan the lobby, how many times had he watched those same eyes look over a situation and then make the right decision; he rubbed his eyes as if Iraqi sand had found its way into their corners…

* * * *

Outside Fallujah, Iraq – Six Years Earlier

"Sergeant," O'Mara said, as she hunkered behind the bullet pitted mud wall. "Move your men there, hold the corner. I'll take my boys, and flank them, there. Ralph, is the drone up?"

"Yes Ma'am, high and loose, screen says six maybe seven outside, can't tell how many inside. Not expecting company."

"Good, let's ruin their breakfast. Gillis, when you're ready let me know, on my count, hit them. Ralph, signal the drone," O'Mara said.

"Roger," Ralph said, satellite phone to his ear.

For the next ten minutes, the two squads moved cautiously, yet expertly to their flanking positions. O'Mara had a 50 caliber machine gun set up on the roof of the central building, its field of fire washed over every foot of open land to the east and west of the enemy's position. The enemy's only option was to move north into the building's shadow, or die.

"That son-of-a-bitch better be there, Gillis. I don't want to shoot this place up and find out that fucking reporter isn't in that building. Those idiots always think they know better, I'm just a neutral guy, just trying to get a story, get the truth. 'So Mr. al-Qaeda, leader sir, can you please tell me why you hate the west, you know we're only here to help you rid this country of Saddam Hussein.'"

Bobby Gillis laughed, "Naïve and stupid, now we have to get his ass out of that hole; if one my guys' gets shot, I will personally cut that SOB's head off." He moved his squad out.

O'Mara sat with her back against the wall and looked into the dusty sky, two vultures circled overhead, she thought of the drone.

"Ralph, ready?"

"Yes, Lieutenant, ready. They have target locked."

"Gillis, okay?" she said into her shoulder mike.

"Five by five. Ready, set, waiting for go."

"At the strike, hit 'em hard."

"Ralph, call it," O'Mara said.

The corporal held the phone to his face, and simply said, "Now!"

From the shelter of the mud wall behind the wreck of house, Ralph's "Now" bounced off a communications satellite overhead, and was relayed through another satellite to a secret bunker in an operations headquarters in the United States. There, a young Air Force pilot, sitting with a joystick in his hand controlling the Predator drone, and two sensor operators verified the target on their screen. The pilot fired the Hellfire missile and, halfway around the world, the missile deployed.

For thirty seconds after the word "now," the scene around the three-story stucco and concrete building was quiet; two men leaned with their guns against the perimeter wall, smoking. It made O'Mara want a cigarette. She waited. The missile from the drone should hit fifty yards outside of the building, the explosion was meant to distract and turn the al-Qaeda toward the explosion, her men would move in from behind, flanking the building. It had worked before, but every day in Iraq was different.

The whomp of the ear-shattering explosion tipped over the old Volkswagen parked mid-way between the target and the building, the two smokers were blown off their feet by the concussion. In a heartbeat, O'Mara's and Gillis' men opened fire and quickly took the perimeter of the building's courtyard, O'Mara saw three of the enemy fall. She looked east and watched Gillis and his men move against the wall where the smokers once lounged, they didn't get up.

She looked at two of her squad holding outside a blown-out window, and nodded. They flipped flash-bangs through the window, more concussions were heard, the other squad members pushed through the door, AK-47s responded from inside. O'Mara continued to watch the perimeter, "Clear Lieutenant, got 'em," Gillis said over the radio.

She moved quickly to the same door, she could see directly through the building to the front and the VW beetle that sat on its roof. Two men, in loose clothing, lay on the floor, blood pooled under both. Three others were on their knees; her corporal was putting Plasti-cuffs on the last.

"Upstairs?" she asked.

"Duke and Bill are checking, no sign of the reporter downstairs."

"Lieutenant, you okay?" O'Mara heard Gillis's voice over her earpiece.

"Yes, use the front. We have two down and three cuffed."

"Four down, the drone cleaned up the area pretty good."

"I'm heading to the front of the house." As O'Mara finished, automatic weapons opened up on the floors above. "Gillis, get your men up there."

She watched Gillis' squad storm the front, and begin to work their way up the stairs, she heard heavy boots, Army boots, on the wooden floor above. Single rifle shots echoed through the building.

"Gillis?"

"Working up, two more dead on the stairs, your men are at the end of the hall, they've signaled us to hold. No sign of the reporter."

"I'm behind you," O'Mara said, as she worked her way to the stair that Gillis and his squad had just climbed.

She reached Gillis, the stair on the right continued up to the last floor. She could hear feet scraping across the floor above.

"Leave two men here with my boys; let's get to the top, must be there. You ready for the charge of the Light Brigade?"

Gillis smiled, "Fucking-A."

O'Mara held up three gloved-fingers, and on a three-count, closed her fist. Two of Gillis' men threw flash-bangs up the stair into the door at the top; she and the five men pounded their way up the stairs; two men covered the door from the landing. At the top the landing served three doors, two were closed. The first room was empty, bedding and clothes covered the floor.

Gillis' men crashed the second door open and found two women huddled in the corner; they wore the heavy black cloak and head-covering of the most devout.

"Search them," O'Mara ordered. Two men headed toward the women, at ten feet, they screamed something and swung AK-47s out from under their garb, the men were ready, and the women never got a shot off.

"And what do we have behind door number three, Bobby? Is it a new car, a vacation, or our reporter?"

"I just don't know Lieutenant, shall we find out!"

She signaled to Duke and on her count he kicked the flimsy door open; it shattered from the frame. Flash-bangs flew into the room. O'Mara quickly followed.

The room was set up with lights and an old VHS camera was mounted on a tripod. Another closed door was on the left, the door heading toward the room with the dead women was on the right. A panel of Arabic scribbles and Osama bin Laden's photo hung on the wall, a plastic tarp covered the floor, and a head sat on the crumpled, bloody body sprawled on the tarp.

"Shit, goddamnit," O'Mara said.

"Weren't us, Lieutenant," Gillis said. "The blood's dry around the edges, been maybe a couple of hours, poor son-of-a-bitch. The tape's missing from the camera, so it's probably on its way to the al-Qaeda news-at-ten station, as we speak, goddamnit." He kicked the tripod holding the camera; it spun through the air and crashed against the photograph on the wall.

"I'll call it in; he didn't need to die like this, shit," O'Mara said, pulling a Marlboro from the pack behind her vest. As she held the lighter to the tip, the door on the left burst open and a large Iraqi, black-bearded and wild-eyed swung his AK-47 up toward the four soldiers standing over the reporter. Faster than a Wild West movie, Bobby Gillis pulled his service pistol out and unloaded five shots directly into the man. He spun back into the door's opening, never firing a shot.

"Nicely done, John Wayne," O'Mara said, as she watched Bobby blowing a plume of smoke off the pistol's nozzle, "nicely done."

* * * *

Now Bobby Gillis stood in the lounge of this hospital, one hundred and fifty miles from his home and half a world away from Iraq, facing one of the most competent, best-looking officers he ever had the pleasure to serve with. He smiled and strode across the rich green lounge carpet, stuck his hand out, only to have it knocked aside. His lieutenant grabbed him by both shoulders, gave him a big kiss, and wrapped her arms around the man who saved her life.

5c

"What the hell are you doing here? You're the last person I would expect to see, especially with all this going on," O'Mara said, pushing back, looking at the face of Bobby Gillis.

"Long story, Lieutenant," Gillis said.

"Bobby, it's Sharon, no bars now."

"Yes ma'am," Gillis answered.

"And no goddamned ma'am either," Sharon said and turned to Kevin. "I'm sorry Bobby; this is my friend, Detective Kevin Bryan. Kevin, Sergeant Bobby Gillis, as you can tell we spent some time together in Iraq."

"Sergeant," Bryan said extending his hand.

"Mr. Bryan."

"Kevin, please. As they say, a friend of Sharon's is a friend of mine."

"Good to meet you."

All Kevin could think of, at the moment, was: how well did he know Sharon, why hadn't he heard about this Gillis fellow before, and, like Sharon, he wanted to know why the hell Gillis was here.

O'Mara looked at Bryan and frowned. "Stop that thinking and wondering now, Kevin." And with that, she cuffed him across the back of the head.

Bobby Gillis smiled, "She was the same in Iraq, tough love, I guess."

"You don't know the half of it Bobby, not even half of it," Kevin said.

"Tell me, why are you here? I saw you at the hotel and it shocked the hell out of me. Sorry, I couldn't talk, my client had some difficulties and I was needed there. But tell me."

For the next hour, over weak coffee and average bakery, Gillis told the two about his blind grandfather, the end of World War Two, and the paintings. He also told her about the tunnels and Merkers and the gold. O'Mara and Bryan were shocked. Three weeks earlier, she barely knew anything about the end of World War Two and now, with what Dumont said and Gillis had verified and fleshed out, she was stunned by the reality of it all.

"I don't think this'll make much of a difference, Sergeant, if I tell you," she said, invoking an unsaid security, "but the man upstairs is Alain Dumont. Your grandfather knew him as Robert Dupont, corporal U.S. Army, infantry, Patton's Third Army. He was not killed, he survived and prospered, he was sure your grandfather was dead. He's the one who sent the ring back to your great-grandmother; he would be thrilled to know that Jimmy Gillis is still alive."

"You know the story?"

"As much as Alain would tell me, he was shattered to learn about Graham's and Jimmy's deaths, broken. But, then again, the world is sure that Robert Dupont is also dead, he would like to leave it that way."

"My grandfather will be very happy to know that Robert Dupont is still alive after sixty-six years."

"Bobby, we now have a problem," Sharon said. "There're others who want those paintings, they're the ones that took them and now want to ransom the art for a case in Mr. Dumont's possession, or I hope it still is. They have already tried to kill Dumont and have killed his nurse; Alain says the Nazis are back. I'm trying to find out more, but I caution you about telling anyone what I've told you, here, I know we have privacy, beyond that, I just don't know. I don't want to put you or your family in jeopardy. They kill just to eliminate a problem, not much different from Baghdad. You'll have to make the decision to tell your grandfather, or not."

"I understand, but the man has been through a lot these last few years. Grams died a few years back and left him alone; he's blind now, ticker's shot, and the only thing that keeps him going is baseball. He will listen to two, three games a day," Gillis said. "Says he don't need to see to watch a baseball game. Besides, he's ninety, says it getting near his time, says he's living his ninth inning. What's next?"

"Paris," Kevin said with a smile. "You know, the City of Light, of love, the Seine, great food, the Moulin Rouge, and Nazi stuff."

"Hell of a time for a vacation," Gillis said to Sharon.

"No vacation," she answered. "Somewhere in that town is a case that someone wants very badly, and my client is now in no position to help. I don't know what's in it, but considering who's after it, it must be very important! We're leaving tomorrow night and we'll arrive the following afternoon, late. There's a lot of work ahead of us. If it works out, we will be back in three or four days. We're open on the backside. Then we'll see what we can do to either make a trade or, as I intend, recover the art and keep whatever is in the case. I don't like hijackers, thieves, murderers, and most especially, Nazis."

Chapter 6

6a

After O'Mara and Bryan left Bobby Gillis at the hospital, they returned to Dumont's Broadway house. Sharon led Kevin to the richly paneled wall; her palm print passed them quickly into the elevator and the vault. They both looked for the notebook and the necessary information; it was easy to find in the early seventeenth century Louis the Fourteenth cabinet, the address and codes were easy to copy, the key to the Paris apartment was made of pure gold. There was also the name, Claudette Leclair; manager was written after her name. O'Mara called the number and a pleasant voice answered.

"Claudette Leclair ici, qui est present," Claudette said.

The notebook also stated that she was president of Clear International, a software company. Sharon explained everything that happened to her employer.

"Mon dieu! Je comprends, Mr. Dumont is more than a business associate; he has been a friend to me my whole life. When will you be arriving?" Claudette asked.

"Late-afternoon the day after tomorrow, we leave tomorrow evening. I will call you when we arrive."

"Très bien, bon voyage."

"We will," Sharon said and thought, as she clicked off her phone, *"Meticulous, the man is meticulous in everything he does."*

"I can't believe this place and the man," Bryan said as he walked through the vault and looked at the art on the walls. "I'm even more stunned by the two bats and the glove in the corner cabinet. They are signed Willie McCovey, Willie Mays, and Juan Marichal, and they are addressed personally to Alain Dumont."

"At some point, he was a minority owner of the Giants, what a life. I think I have everything; we need to get back home and pack. Evelyn said she would stay at the house with Basil; he won't be happy, but he won't have to go to camp. You know, above all people, how much he hates it. She also said she'd give us a lift to the airport," Sharon said.

"Don't I know, since I'm usually the one to pick him up. That'll make it easier, not carrying much. And don't forget your passport!" Kevin replied.

"One time and I'll hear it for the rest of my life."

The Air France flight for Charles de Gaulle airport left precisely at 6:10 the next evening. After three scotches, a snack, and three minutes of reading, O'Mara slept for the next seven hours. Bryan twisted and turned, even the first class seats weren't large enough for his length. When Sharon woke, he had been asleep for a couple of fitful hours but was rested enough; she was ready to go. Bryan knew he would face jet lag and, unlike many, jet lag for him was like fifty-pound weights strapped to his legs, everything for two days would feel like he was wading through a shallow pool, slow and plodding, with the world looking like a fog had settled in around the edges.

Light streamed through the small first class windows as a late breakfast was served. The crisp linen offset Kevin's crumpled shirt. For some unexplainable reason, Sharon looked as crisp as the linen, the seven hours left her refreshed. Kevin just moped about and sucked down coffee.

Two hours before their arrival, as Sharon read the latest Dugoni book on her iPad, she felt a presence in the aisle, a tall blond woman in an elegant suit passed through the cabin.

"Madame, this is not your cabin, please return to your seat, we will be arriving soon," the steward said.

"*Ja, ja, muss ich eine falsche Richtung gemacht haben.*"

"I understand, but your cabin area is that way, please be seated."

"*Ja, danke,*" she said, and glanced at Sharon as she passed. "*Fraulein,*" and tipped her head.

"Who was that?" Kevin asked.

"I don't have the foggiest, but she was looking us over. From the look of her, that woman would never get lost. And I recognize her shape, can't place it, yet."

They arrived in the late afternoon to a brilliant blue sky. Kevin looked beat, the eleven-hour flight and nine-hour time change had done him in.

"Claudette, nous sommes ici," Sharon said into her cell phone as they traveled down one of the escalators that cut diagonally through the disorganized terminal. "Oui, we will meet you outside of Air France baggage, I'm a redhead and my partner is over *deux mètres de haut*, you can't miss us. Oui, oui, merci."

"You speak French?"

"Some, don't you?"

"Right, I have as much trouble with English as the next man, no need to complicate my life."

"You always were a Philistine, Kevin Bryan, a true blue-blooded Celtic Philistine."

"Thanks. Is that French beauty waving at us?" he asked, pointing to woman standing next to a tiny red Peugeot.

"Je suis Claudette Leclair, je travaille avec Mr. Dumont," the petite, raven haired, woman said.

"Bon après-midi, Sharon et Kevin. Nous avons non bagages, tous les bagages," Sharon said.

"It is a pleasure to meet you. I am very sorry about the circumstances. We need to move, they don't let me sit here very long."

"That your car?" Kevin said, eyeing the French automobile.

"Oui, this is my baby," Claudette said. She looked at Kevin and then at the car. "This should be fun; it's only a thirty minute ride. Can you manage?"

"He'll manage," O'Mara said, smiling. "I'll take the back; there may be enough room for Kevin in front."

As Sharon folded herself into the rear seat, Kevin watched a tall Nordic blond walk quickly past the three of them. She smiled at Kevin.

"That's the same blond we saw on the plane," he said softly

to Sharon and Claudette. "I suggest we get the hell out of here, rapido!"

"That's Spanish, Kevin, but I get your point," Sharon said. *"Claudette, je suggere que nous sortir d'ici vite, tres vite."*

Claudette watched the tall woman, "Damn Nazis! Oui, tres vite."

Claudette dove into the miasma that is Parisian traffic. Sharon watched Kevin's knuckles turn to a clenched white as they held on to the overhead strap. She couldn't see Claudette's face, but the look on Kevin's was shear resignation, "Oh, to see Paris, then die!" was all he could say.

Alain Dumont's three-story apartment sat at the center of a T intersection in the 7th Arrondissement, four blocks from the Seine and two from Boulevard Saint-Germaine. Non-descript from the outside, they were not surprised by the elaborate security that Claudette navigated through as they entered the building.

"Monsieur Dumont knew my grandmother from after the war; he has remained close to my family for almost seventy years; he is like my American grand-père. I run a small software company for him here in France. He has always made it a point that we work for our bread."

"Sounds like the Alain Dumont I know," Sharon said.

"Yes, I manage his properties in Paris for him as well; it's not too difficult. But he is an incredible man. I received information that he's doing well, Evelyn Lucca called me."

"You know Evelyn?"

"Oui, her company uses my software. I wrote the program and the code, Mr. Dumont funded it, now it's used by many retailers in Europe, China is next," Claudette said, with just a hint of pride.

For the next hour they settled into the apartment and became familiar with the security system. The walls were hung with great and semi-great pieces of art and, unlike San Francisco, these were American pieces from the Hudson River School and California Plein Air.

"They are here to remind him of home; his home in San Francisco reminds him of Europe; he's always reminded that he's a man of the world," Claudette said.

What didn't surprise O'Mara was the truck in the garage.

"What a relic," Kevin said. "There's still bullet holes in the door, amazing."

The rest of the garage was neat; storage space was minimal, four bicycles were hung from a rack.

"They look old, but sturdy," Kevin said.

"When I was a little girl, Monsieur Dumont and I would bicycle all over Paris," Claudette said. "He was strong and imposing then and we loved to bike everywhere. I try to keep them in good shape; I use them when I'm in town for a couple of days, beats the traffic, even in my little Peugeot."

"I'll bet," Kevin answered; his back was still stiff from the ride from the airport.

They went back upstairs.

"Monsieur Dumont has a safe in his office; I place things in there all the time. I know it's not there. How large is this case?" Claudette asked.

"Not large. Alain described it as a fine wooden box inside a simple wooden box or crate, easily lifted and moved. Maybe a little larger than a case of wine," Sharon said.

"Wine, that reminds me, I'm famished!" Kevin announced.

"Claudette, this man needs food, meat and red wine, any ideas?" Sharon asked.

"Oui, there is a very simple, yet very good small restaurant a few blocks from here. They only serve one item on the menu, well actually two, if you include the pommes frites."

"French fries? I'd kill for a plate and vino rojo,"

Sharon looked at Claudette, "Oui, now you see what I have to deal with. Yes Kevin, meat and potatoes, your favorite food groups."

The restaurant was less than a five-minute walk from the apartment. They sat at an outdoor table. Dinner was all that Kevin could imagine, beef tenderloin with a pepper sauce and pommes frites, especially the all-you-could-eat part. Claudette told them about Alain Dumont's history in Paris, or at least the parts she knew. The breadth of the man's impact on everyone he touched was impressive.

As they were finishing, Kevin looked at Sharon and tilted his head slightly toward the street. Coming up from behind O'Mara and Claudette, a black Mercedes slowly approached the restaurant and accelerated as it passed; it turned at the next corner.

"Yes Kevin, we need to go. If that wasn't a drive-by-check-us-out, I've never seen one. Claudette, we'll leave you here."

"If you go out the rear, past the bathrooms, you will find an alley, turn right and follow the brick. It comes out on the other side of the block, near the school we passed on our way here. There is another alley across the street, it will take you the rear entry of the apartment, you know your way in," Claudette said. "I'll see you tomorrow morning. I'll call. Have a nice evening. *Bonne nuit.*"

With that, the two walked casually through the restaurant and into the alley. Claudette remained out front waiting for two that would not return. After twenty minutes, and another Mercedes drive-by, she paid the bill and left.

6b

Back in the apartment, Sharon poured two whiskies and they settled into the elegant sitting room. The furnishings were colonial American, rich woods and thick oriental carpets; Sharon was reminded of Dumont's San Francisco mansion.

"Tell me the story of Dumont after the war and his arrival in Paris again. I believe that whatever was with the paintings was also on the truck. Let's do it again," Bryan said, his detective skills kicked in, but jet lag was beginning to take its toll.

For the next hour, O'Mara retold the story; Bryan asked her to go over a few things twice to check on her take on Dumont's drive from Germany to Paris. When she finally told Kevin about the transfer of the gold to Switzerland, his interest rose further.

"Do you think he took whatever it is to Switzerland?"

"No, he said we had to go to Paris, not Zurich. It is here. This is where we'll find it," Sharon said.

"I imagine financial rules were a lot more lax after the war," Kevin said. "A few gold bars and other trinkets moving around Europe would not have been unusual. Hell, there were rumors that the Nazis were hiding gold in caves and shipping tons of gold to Argentina in submarines no less. Dumont moving a few dozen bars to Zurich would not have been a surprise."

"And he did it a bar or two at a time," Sharon said. "He only took gold in payment from his customers; that's what he told me. Paper money was worthless; gold, on the other hand, will always open doors and grease wheels."

"And where would he have hidden the rest?"

For a short second they both looked at each other and the same grin appeared on their faces.

"The garage!" they said in unison.

"It has to wait till morning, I'm bushed. Been a long day and I can barely put two thoughts together," Sharon said. "We'll look in the morning. We should be safe for tonight. It was a woman's voice on the telephone demanding the case, I'd bet she was the same woman on the plane."

"Probably, but right now I'm worthless, to bed. I'll take the one on the right, you take the left," Kevin said as he headed up the stairs, the ice rattled in his glass.

"Good night Kevin," Sharon said.

O'Mara was too tired and too wired to sleep, jet lag could be put off; she learned that from years of bouncing back and forth to Iraq. She knew she was good for a couple more hours. *"Who wants this box so bad they'd kill for it?"* she thought. *"Remy, poor soul, must have gotten caught up in whatever game they were playing and they killed him. Dumont knew something and what did he mean by the Nazis are back? Hell, they'd been out of the news for years, the occasional crackpot skinhead waving a swastika was the only reminder, and they were Nazis as much as any tattoo-crazed white man from Idaho was. No, these people were the real thing, direct decedents from the 1940s, of that I'm sure; if they knew about Dumont's apartment, they would have forced their way in by now."*

With that, she rinsed her crystal glass and headed upstairs. Contrary to her head, her body was asleep in five minutes.

The next morning, they stood in the cramped garage, a cup of coffee in one hand and no plan in the other.

"We can't move the truck, they would spot us. We have to try and figure out where Alain dug his vault with that thing over our heads. At least there's clearance," Sharon said.

"There's a mallet over by the workbench, might I suggest tapping," Kevin suggested. "A change in tone might signal something hollow underneath."

"Now I know why I brought you along, get tapping, my man."

Bryan started two feet in front of the truck's grill and quickly tapped the dark red brick, a sharp solid report was heard. He moved one brick closer to the truck, and tapped again; they heard the same sound. He repeated the tapping toward the tires and then back to the truck's centerline, one row of bricks at a time. The sounds were almost identical as he slid under the truck and continued toward its middle. He slid out; dust covered his pants and shirt.

"More coffee, that floor's cold, we're halfway," Kevin said. Sharon handed him a new cup, steam rose toward the ceiling.

O'Mara lit a cigarette, "My guess is that it's forward of the rear axle, the most headroom."

"Why didn't we start there then?"

"And miss you crawling on your belly like a reptile in the dust for the last half-hour; it's something I'll treasure forever."

Kevin raised his coffee to Sharon, "To you and your bizarre ways of being entertained. Well, back to work, I'm going to the axle."

Three rows later, the tap became a clack. The clack changed to a fuller more hollow-sounding clunk.

"I saw a chunk of carpenter's chalk on the bench, get it for me," Bryan said.

He marked the first brick and then the successive bricks that responded with a clacking sound. When he was done a rectangular shape, about two feet wide and four feet long, was marked on the bricks. O'Mara shined a flashlight over the surface.

"They've not been moved for years, the dust is deep into the sand joints."

"My guess is one of these should be easier to pull than the others, then we can remove the rest," Bryan said, looking closely at the surfaces of the marked bricks, he brushed his hand over the rough surface; in the corner, he spotted a small cross cut in the edge of one brick. "Got it, X marks the spot. Two screw drivers please."

Slowly, digging out the sand along the joint, he found a groove cut into the brick's rough side; continuing on the opposite side, he found another groove. Wedging the two screwdrivers into the grooves, he slowly pushed them down, the brick rose. O'Mara, joining him under the truck, gripped the brick and lifted it out. For the next half-hour, they pulled out the remaining marked bricks. They stacked them to one side, but still under the truck.

"Would be easier without this damn thing over our heads," Bryan said.

"No kidding, but this is what we're stuck with. How deep is the sand?"

Kevin pushed the caked sand with his hand; it cracked and broke into thousands of smaller pieces, and two inches down he found an iron surface.

"Not deep, I got the top."

She found two large mason trowels and two small metal buckets under the workbench.

"Perhaps these are here for the same reason we need them," Sharon said.

Using the trowels and buckets, they transferred the sand from under the truck to a growing pile just outside the rear wheels. Sharon passed the light over the steel cover.

"Looks like doors, no locks," Sharon said.

"Figures, if you got this far, a few locks wouldn't exactly

stop anyone. The cover's split in two, seam down the center, handles there and there, hinges opposite. I'll give the right side a pull."

A tug loosened the lid, another gained it six inches; Bryan pushed it open until it banged against the drive shaft of the truck. Sharon scanned the vault with the flashlight, small metal boxes sat on the vault's floor, five World War Two ammunition boxes.

They pushed up the other lid; it banged against the truck also, but the opening was clear. With the vault fully open, the two were stunned to find nothing. The ammo boxes were all that remained in the vault.

6c

"No box, what the hell?" Bryan said.

"What's in the ammo cases?"

They pulled out the World War Two relics; each weighed a lot more than twenty pounds. Sharon opened one and was not surprised to find it half-full of gold and silver coins.

"There must be thousands in gold and silver, quite a treasure, but not exactly something to kill people over. These people are after something much more valuable," Sharon said.

"Agree, what's next?" Kevin asked as he slid out the last ammo box. Twisting about, he accidentally knocked the mallet into the vault; it hit the floor. The sound was like the ringing of a bell.

"You hear that?"

"Sure did, I don't think we're done," Sharon answered.

Sliding back to the vault, she slowly ran the light along the seams and edges; a small hole appeared in the middle of the floor; it could have easily been missed.

"Now what?" Kevin asked.

"I need a strong wire hook, what do you suggest?"

He scanned the garage, his eyes settled on the buckets, "Of course!" he said.

"What did you find?"

"One minute," he said, as he twisted the wire handle out of one of the buckets. "Try this."

"Should work," Sharon said.

She slid the open hook into the hole and twisted the handle; the wire caught the false bottom. Pulling it, the floor opened like a door.

Sitting in the center of the new vault was a rough-hewn crate, the name of a vineyard printed on the top and the sides. No locks, no hinges, just a simple wooden wine box. Next to the box was a muslin cloth bag as dusty as the crate.

"Got to be it," Kevin said. "I suggest we get out of this hole and move it upstairs where it's a bit warmer and dryer."

"Excellent idea, we can clean this up later."

Kevin pulled the bag out first. They could hear the unmistakable muffled sound of metal on metal.

"Pistols and other weapons, I think," Kevin said as he handed the bag to Sharon. The crate was next.

As he put the dusty box on the elegant marble table in the kitchen, her cell phone rang.

"Bonjour, Claudette . . . Oui, yes we slept well, yes, I think we found it. One hour, we'll wait . . . au revoir."

"Let's start with this," Kevin said as he reached inside the muslin bag and withdrew two Lugers and two Browning Colt .45s, all four were well oiled. Kevin slid the slide back on the Colt and inspected the Lugers. "If the bullets don't blow these up, they seem to be in good working order."

"Good, hope we don't need them," Sharon said. "I have felt a little undressed since we left San Francisco."

"Me too, a couple of pounds under your jacket begin to feel familiar," Kevin replied. "I think the coins were a red herring. I certainly wouldn't have looked any further."

Kevin turned the box to face them. As he started to turn the clasp, the door chimed, a panel over the kitchen instantly flashed on and showed Claudette standing in the vestibule of the door. She was looking over her shoulder.

"I'll go to the door, hand me one of the Colts," Sharon said.

"May not work," Kevin said.

"But still scary."

Sharon returned to the kitchen with Claudette.

"Bonjour, Kevin."

"Mademoiselle, bonjour."

Claudette didn't reply; she could only look at the box. She crossed herself.

"I can still feel the evil. I was born thirty years after the Nazis were defeated, yet the family stories gave me *cauchemars*, how you say . . ."

"Nightmares," Sharon offered.

"Oui, nightmares. I still think about it and what they did to my country. Now this," Claudette said, resting a paper sack on the counter, the aroma of croissants filled the room. Kevin, still famished, devoured the pastries.

"Without a doubt, the finest bits of butter and flour I have ever eaten, wonderful," Kevin said. "Thank you, Claudette."

"You're welcome, Monsieur," she replied with a smile. "Have you opened it?"

They turned their attention back to the box.

"I believe the vault was set up to make thieves think that's all there was," Sharon said. "They would have taken the coins and left happily. The people looking for this box would not have stopped. The box is from a vineyard in Germany, says 'Trittenheim and Mosel' on the side. Don't know the wine or the region."

Sharon retrieved her iPad, took a photo of the box and typed in Trittenheim, a wiki site for the village popped up, as well as a list of vineyards.

"Riesling grapes," Sharon said.

"Too sweet," Kevin added, "like drinking perfume."

"You need to broaden your horizons, but yes, give me a good cabernet," Claudette said.

"Do you think the box labeling has anything to do with what's in it?" Kevin asked.

"You mean wine or something?" Sharon asked.

"Yeah."

"Doubt it, probably a convenient disguise or ruse."

Kevin inspected the top of the box, small tacks held the lid tight to the box itself. Taking a screwdriver, he slid the point under a corner and levered it up about half an inch, moving to the next corner, he did the same, with one end up, he pried the top off. Heavy dark green felt, lightly dusted by fifty years of time, filled the interior.

"Mystery inside an enigma," Kevin said.

"Something like that, let's get it out," Sharon said.

Kevin pulled on the felt, releasing it from the wine box, the felt filler turned into a sack as he drew it out. There was another case inside the felt bag. He placed the bundle on the marble, allowing the felt to fall away, revealing a lustrous oak case. Expertly carved into the broader sides of the ornate box was a black swastika set in a circular pattern of white and red.

"Seems the story Alain told me was true," Sharon said. "In amongst the things they took from the mine, besides the gold and the art, was a rough box, not sure why, maybe he doesn't remember either, but here it sits with all the evil it represents. You ready for more?"

"Oui, but I think that opening this box will, how you say, open a Pandora's Box, release great evil," Claudette said.

"Maybe, but we will deal with that later. Kevin, are you okay?" Sharon looked at the man, his fingers rubbed across the box's surface.

A stunned Kevin Bryan quickly pulled his fingers back, as though he'd felt a shock. The carving covered the whole box; the clasp and hinges were still bright.

"Those are gold, no tarnish," he said, recovering a bit. "The Germans were famous for their oak work, only a master carver could have produced such a case. No lock or key required, simple and easy to open. Shall we?"

"Slowly, may be a booby trap," Sharon answered.

Kevin turned back to the oak case and turned the clasp; he raised the lid until a sliver of light from Sharon's flashlight could pierce the gap.

"No wires or trips that I can see. You girls, move out of the room before I open it."

"Right! Open the damn thing. I'm not leaving the room," Sharon said.

"Me neither, *Monsieur s'il vous plaît ouvrir le boîtier*."

"Huh?"

"Open the damn box, Kevin."

He quickly flipped open the lid, a gold chain prevented it from opening completely. A piece of parchment hid the contents, a swastika, crudely painted, covered the translucent paper. He took the paper by the corners and set it on the marble.

"There's a pencil signature scrawled in the corner," Claudette said. "*Mon Dieu*, it's Hitler's. He painted this, looks like the work of a child."

"Maybe he was a child when he painted it," Sharon offered.

Kevin pulled three more small paintings from the box; each was of a house, a German house.

"Same, but a more mature signature," Sharon said, looking at the watercolors. "Good God, these are his work."

Next, Kevin pulled out a packet of photos; in the first photo, Hitler and a young woman were dressed for summer.

"Family pictures, look, the man is playing with his dog, couldn't have been too bad," Kevin said sarcastically, as he found a small bag that rattled about, "Look, I found his marbles!"

"Stop the commentary, Kevin," Sharon said.

He withdrew a number of small ornate boxes; each held a specific medal attached to ribbons.

"I'm guessing that he was the only German soldier to receive any of these, they gave out lots of medals, they loved the pomp and circumstance," Claudette said.

A gold Luger with a carved ebony handle was the next item in the box, still in its holster of oiled leather; it looked new. Three books were taken out next; two had red covers, *Mein Kampf* was written across the blood red cover. Sharon quickly looked through the well-worn books; she noted they were both signed and there were pencil notations covering the interior pages.

"He took notes on his own work," she said, looking through the two-volume set.

Another object, square-shaped and wrapped in black felt, sat on the bottom of the oak box. Kevin sat it on the marble countertop. He unfolded the wrapper, laying each piece of cloth out until another oak box, also carved, sat on a black napkin.

For two long seconds, the kitchen was quiet.

"More carvings," Claudette said. "SS work there in the corner, a death's head figure carved there, and the swastika there, excellent work, considering the subject matter."

Kevin opened the box. The interior was divided into two rectangular panels, each the same size. The inside of the lid showed another swastika carved in a circle. Only the upper half of the box held anything, a sleeve of red silk cloth held something. Sharon removed the bag.

"Hard, metal, thin, but very heavy for its size." She slid the plate out of the bag, gold flashed in the morning sunlight streaming in the window. The plate was simply carved with a frame at its edge, a swastika etched to the right and four numbers across the center of the plate.

7 53 37 72

"Lottery numbers?" Kevin quipped.

"I'll buy a ticket when I get home," Sharon said looking a Kevin. "I really doubt it."

"It's obvious that the other half of the box was meant to hold a similar plate, maybe with numbers," Claudette said.

"Or instructions," Sharon said.

"Maybe."

"Whatever this is, it's the reason the Nazis hijacked the art, killed Remy, tried to kill Alain, and are chasing us now."

"Two halves make a whole," Kevin offered.

"That's it," Sharon said. "They want this half to match up with one they have. With the pair they can access something squirreled away for more than half a century. The only thing that's worth the wait is money, lots of money. So this is a partial account number for a bank account or a combination to a safe or something."

"Could be a lot of things, Sharon," Kevin said.

"Mon Dieu," Claudette said. "If these Nazis are still organized, accessing this money could do frightful things to specific governments or even to the world. The Nazis had alliances during the early years with very nasty Middle Eastern regimes, many still carry their ideas. South American countries are now on the brink of economic collapse; a well-financed effort could help take control of one, like Argentina, and cause great *malice*."

"Mischief?" Sharon asked.

"Oui, mischief."

"Properly done, they can throw the world into a panic," Kevin said. "Look what a few cartels in Mexico are doing to their own country and to us, and they're just thugs. An organized group, well-educated and well-financed, and with almost a century of experience, is formidable. People need hope to move forward, and even though this is the most evil man can create, it's hope to many. Hitler did that in the 1930s, that's why a whole country followed him into hell."

Sharon ran her finger across the polished face. "We could destroy it, melt the damn thing right here, right now," she said, looking at the ornate fireplace in the kitchen's corner."

"Or try and find the other plate and make that money work for peace, save a country instead of destroying one," Claudette said.

"Maybe, but if this is the only one and these are the only numbers, and we have to assume that it is, we need to make it safe since its now seen the light of the Twenty-first Century."

"Back in the hole?" Kevin offered skeptically.

"If we found it, they can find it. And they know we're around here so if they find this house, they will take it apart brick by brick, how about a bank vault?" Sharon suggested.

"My company uses a private bank and it's close and very

secure; we keep original copies of software in their vaults as well as hardware prototypes, my family and Alain have trusted them for almost fifty years."

"Software, of course," Sharon said. "I saw a scanner in Alain's office, I suggest we scan the plate and email it somewhere safe. No photos, they might be found. We can then stash the plate in your safe deposit box at your bank. It frees us up from having to carry the cursed thing around."

"Use my Lafayette police account, it's extremely secure due to the press and all. I can't even access the account remotely; I have to be at one of the station's terminals. It should work."

They gathered all Hitler's personal materials, except for the golden plate, and placed them back in the oak box. It fit into the safe secured in the floor of Alain Dumont's office. Then they sent the scan to Kevin's police account.

"Lafayette?" Claudette asked. "You live and work in a town named after our Marquis de Lafayette; you Americans amaze us. We French would never name a town after one of your leaders. Can you imagine a French city named Roosevelt or Eisenhower, or even Obama? Yes, you are a strange people."

"Yes, we continually amaze ourselves," Sharon said. "It's almost three o'clock; we need to get this to your bank. Claudette, there's something in the garage you need to see."

When they returned to the kitchen, they were able to combine the five ammo boxes into two, and, though heavy, they placed them in the safe.

"I'll replace the brick and cleanup after you leave. There's no rush," Claudette said. "There's a quiche in the refrigerator and a bottle of Chablis, may I suggest a quick bite."

"We can't go back to that place where we had dinner last night?" Kevin asked, looking wistful and very hungry.

"No, we need to keep a low profile until the plate gets put into the bank," Sharon admonished. "Then we're heading back to California. Quiche sounds great."

They discussed the implications of the numbers and what they might mean while eating quiche and drinking Chablis, the conclusion was no conclusion, without the plate's brother, nothing could be resolved.

"Assuming there is one," Kevin offered. Speculation was just that, speculation.

"Traffic is just awful, and it's nearing four o'clock. It will be easier to go the ten blocks to the bank on bikes. From there, we can get a more substantial meal and then head back," Claudette said.

"Haven't been on a bike in years," Sharon said. "I did notice the kiosks and bike racks as we drove in."

"Our government's idea to help the citizens and maybe pull a few more dollars from tourists' pockets; it's called Vélib," Claudette said. "The bikes, quite ugly if you ask me, are available to anyone with a credit card. You pay when you take a bike and then check in when you return it. Cost millions of euros to start and, in the first weeks, thousands disappeared. Some were found at the top of lamp poles; God knows how many are in the Seine. But they keep putting more bikes out and moving them around Paris. It's just one more reason why we're going bankrupt."

"Patrolled on one a few years back when we helped during a festival," Kevin added. "I have a feeling my butt's not going to appreciate this but it's better than walking with that Mercedes cruising the streets.

6d

With the plate in a Bon Marché shopping bag stuffed in the wicker basket of Sharon's bike, the three left the apartment and headed toward the river. Sharon threw her backpack over her shoulder. Claudette's bank, a very private, very secure institution, faced the river; the Orsay Museum was three blocks away. The bank sat on a corner; tall pillars flanked the ornate bronze doors, broad stone steps climbed to the terrace at the base of the columns. Two armed guards stood near the doors and watched as the three stood their bikes near one of the Vélib kiosks; Kevin noticed that many of the city's bicycles had flat tires.

"Hard to rent those," Kevin said, as he kicked the stand under his bike.

"Not sure how this would fly in the U.S., armed guards standing outside banks were done away with years ago," Sharon said, looking at the bank.

"They're used as a deterrent here, bank robberies are rare with the mantrap doors we put at the entries to our banks, but they do happen," Claudette said. "It's also a paternal thing, shows our customers that we care."

"Yes, banks, you just gotta love 'em," Kevin said.

"We can place the plate in my personal safety deposit box; it's much easier than trying to open an account," Claudette said. "If you don't have the time and the necessary paperwork, opening an account is impossible. Banking is very complicated here, for some reason, the government thinks you may be trying to hide something, banks are overly cautious."

"Yeah, Kev, you gotta love 'em," Sharon said.

"I'm with the bikes," Kevin said. For some reason he felt more comfortable now, maybe it was the Colt 45 jammed in the small of his back, even though, after the bike ride, he knew he'd have a bruise just above his belt. He saw no black Mercedes following them. He watched the street as the girls mounted the steps.

The goings-on at the Vélib stand amused him, tourists of all types tried to figure out the system. As with much of Paris signage, French is pre-eminent. Kevin could spot the Americans; he overheard one say it was just like another ride at an amusement park. He froze when a woman's voice whispered in his ear.

"Herr Bryan, please do not move, when the women return, I want what they removed from the bank. It's ours."

Bryan slowly turned and took a step back, the blond from the plane stood directly in front of him, her dark blue eyes cut sharply into his. He saw a very large man, obviously German from the look of his dark blond hair and crisp jaw line, standing behind her and to one side. The man had his hand inside his coat, he smiled at Kevin. The man looked like a six-foot-four inch Teutonic Napoleon. He was a bit shorter, but he had fifty pounds of muscle on Bryan.

"Nazis in Paris, again," Kevin said. "Don't you ever know when to quit?"

"The gold plate, Herr Bryan; that is all I want. We will even return the Jew's paintings for nothing. Just give me the plate."

"I'm just here for the food, not sure what you're talking about."

"Do not play me for the fool."

"Great line, but I know you can do better," Kevin said, adjusting his stance. The Nazi moved his hand, "Don't," he added, looking at the man. He caught movement on the stairway.

They both turned to watch the two women walk down the steps, Sharon's eyes never left the woman; she still carried the Bon Marché bag, her leather backpack hung loose to one side. Reaching the sidewalk, Sharon quickly walked to the pair, briefly looked at Kevin, winked, and immediately threw a hard right into the jaw of the woman, knocking her to the sidewalk. As she fell, Kevin pulled the Colt from his waistband, and pointed it directly at the guard.

"I said, don't!" as the guard reached into his coat. "Don't, finger tips only!" The guard slowly removed his hand, his automatic held loosely between his fingers.

"On the ground now!" Kevin ordered. His Colt looked like a canon, compared to the automatic. "Slide the gun toward me."

The man quickly went to the sidewalk and did as he was told; he watched his boss, still on the sidewalk, squirm under the foot that Sharon had put on her chest. The black Mercedes slid to a stop in the street, the driver exited and stood at the door. Kevin waved the gun at the man.

"Leave it. You," Kevin yelled at the car. "Here. Hands up. Up!" The man walked to the sidewalk, raising his hands. "Down!" He settled in lying down on the pavement next to Napoleon.

Claudette scanned the area; she saw that the guards at the top of the stairs were starting to move toward them, she heard a woman scream, it all seemed like she was staring, like tunnel vision; what was happening in front of her was the only thing that mattered.

"We need to get out of here now," she said to Sharon. "And I mean right now."

"Got it. Name?" she said looking at the woman on the ground. "No fucking games, your name."

"Fuck you," the woman spat, as she looked at the bag, "Now you'll never see the paintings. Get away from this; you're nothing to us. Give us the plate and they'll be returned and the old man will live. I could have killed him once, I will the next chance I get."

"Sharon," Claudette said watching the guards; they were halfway down the steps, their actions, tentative, rental cops.

"Take their guns, Claudette. Throw them in the sewer; pull the keys from the Mercedes. We'll take the bikes." She looked down at the woman, "Fräulein, don't fuck with me. I know what you want. If Mr. Dumont is threatened again or the paintings damaged, I will make sure the golden bauble is lost again, and this time, forever." She waved the bag over the prostrate woman.

Margrite focused her gaze on Sharon, "You wouldn't!"

"Believe me sister, I would in a second," she rattled the bag. "Don't move. More than one can play the ransom game. Kevin, Claudette, we're out of here."

Claudette pushed the pistols through the sewer grate; the keys joined the pistols. She and Sharon mounted their bikes; Kevin mounted his with extreme care; his Colt never left the figures on the ground.

"Vite, vite, now, we must go!" Claudette said.

They turned their bikes up the street and pedaled hard. Sharon looked over her shoulder as the gendarmes reached the three, quickly rising from the ground. Speyer pushed one of the men away; Napoleon pulled a pistol from his pants cuff, the driver pulled a second pistol; the rental guards froze. Sharon turned her attention back to the street and pedaled harder.

"Messieurs, I suggest you do not move," Margrite said to the three men. "Olaf, keys?" The driver pulled another set from his pocket.

"Good. Derek, get bikes," Margrite said as she looked at the typical gridlock of mid-afternoon traffic.

The big man quickly walked to the Vélib station where two obvious Americans, stunned and frozen by what had just happened, stood next to their newly rented bikes.

Derek waved his pistol at the tourists, *"Madame et monsieur, je veux vos vélos!"* They didn't understand French but they understood the meaning, they released their hands, and stepped back. Margrite and Derek mounted the bikes and watched as the three turned right at the next corner. The driver, still pointing his pistol at the guards, quickly got into the Mercedes, found a break in the traffic and accelerated fast toward the Boulevard Saint-Germain. The stunned guards stood silently as the chaos disappeared, as quickly as it started. Only the Americans, arguing with each other, made any noise. "You shouldn't have just given the bikes to them Michael, now we're going to be charged for them. It's been like this the whole trip, London, then Rome and now here. This trip is just one disaster after another," the woman said as one of the guards talked into his headset.

"At the next corner, we split up," Sharon said as they pedaled hard toward the Seine. "Claudette get back to the apartment, I'll call you later. Kevin you meet me at the Pont des Arts, they can't follow us all. We need to get out of Paris."

After Kevin and Claudette turned at the next intersection, Sharon headed straight toward Quai Malaquais; she knew the woman would follow her and maybe her bodyguard would too. All she knew was that she needed to get over the river. She cut through the plaza at the Orsay Museum and turned hard right onto the boulevard paralleling the Seine. The traffic was aimed directly at her, she wove between three honking blurs of color; to her left, one of the famous river bateaux churned upstream; she took a quick look at the upper deck crowded with tourists. Looking forward, all she saw were cars and trucks and chaos, people, eight deep, walked along the sidewalks; she had to stay in the street. She knew now how a salmon felt swimming upstream. Looking over her shoulder again, she caught the blond and the bodyguard turning onto the boulevard from the Orsay before they disappeared behind a truck; Sharon pushed harder. The Pont des Arts was visible between the trees; she bolted across the traffic to the bike and bus lane, still fighting the one-way traffic.

"Sharon," a familiar voice yelled over her shoulder, Kevin pulled up next to her. "Good thing I remembered the Pont des Arts, got lost for a block but a cop pointed me in the right direction."

"They are both on my tail, three, four blocks back, we will cross here and hope none of the famous Paris gendarmes are waiting for us on the other side," Sharon gulped deep breaths. "I really need to cut back on my smoking," she said to herself as they bolted up the steps, carrying their bikes onto the bridge.

"Fast, I don't think bikes are allowed," she said to Kevin.

Pedestrians threw up their hands and screamed at the two as they weaved in and out of the human obstacles walking over one of the oldest bridges in Paris. The empty Bon Marché bag, caught by a river breeze, flew out of Sharon's basket. She slung the remaining strap of her backpack on her other shoulder.

Two thirds of the way across, Sharon quickly jammed on her brakes.

"What?" Kevin said. "We need to keep moving."

"Your gun, toss it. If we're caught by the police with that pistol we're in more trouble than what that Nazi can do. Toss it, now."

Kevin reached in his waistband and, without a thought, pitched the Colt over the rail into the river, "Now can we go?"

"Vite, vite, that-a way," she said, pointing to the Louvre that loomed up ahead of them. "Right, then turn left at the next corner."

"Where?"

"We need to get out of Paris, Gare du Nord, if we get split

up. Catch the Eurostar to London; she'll have people watching the airport."

"What about her? She's climbing up the steps to the bridge and that bodyguard has caught up too," Kevin said pointing.

"All the more reason to hurry, go, go, go."

They continued north through the maze of streets and alleys, twice they thought they had shaken the pair but at Boulevard Saint-Denis and Boulevard de Sebastopol, their luck ran out. As they approached the intersection, the woman crossed Saint-Denis ahead of them. They slammed on their brakes as the Nazi swerved into the intersection and took command of one of the corners.

"She must have taken a short-cut," Kevin said breathing hard, but not as hard as Sharon. "Now where? They can cut us off from the station!"

"We'll just have to beat them there and hope for Irish luck!" Sharon said, as she watched the bodyguard sweep into the intersection ten seconds behind the woman.

"Well, I could just ride up to them and shoot them. Oh yeah, I don't have a gun, should always remember to carry a gun, had one but it now sleeps with the fishes, cause *someone* told me to toss it."

"Quiet, I'm thinking!" Sharon said, watching the two straddling their bikes a block ahead of them; they had not spotted Kevin and Sharon.

"Turn here," Sharon said, pointing to the Rue du Faubourg, "This should take us near the station."

"Our secret's out," Kevin said as the bodyguard spotted them. "As you said, vite."

He watched as the blond went one way and the guard peddled hard toward them. *"That hulk of a man has to be fit,"* Kevin thought as he watched the man pull hard into the parallel traffic. Focused on the two only, the bodyguard swerved to avoid a panel truck and tried to duck between a bus and another delivery van. Unfortunately, he didn't see the boy with the hand-truck stacked with Perrier boxes step into his path. One second the man was upright; the next he was sprawled across the Boulevard Saint-Denis. He was lucky, but his rental bike wasn't as a FedEx delivery van crushed the Vélib as flat as a Parisian crêpe, now the Americans would be charged for the crushed bike as well.

"One down," Kevin said.

"One to go, she's paralleling us," Sharon answered. "The sign said the station is ahead." They continued to weave in and out of the oncoming traffic.

"When are we gonna go with the flow, this is crazy," Kevin said as he dodged another van heading directly at them.

"Now, turn left, she's found us," Sharon yelled at Kevin as she turned onto the Rue des Petites Ecuríes. The narrow street left little room to maneuver between the bikes, scooters and cars parked on the right side. They struggled to stay ahead of the woman but, at least, the traffic flow was in their direction.

She was now a half block away; Sharon gauged the space between the two delivery trucks, just wide enough to squeeze through.

"You sure," Kevin said.

"No option, take a deep breath!"

The two jammed their way between the panels of the trucks; diesel fumes filled the air, the noise was deafening. They exploded out of the space and flew past the stunned drivers.

"Shit," was all she could say.

"Where?" Kevin yelled.

"Next right," the blue enameled street sign stuck to the wall said 'Rue d'Hauteville'. "Hard, hard."

"Yeah, yeah, I know, vite, vite!" Kevin followed Sharon, peddling hard into the narrow alley, just missing one of the short iron stanchions that lined the street. A dramatic colonnade commanded the far end of the street; a tangle of traffic blocked the onrushing intersection, red taillights flared.

"Shit," Kevin said.

"What?"

"Ahead."

"Shit."

"Construction, suggest a right."

"Right it is," Sharon answered; the sound of jackhammers filled the canyon of windows and iron balconies. She turned to take a quick look; the blond was a half block behind them and gaining. Sharon saw the unmistakable flash of chrome. "Gun."

"Where?"

"She's got a gun," Sharon said.

"Now don't you wish you didn't tell me to pitch the damn thing? She didn't throw hers away when she crossed the bridge."

"Shut up and pedal."

Sharon took one last look down the street. The woman pedaled hard, intent on O'Mara, her left hand gripping the handlebar; her right held the pistol. But then she made the mistake most urban riders fear; she failed to notice the door of an old Renault swing open, directly into her path. No time to brake or even say a quick prayer to Oden, the woman hit the door mid-panel, collapsing her tire and jamming the handlebars into the open window. Sharon watched as she did a complete three-sixty in the air before tumbling into another van being unloaded. The Algerian delivery boy spit out his cigarette and it spiraled into the air as Margrite slammed into his hand-truck full of wine boxes, her pistol spun over the cigarette in a bizarre dance and slid under the delivery truck. She tumbled over the rough pavement, out cold.

"Good," Sharon said, as Kevin backtracked and caught up to her.

"Now can we leave? I am not enjoying my stay in Paris. I'm hungry and pissed. This isn't the city of love that everyone says it is."

"England is much more romantic; let's go before someone puts her and us together." Sharon watched the woman sit up, blood streamed down her face, the young Algerian was talking to her, the dapper man from the Renault was waving his hands about and three people stood nearby talking into their cell phones, a claxon could be heard echoing down the centuries-old walls of limestone. The Americans would not be happy when they find this additional Vélib charged to their bill when they returned home.

Sharon and Kevin passed the colonnade of the church of Saint-Vincent-de-Paul and turned toward the station. The Gare du Nord was four tourist-filled Parisian blocks away.

Chapter 7

7a

The Eurostar was one of the few joint efforts, other than World War Two, between the French and English, which actually succeeded, almost beyond even their own expectations. Sure there were the fears that rapid foxes would find a way to sneak under the English Channel and invade the relatively rabies-free island; even these passed because of all the revenue the rail line created. But, in many respects, the system is like two international airports at each end, very little between London and Paris gained much financially from the new high-speed rail line. Instead of flying over the countryside, the trains flew through it.

O'Mara and Bryan found the ticket counter and purchased two first class tickets for the last train leaving for London, they had thirty minutes to spare, or, as Kevin said to Sharon, "Thirty minutes to lay low and try to stay out of sight."

Once on the train, they spent the first fifteen minutes making sure they weren't followed or being watched, a little difficult with his six foot-six inch height and her red hair and their obvious Irish look. They each ordered a scotch and settled in for the two-hour ride.

"She'll have someone waiting for us in London and Heathrow; I just know it," Sharon said, looking at the simple map in the seatback packet of documents. "We'll get off at Ashford."

"I'm exhausted," Kevin added. "I'm still jet-lagged and need sleep, till then I'm worthless."

"That goes without saying, but I agree, I'm dragging too."

"There's got to be a hotel near the station," he said, as he watched Sharon leaf through the Eurostar magazine; an ad popped up for a small hotel a short walk from the station.

She pulled her cell phone from her pack. Ten seconds later

she was connected, one minute later they had a confirmed room, with a shower.

"One room?" Kevin asked.

"One room, we're economizing and it's safer, besides, I'm too tired and I'm developing a headache."

"You always say that."

"You make me tired, get some sleep. I'll wake you up when we pull in."

For the next hour, Sharon fought to keep her eyes open, but eventually failing, the arrival announcement for Ashford was intentionally loud enough to wake even the dead. The train had experience with travelers sleeping through their stop.

The hotel was a short cab ride from the station; they collapsed on the twin beds, only the sun punching through the window at five a.m. woke them.

"Please shut the blinds, Kevin."

"Gladly."

He reached up and drew the curtain across the window; when he awoke, it was nine a.m., the shower was running and the electric kettle was boiling away. He dumped a packet of Nescafe into a cup and poured the hot water over the mixture. Tapping on the door he said, "I'm up."

"Coffee?"

"Just made it, want a cup."

"Yes, I'm out in five."

He slid the curtain aside and stared at the strangest landscape he had ever seen. A hundred sheep stood there looking at him, it was raining, they were soaked but didn't care; suddenly, they all turned and started to walk away.

"Was it something I said?" Kevin asked as he watched their tails twitch in the damp morning light.

"What?" Sharon asked as she left the bathroom, wearing a robe, with a towel wrapped around her head.

"Nothing, I'm next. Wasn't a razor in there, was there?"

"No, but the day-old beard gives you such a Euro-trash look, why don't you go for it. And the shower's not bad by English standards."

"That's aiming low, breakfast after and then we're off," Kevin said.

"Yes, we need to get our schedule together, maybe find some clean clothes and dump these."

"Yes, I'd kill for clean underwear after yesterday."

"Thanks for the update."

By eleven, they'd had breakfast and found some interesting clothes, no high-end boutiques in Ashford, but they were serviceable and, above all, clean. For the next hour, Sharon looked for the best routes home, everything seemed to leave early in the morning.

"You want to stay another night?" she asked.

"No, at least, not here. London, sure. But here, not if I don't have to."

"Alternative is taking a chance at Heathrow and, after what we did to that woman, I'm sure there's people watching for us. Sadly, it's Gatwick tomorrow morning to Orlando, then Southwest to Oakland. We should get in about 6:30 tomorrow evening, will that work?"

"Do I have a choice?" Kevin asked as he looked out the restaurant window; it was still raining.

"Done," Sharon said five minutes later.

"Why do I feel as though I'm in an English holding cell?"

They took the local train and stayed at a hotel near Gatwick Airport; at least they had separate rooms and Kevin found a razor. Sharon's last call, before they went to bed, was to Evelyn Lucca. She brought her up to speed, found out that Dumont was much better, inquired about Basil, and then asked Lucca to pick them up in Oakland. Sharon and Kevin slept through most of both flights, including the endless parade of stupid movies and shows across the Atlantic.

Precisely at 6:45 p.m., they walked into the baggage area of the Oakland airport; Evelyn Lucca walked up to Kevin and gave him a kiss on the cheek, she hugged Sharon.

"Thanks for picking us up; we're bushed, even with a nap on

both planes," Sharon said.

"It's good to have you back; there's been nothing new since we talked yesterday, no calls to Alain's house or even the police. Nothing," Evelyn said.

"Since Paris, I would think so. The tumble that woman took was serious," Sharon said.

"I need a cocktail, a real drink, a Jameson would be perfect. Do you know any place nearby where we can stop?" The girls both looked at Kevin and smiled.

"I suppose you know somewhere?" Sharon asked, looking at Kevin.

"I miss Gina," Kevin said. "Evelyn, a quick stop at her place, then I'm home, a bite to eat and then sleep. Captain wants me at my desk tomorrow, some of us have to work," Kevin said. "He's getting moody about my globetrotting."

"Gina's it is," Evelyn said. She had met the number one bar-tender in Lafayette at a dinner party at Sharon's after their last collective adventure.

They walked into the half-full bar a little after 8:00 p.m.; Gina hugged and kissed all three. Within thirty seconds, a Jameson on the rocks, a Red Label rocks and a Pernod rocks sat on the bar. They settled in and, for the next half-hour, O'Mara told Cavelli everything about their adventure in Paris. Gina owned one of the best bars in Lafayette, Geno's, handed down to her by her father. Well known and liked in the community, Gina had known Sharon and Kevin for years and had listened to their tales of woe and happiness. She was better than a shrink; she cost less, provided better results, and served refreshments during the sessions.

"Son-of-a-bitch, you mean the Nazis, those goose-stepping assholes that tried to take over the world?" Gina exclaimed. "Good God and a bike chase through Paris. I'd have bought tickets to see that man," she pointed a stick of celery at Kevin, "on a bike pedaling his ass up the Champs-Elysees, all knees and elbows; it would have been a sight."

"It was," Sharon said. "But he's such a baby when we travel, always complaining about the food, or lack of it."

"Not that steak house, or whatever it was," Kevin said. "That meat and sauce was so good Gina; I wanted to go there for lunch the next day, but no-o, we had to get back home. Who goes to Paris and spends one day?" He hooked his thumb toward Sharon. "Her. She owes me a real trip back there, and soon. And this time, no bikes!"

"Another?" Gina asked, pointing at the drinks.

"One's enough tonight Gina," Kevin said. "Work tomorrow. Boss is getting touchy. Should we get together late tomorrow?" Kevin added looking at Sharon.

"Seven o'clock okay?"

"Seven it is, barring unforeseen events."

"You always say that, can't you commit?" Sharon asked.

"There are always unforeseen events." Kevin smiled and took his things out of the trunk of Evelyn's Maserati sedan, slid into the front seat with his bag on his knees. "Hopefully, the few clothes I left in Paris will get here; I already miss my favorite shirt."

"Claudette said she'll send it all," Sharon added.

"She's an excellent business woman," Lucca said. "When I'm in Paris, at the designer shows, we have dinner; she's a delight and she's tough. She reminds me of a more petite version of you, Sharon."

"That's not what I was thinking," Kevin said, as he told Evelyn to make three left turns after they passed under the freeway. She pulled up in front of Kevin's bungalow.

"Nice house, Kevin, very neat and comfortable-looking from out here," Evelyn said, complementing Kevin on his choice of home's.

"Looks can be deceiving, the inside's a disaster," Sharon said.

"No need to tattle. It is a bit unkempt, a lot like me. But I know where everything is and that's important. Good night girls, Sharon, tomorrow night, seven." As he unlocked the door, he watched them turn the corner and head back toward the freeway.

Kevin sat his one bag on the front hall chair and pushed his way through the loose mail strewn on the floor below the mail slot. *"Really need to put something under that thing someday,"* he thought out loud. Gathering the debris, a local pizza joint's colorful advert card popped out. Till then, all he had eaten for the last two days was a bad omelet and a worse sandwich. Pizza, he'd kill for a double pepperoni. A quick call, a check around the house, and water splashed on his face refreshed him enough for the five-minute walk to pick up dinner. Unconsciously, he slid his service revolver into its halter and pulled his jacket on. *"Much better,"* he thought, *"much better."* Pleasant but cool, the walk helped to relax the tightness in his legs after fifteen hours spent sitting in a plane seat.

Franco's Pizzeria had been a staple of the neighborhood for years; good pizzas and quick Italian food fed almost everyone for blocks in every direction at least once a week. Kevin had been eating there since the first night he moved into the bungalow. All he needed was a double pepperoni and a Harp Lager; he could live on that. A dusty beige Cadillac parked directly in front of the door. As he passed the driver's side, one man slid further down in the driver's seat, noticeably trying to hide in the car's interior shadows.

"Evening Franco, nice night," Kevin said, walking into the pizzeria.

"Good evening Clint," Franco said, with a tense-sounding voice.

"Clint," surprised Kevin, instantly on guard, he scanned the small room. Six tables lined the windows, every one empty except the corner one, where three young men sat hunched over. One watched him through the mirrored reflection of the window. All three did not fit the profile of the suburban teenager; they said **Oakland** in large letters.

"Thanks, Franco, pie ready?"

"Five minutes, we been real busy, Clint, real busy." Franco's eyes darted toward the group, then back to Kevin.

"Is their pie ready?" Kevin asked, pointing to the boys.

"Almost, but glad you came in, not seen you for a while."

"Out of town for the last week," Kevin said as he slowly turned toward the corner table, pulling the revolver from his shoulder holster.

The first boy, the one against the glass, jumped up from his chair, it tipped, fell, and slid across the floor. He swung a chrome cannon upward, the action looked almost funny due to the size of the gun and the kid's small hand. But it immediately set the tone of conversation.

"Motherfucker, why d'hell you 'ave-ta come in, we was almost out, goddamn mother fucker!" the teen yelled.

"I'm Officer Kevin Bryan, asshole, just drop the gun or I *will* have to kill you. Drop it, and go to the floor," Kevin said, standing against the counter; Franco had already ducked below the countertop; Kevin heard the rear door slam as the employees ran out the back.

"Drop it now, I'm a cop. You don't want to do this."

"Com-on Darryl, we need ta get outta here, been too long already," one of the sitting boys pleaded.

"No, this fucker's gonna get us our cash; tell that asshole to give us money and we're gone. Now!'

"Can't do that Darryl, just can't," Kevin said. The lights on the beater Cadillac flashed on. "Just drop the canon, no need for it."

"Fuck you, get me the fucking money!"

"Can't, Darryl, just can't. You boys lie down on the floor and this'll be over. The gun, on the floor! Now!" The faintest sound of sirens could be heard in the still suburban air.

"See, in two minutes, there'll be more black and whites' here than you can count and either you'll be on the floor alive or you'll be on the floor dead, what is it to be?"

"Fuck you!" the kid started to tense up. Kevin knew the signs. In the next second, the glass wall of the pizzeria exploded as the Cadillac crashed through the front window and then backed up, the two sitters bolted, ran through the busted window frame and jumped into the car. Darryl, as startled as Kevin, pulled the trigger; the gun's weight had lowered his arm toward the floor. The bullet hit the tile and ricocheted up into Kevin's thigh. He managed to fire one shot, hitting the boy in the upper body, Darryl spun into the broken glass blown across the floor. As Kevin began to slump, he watched the Cadillac reverse out into the parking lot, acrid smoke exploding from the squealing tires; it's trunk crashed into the side panel of the first police car. Kevin looked down at his right sneaker; it was turning red.

7b

"Good morning, Margrite, you do look better. The swelling has lessened and your black eye is now just a delightful dark brown," Otto Speyer said. "Breakfast?"

Margrite Speyer lay in bed, propped up against a stack of brilliant white pillows. The contrast made the mess of her face even more evident. She tried to smile through her split lip; a tooth was missing.

"Breakfast would be great; I'm hungry, but make it liquid, maybe a shake. My jaw is still too sore to chew."

"You were very lucky my dear, very lucky. That tumble could have done more than damage your face, but it's not too bad. The doctor says it won't be noticeable in a week or two and the tooth will be replaced. The paintings, are they still safe?"

"Yes."

"We can only assume that the O'Mara woman has returned to the states; she will be looking for the paintings and for you."

"She still doesn't know who I am, and who we are, but she isn't stupid and she is skilled. The tall fellow with her also handles himself well, these are not amateurs."

"Mr. Dumont would not have done it any other way. Our research shows the man is very wealthy and has extensive resources. What has happened probably surprised him, they'll be on guard now and this will be more difficult."

"Yes, grandfather, much more difficult." She had only arrived from Paris a day earlier; she thought about how lucky she had been.

A Parisian ambulance took the semi-conscious Margrite Speyer to the nearest hospital; her passport identified her as a citizen of Argentina. There was also a business card in the clear passport holder found in her pocket. They placed a call to the number on the card; it was for the Argentine winery. Otto Speyer quickly took the call, within thirty minutes one of his agents was at the hospital, taking charge. Senorita Speyer was recovering and, other than the slight damage to her face and cuts to her hands, was well enough to travel; she left the hospital the next morning. An hour later, she was on a private Gulfstream headed home to Argentina. She arrived at the Mendoza airstrip three hours before Kevin and Sharon arrived in Oakland.

"I'm sure they found the plate, Grandfather," Margrite said. "I believe they left it in the bank, probably in a safe deposit box. It will be difficult to get. There was also another woman with them, French, I'm sure. We're trying to identify her. She went another direction and I didn't have someone who could follow her, she will be found. We also don't know where they were staying but it had to be near the bank, somewhere in the 7th Arrondissement."

"The original plate is important but not totally," Herr Speyer said. "They probably made a copy of some kind. It was with them when they left Europe and we still have the paintings. My guess is the Jews that were going to receive the paintings will make a fuss, they always do. This O'Mara woman still has to find the paintings and we can still use them as bait. You get some sleep; I have a call to make."

7c

Sharon took a long shower, put on shorts and a loose tee shirt, spent a quality half-hour with Basil, and made dinner of frozen leftover lasagna. She washed it down with a good cabernet. She fell into bed at midnight; Basil stood guard at the door to the bedroom and his eyes never left his mistress.

At 2:30 a.m. her phone rang, it buzzed through her head like the Parisian jackhammer she was dreaming about.

"This better be good, damn it," she said.

"Sharon, Gina here, you awake?" Gina Cavelli asked.

"Gina, you okay?"

"I'm fine, but Kevin's been shot, wounded in a shoot-out at Franco's Pizza. He took a bullet in the leg, lost a lot of blood."

Sharon was more awake then she had been in a week.

"What? Repeat that, shot? How bad?" Basil stood next to the bed, he knew the tone of his master's voice and she needed help.

"Bad, but not life-threatening. He's at John Muir. Tried to stop a hold-up, put one kid in intensive care; they caught three others trying to escape. The cops were all over the place; he was in an EMT van in ten minutes, didn't hit an artery."

"How'd you find out?"

"Two of his people stopped here after they left the scene, they remembered that I knew Kevin, told me what happened. I'm at the hospital, in all the chaos I asked if anyone had called you, they didn't know."

"I'll be there in ten, see you in the lobby."

As Sharon walked up to the emergency entry at John Muir Hospital she looked through the glass door and saw Gina Cavelli pacing about the room.

After a soulful hug, Gina told Sharon everything she knew. "He's still in intensive care and sedated, no visitors until morning at the earliest, he's lucky, the bullet, or at least a part of it, had cut into his leg, probably a ricochet. The kid had a 45 caliber cannon; a full slug would have ripped half his leg open. Nice welcome home and all for a fucking pizza. Our boy was very lucky; you two should have stayed twenty minutes longer last night."

"But then who knows what would have happen at Franco's; sometimes things happen for a reason. And yes, he was lucky, very lucky."

Sharon found a relatively comfortable lounge; Gina found a serviceable cup of coffee, and curled up in the opposite chair. In fifteen minutes, they were both asleep.

The first rays of sunlight were streaming through the lobby when Sharon's phone began to buzz in her pocket; it startled her awake.

"O'Mara here."

"Miss O'Mara, I hope that I have awakened you from a deep comfortable sleep," the German accent said. "You have something that we want, and you and I need to find a way for it to be returned to us."

"Look, you Nazi thug," Sharon said, holding her hand up toward Gina, "there is nothing to talk about, sure I have *what* you're looking for, but, as I told that blond bitch, I will destroy it before you get your hands on it. Do you understand me?"

"Please, please don't be so hasty," Otto Speyer said. "There is always room to negotiate about such things."

"No there fucking isn't, *auf wiedersehan*." She clicked the phone off. "Fucking Nazis."

"Your language my dear, please," said a familiar voice from behind O'Mara. Evelyn Lucca walked across the lobby, heading toward the two women, "Coffee?"

She held up a paper tray with four coffees on it, "There's one decaf, wasn't sure."

Sharon and Gina looked at each other, "Regular!" they both said.

After ten minutes, Evelyn was up-to-date on Kevin's condition, she was also told about the call from a man with a German accent.

"I talked with Claudette on my way here," Evelyn said. "She wishes the best for Kevin; she seems to have been smitten by the big guy. Sharon, she wants you to call her later, they have repaired the garage and secured everything in the apartment, and it's being monitored. There has been no black Mercedes; she said you would know what that means."

"I'll call her as soon as I can, she was a great help, Dumont seems to have a lot of good women around him," Sharon said.

"I have been told that has been his professional trademark,

but to all of us, he is more like a grandfather," Evelyn answered. She nudged Gina when a grey-haired man turned the corner of the lobby and walked directly toward them, his light green scrubs and tablet computer suggested he was a doctor.

"Good morning, Dr. Abraham, how's Kevin?" Sharon asked.

"Good morning, Sharon, he's doing better than we expected," the doctor said. "The structural damage was minimal, he just bled a lot. But he'll be walking later today; we need to keep him moving about. If he can be kept quiet and restful, he can go home in a couple of days."

Sharon had been in and out of John Muir Hospital a few more times than she wanted to remember. The last official visit was with Basil when he had been shot, Dr. Abraham was on duty then as well, and he patched up the Shepherd-Rottweiler mix, the honorary police dog tags helped him get through the doors.

"Can we see him?" Gina asked.

"Give him an hour, then be brief, he seems exhausted and it's not from just the hole in his leg."

"We've been traveling," Sharon said, and told the doctor about the trip, at least the more pleasurable, less dangerous parts.

"That explains a lot, jet lag on top of being wounded, no wonder his body wants to just sleep. One hour, then in and out. I'll call you later."

Kevin could barely keep his eyes open when the girls walked into his room; he smiled and waved the arm that was taped up with IV's.

Sharon flashed on Alain Dumont and the last time she saw him, *"This is getting way too messy,"* she thought to herself.

There was little to tell him, Sharon kept the German's call to herself.

"We've been talking," Sharon said, pointing at the girls.

Kevin rolled his eyes, and through his raspy anesthetized vocal cords said, "Great, now what?"

"Quiet. No talking. You'll stay at my place, in the extra room.

All three of us will be your nurses till you're back on your feet."
Kevin started to object. "No talking, doctor's orders, it's settled.
I have a lot of things to do, and you're on injured reserved for
the next few weeks; I need to know you're safe, and with these
leftovers from World War Two about, I need to be sure you're
okay. And my place is as good as any."

Resigned to his fate, Kevin nodded.

"I'll be by later this evening; I need to get some sleep as
well," Sharon said. As they left, Gina and Evelyn gave him a kiss
on the cheek.

They parted in the lobby as Kevin's captain walked through
the automatic doors.

"Captain, good morning," Sharon said.

"Good morning, Sharon, how's our boy?"

"Doing well, may be out in a few days, lucky, he was."

"Very lucky, just a case of wrong place, wrong time. But
what he did probably saved Franco. The kid was a banger from
Oakland; we think he was trying to make his bones with the
gang. The others have long records; he might have been told to
shoot the man. Kevin stopped it. It was a good shooting, if there
ever was one."

"Good. The other boy?"

"He's upstairs, his shoulder's busted up from Kevin's slug.
They tell me an inch lower and he'd be in the morgue; he was
lucky too. All of them will be going away for a long time. Kevin identified himself as a cop, they shot him, we caught them
on site, and Franco is a good witness, it's all clean and well-
wrapped."

"Another bunch of thugs off the street," Sharon said, trying
to catch up with the girls as they went through the door.

"Yes, but tell me why Kevin needed a week off to go to Paris
with you; you two getting serious? No one goes to Paris without
being serious about something."

"What? The two of us, you've got to be kidding. Kevin was
helping me with some things I'm involved with."

"The hijacked paintings, perhaps?"

"How'd you know?"

"I can read a paper and Kevin's in a bit of trouble for not telling me he was there; I heard it from a friend on the SF police. Sharon, I don't like those calls when they concern my men; you two have a history in my town and it's been a mess to clean up now and then. I can't tell him to stay away from you, but you need to take better care, there's a lot on the line for him. He's very good at what he does and these escapades can cost him a lot of support, my support, if you know what I mean, *capice*?"

Sharon, never one to be lectured at, could only shake her head. *"He's right,"* she thought. *"I've put Kevin in a tough spot, he would do anything for me and I just let him go along, it's not fair. And the captain thinks we are more than just friends, but that's what a lot of people think. Shit!"*

"Do you understand me, Ms. O'Mara?" the captain repeated.

"Yes sir, I do. I'll keep him out of my professional affairs, that's the least I can do. Acceptable?"

"Acceptable, he won't be happy about it but I need to protect him . . ."

"From me?"

"I didn't say that, we need to protect him from himself, he would do anything for you and that's his problem, so, *understood*?"

"Yes."

Sharon took Basil for a long walk around the neighborhood; they made quite a pair and more than one tradesman's van slowed to check them out. "Nice dog," one said, as he unloaded his truck. Basil looked hard at the man; he backed away a bit, "Real nice dog." Sharon could only smile.

Basil had been with Sharon since he was whelped. He was the best product of another failed police marriage between two professionals, a German Sheppard and Rottweiler, when they slipped their handlers and disappeared for ten frantic minutes. Sharon had the choice of the litter; even that first morning, Basil's eyes never left her.

Sharon took a one-hour nap, ate a late breakfast of scrambled eggs, showered, slipped on a tank top over her shorts, and sat down at her computer. She flipped open her iPad and found the photo she'd a taken of the box; she emailed it to herself to get it on her computer. The outside said 'Trittenheim' in black Germanic script, still bright from being hidden in the dark for over fifty years. She typed in the name and the wiki site popped up. Scrolling down through the various entries for the town and the area in Germany, her eye caught the name Speyer and a winery in Argentina. She clicked on the winery's name, Trittenheim, same as the box.

"A coincidence boy? I don't necessarily believe in them."

Basil lifted his head and then slowly sat his chin on the edge of his bed.

The business website for the winery opened, a very professional and obviously successful operation. There was a box for customers to sign in; a password was needed. There were lists of their wineries; they covered the globe. The Trittenheim label boasted appellations from Europe, Australia, South Africa, Napa, and Argentina. She vaguely remembered an Australian wine with the same bold label; she went to her pantry and, from a small stack of bottles, found the red Shiraz.

"I'll be damned," she said, looking at the large black Germanic 'T'.

Back at the computer, she clicked on the events button, a long list of tastings appeared. She randomly selected a date from six months earlier, it said birthday. A brief description announced that this event was celebrating the ninetieth birthday of the winery's founder, Otto Speyer. She clicked on the photos button, ten images appeared. An elderly man, still strong and erect, stood holding a glass of wine, obviously saluting the crowd; next the man was standing among posed pictures, the kind that successful people hang in their offices, a politician is standing in the middle usually. She felt her shoulders shudder; even Basil changed his position on his bed, as if he'd been disturbed.

She clicked on the next picture and it filled the screen, "My God, it's her!" Basil lifted his head.

The photo showed the old man and a blond woman kissing him on the cheek; it was Sharon's Parisian blond, the bitch on the bike. The caption said, "Margrite Speyer kisses the cheek of her Grandfather and winery founder, Otto Speyer. Margrite is the CEO of the Trittenheim Winery Group."

"I'll be damned, and she's a rich bitch to boot. Basil old boy, now the Nazis are into wines and mayhem. We've got our work cut out for us."

7d

Late in the afternoon, Sharon called the hospital to check on Kevin, a familiar voice answered the phone,

"Detective Kevin Bryan's room, nurse Cavelli here."

"I thought you went home," Sharon said, not surprised.

"Did and got four hours of blissful sleep, but I have a business to run and I'll be out of here at 6:30, just checking on our boy."

"How's he doing?"

"Actually good, not as groggy, still raspy, and getting his attitude back, says he's still owed a pizza!"

"Can I talk with him?"

"How's my fellow traveler?" Kevin said pausing as he caught his breath. "What a piece of business I walked into, all for a slice.

Dammit, now every time I see a pizza, I'll also see a chrome-plated 45, takes all the fun out of it. You ok? Now it's your turn to be nursemaid after all the times I took care of you!"

"I'm fine and it's good to hear the strength in your voice. You know I'll always be here for you. But I have some news; I know who blondie is, you ready?"

For the next five minutes, Sharon walked Kevin through the process that ended up with the Internet picture of granddaddy Nazi and his heir apparent. Once she had a name, the rest wasn't hard. High profile people may try to hide their tracks, but it's impossible, especially when someone needs the news and papers to help sell their products, and wines are international. She found Margrite Speyer's remarks in the Melbourne papers, Johannesburg, and Rio de Janeiro, presentations at competitive tastings in London and Berlin, and donated cases of wine in the Napa wine auction; their winery was in Yountville. Her face was everywhere, a private and secretive person she was not.

"My guess, she's part of the new glue holding together whatever they're now calling this organization, not only is traveling a good cover for her, she even makes a few bucks along the way."

"The old man called me after we saw you this morning; he wants to make a deal of some kind and I'm letting them stew. We'll wait and see what happens; I think she's recuperating at their Argentine winery, it's near Mendoza, a region famous for Malbec."

"Is it red?"

"Yes."

"Then they're not so bad, if they were only making that Riesling crap, I would get out of this bed and shoot someone or at least arrest them, but red wine, now that's a different matter." Kevin coughed.

"You okay?" Sharon asked, hearing the pain rasp in the sarcasm in Kevin's voice.

"Yeah, I'm fine. They want the gold plate," Kevin added.

"Yes."

"And we are *not* going to give it to them, correct?"

"Yes, that's correct."

"Good, after what they did here and in Paris," Kevin paused. "Damn, forgot about the files on my computer at work, and there's no way you can get to them, only me, another reason to blow this joint."

"Hang tight; I don't want you anywhere near all this. It might jeopardize the case against those bangers, and the files are fine where they are," she said, trying to keep Kevin at more than arm's length now and keep his captain happy. "I am going into San Francisco to see Mr. Dumont, need to report everything that has happened. Evelyn says he's doing better than you and is twice your age, so buck up, buckaroo."

"You know I hate it when you say that."

"That's why I do it, say goodbye to Gina for me; tomorrow," she hung up.

Alain Dumont had been transferred to a private hospital that he had funded and built; it was not only for very wealthy clients wishing for extreme privacy, it was also one of the world's finest children's hospitals for victims of war and other depravities of man. The damaged families do not pay one penny, euro, or Central African franc; it was through the benevolence of the wealthier patients in one wing that these children, in the other wing, would now have a future. Those clients paid through the proverbial nose for the doctors that worked in this hospital who, in the morning, might be repairing a disc or knee, and, in the afternoon, operating on a three-year old land mine victim. They paid for the privilege, and Dumont made sure that, if they bitched, it was their last visit. Few bitched.

Sharon looked around the door of the well-appointed room slowly; Alain Dumont was sitting in a chair, reading; his smile changed the whole day for her. She wore a paisley top over black slacks, a green bag over her shoulder, her red hair was down passed her shoulders and black flats finished her look. He waved her in.

"You look well, very well, my dear, and I like your hair

down. Paris is a magical city, is it not?"

She was shocked and distracted by his comment, "Don't you know what happened?"

"I know everything; Claudette called and filled me in. No, Paris had nothing to do with your little misadventure. She is what she is; maybe I'll be buried there, next to that Morrison fellow, always liked his style, shitty way to go though."

The non sequitur took her back for a second, "He was dead before I was born, but I have all his records."

"Records or CDs or those digital things, which?"

"I bought a ton of records at flea markets when I was young, I was alone a lot, helped to pass the time, now they're on my iPad and iPod. Wait a second, you're distracting me."

"Intentionally, see there're lots of other more important things than Nazis and art, but I guess we have to come back to reality. These are very real, very bad people, poor Remy found that out."

Sharon told Dumont about the thread of evidence leading back to Speyer and the winery operations.

"Makes sense, do you have pictures?" Dumont asked, looking at the expensive handbag Sharon carried. "Nice bag, STIA I see, Evelyn and her family are doing well. Sharon, always do what you love, only great things come from a great love of what you do." Dumont sipped some water, his eyes never looked at her handbag; they looked only at her.

Sharon extracted a manila envelope from her bag and slid out a small stack of printouts from her computer. She handed them to Alain.

He held the images by the corners; old habits from the days of real photography die hard. He leafed through them one by one. Halfway through, he stopped and held up the first image O'Mara had found: Otto Speyer toasting his birthday crowd.

"It's been a long time, but I know this man, don't remember where, yet, but I will. I've seen him before; we were younger, much younger." He turned the picture toward Sharon. "Just give me a little time; I *know* this son-of-a-bitch!"

Chapter 8

8a

After the hijacking and his conversation with Sharon, Bobby Gillis returned to Bakersfield. His grandfather still sat in the large leather chair, sipping bourbon. The heat of summer had raised the temperature to over one hundred degrees; inside, it hovered at a dry comfortable eighty-five. It was also dark; the shades were drawn to keep out the insistent sun, to Jimmy Gillis it didn't make a difference; he was blind.

"Grandpa, it could be him, your old buddy Robert Dupont, but he calls himself Alain Dumont now," Bobby said opening the refrigerator, the cold light cut through the gloom for the few seconds he needed to pull out a beer.

"Dumont, I know that name. He's been in California for a long time, tech or something. Some of his software helped to run the farm here maybe fifteen years ago, when we were successful, before the Feds took away our water. You were still in high school I think," Jimmy said.

"Don't remember, more into football and women then."

"Both can hurt you bad, but you know that now. What else?"

"Seems after the art was stolen, a lieutenant I knew from Iraq popped up. She was in charge of the operation, it blew up; not her fault but there's a connection to Paris. She's going there with another fellow, Kevin Bryan, he's a cop. May even be there now."

"You said that Robert Dupont and this Dumont is the same guy?"

"That's what the lieutenant said, no reason for her to say

otherwise. Told me that Dumont said you and Graham were dead, killed in the war. It was his decision to take the truck. It certainly turned his life into something."

"That much loot could have turned someone into a rich man or a fool, glad to see he took the better road. Did you talk to him?"

"No, when I left the hospital, he was still in a coma. Sharon says he's touch-and-go. I came back to tell you what I know."

"Good boy, your dad would be proud. Still it's a wonder that, after all these years, I'm still alive to see all this happen. Oh what a fool I could have made of myself with that gold, and now it's the paintings that are causing all the fuss. Strange times is all I can say, strange times."

"You've been good gramps, good family, been a rock. You never know what'll happen."

"That's for damn sure boy," Jimmy Gillis said as he rubbed the small piece of his upper arm left from the war. "That's for God damn sure."

A few days later, Bobby sat at the breakfast table in the kitchen of his small home nestled snug on the edge of his quarter section of almonds, reading the Bakersfield *Californian*. In the lower corner of page three, under Northern California News, was a small story.

Lucky to be Alive
Lafayette, California

Officer Kevin Bryan, Lafayette detective, while picking up a pizza, broke up a strong-arm robbery that was underway when he entered. Bryan, severely wounded in the leg, managed to shoot one of the robbers. Three others tried to escape but were blocked in by police cars. Bryan's injury isn't life-threatening and he is expected to survive. Bryan's captain said, "Bryan is a shining example of the type of people we have on our force, men and women who, when not on duty, are still on duty."

Gillis punched in O'Mara's number on his phone.

"O'Mara."

"Lieutenant, Bobby Gillis. What's this about Kevin? He ok?"

"Bobby, damn it, please call me Sharon. And yes, he's going to be fine but he's out of commission for the next three weeks at least. Lucky, a ricochet off the floor caught him in the thigh. How's your grandfather?"

"Surprisingly pretty good, he lives in a very small world now, but this news about Dumont has opened some windows for him. Seems much brighter, best I've seen him since grams died. Strange news, but it's helping him a lot."

"Good," Sharon said, she paused.

"You okay?"

"Fine, Bobby, just thinking." She paused again. "Bobby, what are you doing right now?"

"Reading the paper, then not much to do for a month, almonds are okay, my boys can watch the water, won't shake the trees 'til mid-September at the earliest. Why?"

"Need a man, Bobby," Sharon said.

"Best offer I've had in months, maybe years," Bobby said with a laugh.

"Dream on, soldier," she answered. "I need some help, with Kevin out and his captain giving me the heads up that he's in trouble for hanging out with people the likes of me, I need someone to watch my back. There's trouble ahead; I know you and respect your skills. And there's a good per diem."

"Tell me more," Bobby answered.

Sharon told Bobby everything, about the hijacking, the death of Remy Adler, the trip to Paris, the box, their return, and the last phone call from Otto Speyer.

"Just a sec, Sharon," Bobby said.

He opened the box containing his grandfather's photos he had sat on the kitchen table. He found the picture of the two men on the truck, the painting behind them. Off to one side, sat a small box, it was inconsequential; he never paid any attention to it. It was the painting that he had always looked at.

"Does the name Trittenheim mean anything to you?" he asked.

"How do you know that name?"

"I have a picture of the painting with my grandfather and another man, gramps says his name was Graham. On the back of the truck, next to them, sits a box, the box says 'Trittenheim' on the side."

"Son-of-a-bitch, I was crawling around under that same truck last week, I saw that box; I know Trittenheim. Damn. Now, are you interested?"

"Lieutenant, I see an operation coming up. Just like old times. Good guys versus the bad guys. The world is such a simple place."

Sharon didn't correct him calling her lieutenant again.

8b

"Good morning, Zoe," Sharon said, answering her phone. Dr. Zoe Goldfarb-Binder's name glowed on the screen. "Everything okay?"

"It's you I'm worried about, seems that the connection between Officer Bryan and you has been made by a reporter here in LA," Zoe said. "And how's Officer Bryan? We never met him but he was with you that day."

"Kevin's fine, what do you mean, connection?"

"The *Times* has been dogging this story since the paintings were hijacked; one of their people was up there that day, tall blond fellow, his name is Trent Smyth."

"I remember a tall blond, real So-Cal type with a mini tape recorder, never talked to him."

"He's still upset about that from what I understand. Has known Saul for maybe five years, worked the Hollywood scene, my thinking is he's a disappointed actor, turned newsman."

"Hear there's lots of that down there," Sharon said.

"Yes, come to LA, become a star. At least he's found a job. Anyway this guy Smyth has strung all the events together, and now, with Kevin being shot, the story is only getting juicier. Saul is feeding him stories; some are just imagined, trying to make more out of all this than it is."

"Zoe, there is a lot more to this than even Saul and you know," Sharon said.

"More?"

"A lot more, and even though I want to tell you, I have to keep you in the dark for a while. It's best for you and your family; I really mean it. The people that hijacked the paintings are in this, not for the art, but for other things, more valuable things. Please understand."

"I will try and I'll try my best to keep Saul under control," Zoe said.

"Good luck."

Sharon closed her phone and looked up the article, Los Angeles *Times* streamed across the web page; she read the story about stolen Nazi art, the bi-line was Trent Smyth. It was an accurate tale of how many of the great pre-war private collections were stolen by the Nazis, especially those collected by Jews. It followed the sordid stories of art through galleries that didn't care about the art's ownership, only their commission. It also mentioned some of the great museum battles and acquiesces to the rightful families who owned the art; few paid fines or penalties, even fewer went to jail. Smyth was trying to gin-up the story of Dumont's art into one of these tales.

"This may be one of the best, Trent ol'boy," Sharon said. "This may be one of the greatest stories and you don't know the half of it." Basil looked up at Sharon and harrumphed, as only a very disinterested dog can do. His mistress was home again; that's all that mattered.

As O'Mara clicked on the Arts & Culture button to follow the story, she noticed the *Times* header across the top of the page, the T in *Times* looked remarkably like the T on the label of the Trittenheim wine that still sat on her kitchen counter. *"Not a chance,"* she thought to herself. *"Not a chance, but still, you never know."*

She looked at the clock, did a mental calculation and punched in a number. Five seconds later, a pleasant and very professional voice answered in unmistakable French.

"*Oui, J'suis Claudette Leclair ici.*"

"*Claudette bonsoir, comment allez-vous?*"

"Sharon, I am very well and finishing an excellent dinner; it has been a long day and the adventures that Monsieur Dumont and you have created have also made it a very exciting day, or, should I say week," Claudette said.

"Sorry about that, but I can't deny that the days do go by very quickly. Have you talked to Mr. Dumont today?"

"Non, but I did yesterday, after you left him. He asked if I recognized the name Otto Speyer, I said no. He mentioned the winery Trittenheim and I asked if it was about the box in his safe, he said yes. Well, *mon cherie*, now I have a story to add to your story."

"Do tell, Claudette, do tell," Sharon said curiously.

"I asked our Rio de Janeiro people whether the name Speyer had popped up in their business relationships, especially in distribution and logistics. I was sent to a gentleman who has been with me almost ten years and has been an important part of Mr. Dumont's companies in South America much longer than that. He said he would call me back from a different phone."

"Strange."

"An hour later, he called from a cell phone; he said he had just bought it. I'll make it short for right now, and will add a lot more later. It seems that Herr Otto Speyer has been involved, quite quietly, with a well-organized group of ex-Nazis for the last fifty years. They have political influence and are paid great respect by the politicians in that crazy country. Their money has comforted many politicians. But the old guard is dying off one by one. Twenty years ago, it was rumored that the Israelis helped to cull the herd, but more recently it has been attributed to old age. Speyer is the oldest survivor and the most coherent. My man says the younger generation, in their fifties and sixties, are not as involved as the older men had hoped. But he says that there is now a more radicalized younger group led by our close friend and fellow bicyclist, Margrite Speyer, that's beginning to be very vocal and, as my man says, impatient. He doesn't know how or why, but with all the turmoil in the Argentine government, there are opportunities available now that have not existed since the Juan Peron days."

"Overthrow a government?"

"Possibly, or certainly control large and important parts of it."

"And a couple of billion dollars wouldn't hurt."

"Sharon, as you well know, money can help solve a lot of problems."

"Or cause them."

Sharon spent the remainder of the day at the gym and the pistol range. The stretching and the weights helped to tone muscles that suffered from the hours spent sitting in a plane; the range not only honed her eye but also helped her concentration. As always, she scored well. The pudgy middle-aged boys on the line could only smile, nothing like a hot chick with a gun to start a man's mind racing.

She stopped at John Muir Hospital on the way home; the change in Kevin's attitude was refreshing.

"Any more news?" he asked, "and do I smell cordite?"

"Can't fool you, no, not much yet, but I think the storm's gathering. They're getting impatient, and that's good. Impatience can make for mistakes." She also filled Kevin in on Claudette's news.

"Be careful, I'm not much help these days. Tried to walk to the can and it hurt to bloody hell, just made it back without an accident. But the good news is I'm out of here the day after tomorrow. Then your place; I hate to do it. I can still go to mine, it'll work."

"You have no choice. Basil's a good guard; he'll take care of you along with Evelyn and Gina, it couldn't be better."

"Where're you going?"

"Who said I was going anywhere?"

"You did, you never said you'd be there to take care of little ol' me, tell me."

"I need to go to LA to take care of a few things with the Goldfarbs; there's a story building that I need to slow down, the story will help us in the long run but right now I need to lower the pressure it can cause."

Sharon told Kevin about the news reporter at the Times and the thread he was building. She also told him about her idea to perhaps smoke these people out.

"Might work, back-up?"

"My old sergeant from Iraq will be with me."

"Gillis?"

"Yes."

"Trust him? He's got more than Iraq wrapped up in this now with his grandfather and Dumont's history. Maybe he sees more in this than what he lets on."

"It's possible, but I trust him as only one soldier can trust another. You know what I mean?"

"Yeah, but still be a careful, the setup you laid out may work or it could back-fire, and, if that happens, I hope he's as good as you remember."

"He's better," Sharon answered as she looked at the IV tube still connected to Kevin's arm, a steady flow of clear liquid passed along the tube to his arm. "You get better; we'll get you out of here and take you to the house. Then I'm going to LA."

8c

O'Mara sat in the tight corner table that overlooked Santa Monica pier. Tourists and beach bums hung out along the old wooden railing, a beer in one sunburnt hand, a cigarette in the other. *"Wait until the smoker vigilantes catch them,"* she thought to herself. *"Santa Monica's famous for their opinions on personal habits, at least those they deem wrong."* She ached for a Marlboro.

She called Trent Smyth with the number Goldfarb-Binder gave her after she left the hospital. She wasn't surprised that he didn't pick up; she left a message. How quickly he returned her call did surprise her.

"It's good to talk to you, I'm sorry we didn't have time that morning in San Francisco," Smyth said.

"Me too," she answered, with her most sincere voice. "Zoe Goldfarb suggested I call, says that you have been meeting with some of the family, trying to find out what's going on. Since they really don't know anything, I thought we might get together and maybe I can answer a few of your questions."

There was a pause. Sharon waited a three second beat, "Well?"

"I'm surprised and a little shocked," Smyth said, as his voice went up an octave.

She scrunched her face at the sound. "I liked your article in the *Times* about World War Two art and the difficulties the original owners and families are having proving ownership. So maybe I can help you flesh out your story."

Another pause, "Well, okay. What about an interview? Maybe over the phone or maybe I can get my editor to spring for a ticket to Frisco."

"It's San Francisco, and I'll be in LA Thursday. Meet me for lunch at The Lobster, 1:00 p.m., you're buying."

"Okay, 1:00 p.m. at The Lobster. Is that the one at the end of Santa Monica pier?"

"Yes, the east-end, near the street."

"Okay, 1:00."

It was 1:10 and he still hadn't arrived. Sharon was impatient and the meeting with Saul Goldfarb was three hours away. *"That'll be fun,"* she thought. She saw Smyth reflected in the glass, tall, very blond, good tan, nice shirt and young.

"Ms. O'Mara," Trent Smyth said as he weaved through the tightly placed tables.

"The one and only," she answered. "Sit," came out more as an order than a request.

"Sorry for being late, I could offer the usual excuse, traffic, but if you live here the excuse gets stale. Me, I'm just plain running late. Sorry."

"No problem, like the honesty, besides, the chardonnay you

bought is very good. Want a glass?"

"My boss says there're rules about drinking on the job, so I'll hold off."

"You'll get over that if you stay in this profession of yours, comes with the territory."

She took a sip and waved to the waiter who had already tried to get too friendly, "Bring my friend a glass."

The waiter sized-up Smyth and she watched him return the once over; she shrugged.

Over the next hour, they finished one bottle and were well into a second. The lobster salad was the best she could remember. The talk was about career choices and the future. She surprised him with her Iraq experience; she found that outside of some naïveté, he was not such a dunce. And he could actually write.

"UCLA journalism and acting, wanted to cover my bases."

"Strange pair," she said.

"Well, I knew that acting wouldn't last long, even if I got a gig, so I thought, like an athlete when their career is over, go into broadcasting. I'm still in the game but on the edge. Working at the *Times* is about the same grind, was able to get into some interesting places, pulled together a few good stories, and, after a couple of years, moved up, wasn't easy, but I'm still here."

Sharon raised her glass and saluted, "Here's to persistence."

"Persistence," he echoed, "now for some questions."

"Shoot."

"Was Saul Goldman telling the truth about the paintings?'

"What did he tell you?"

"That after a great deal of research, he found out that Mr. Dumont had the paintings and that, through his own efforts, he convinced Dumont that they be returned to his family."

"Yes, that's how Saul would have framed it. Would be a much better story than the, 'I'm a lucky son-of-a-bitch' angle."

"I take it that's not what happened."

"Trust me, Trent, Saul never gave those paintings a thought until my call, on Mr. Dumont's behest, and I told the family about them."

"Thought as much, but that's still a good story, like winning the lottery."

"Yes, except for all that concentration camp Holocaust and millions dying stuff. It's not a lottery that most Europeans would have wanted to win."

"I get your point," Trent added. "But is there a story?"

"Yes, Mr. Beach Boy, there is a story," she answered. She watched him blush.

Through the rest of the bottle, she told a CliffsNotes version of the paintings and their travels. She left out the tunnels, the gold, the truck, Paris, and the Argentines. She threw in some speculation about the hijacking; she was hoping that Smyth would leave it lie as told, especially the part about a ransom demand for millions. She wanted the real story known only by a few people, but, with Smyth's help, maybe the story would tease out the Argentines a bit more, get them anxious, make them make a mistake. She was counting on it.

After she left The Lobster, she headed east up Wilshire in the electric toy she had rented at LAX. It hummed along, but the computer screen kept distracting her by changing its little arrows and numbers every time she slowed and sped up. She wasn't impressed. The usual slow down as she neared Beverly Hills pushed her off Wilshire, she headed up into the rolling streets near the Polo Lounge; Saul Goldfarb's estate was off Rexford. O'Mara was impressed by the baronial mansions buried behind ten-foot high iron fences and ivy covered walls. The palm trees seemed especially well suited for lining the streets. At the address Saul Goldfarb had given, she punched in the only button on the panel, a light flashed and then a voice offered, "Who is calling, please?"

"Sharon O'Mara."

The gates began to open slowly. She thought to herself, *"I wonder if this is how easy it'll be to get into heaven. 'St. Peter, Sharon O'Mara here, been a very good girl, is the Boss in?'"*

A lot of very expensive real estate had been lost to build the road up to the French limestone of the Goldfarb mansion; ten typical Los Angeles homes could line the lane, five on each side. A large fountain anchored the cul-de-sac in front of the double doors that looked bronze. Saul Goldfarb stood at the top of the stairs looking like a character from central casting, *"I need someone to play the dwarf, have him wear a bad Hawaiian shirt, lots of gold jewelry, one of those Rolexes with the blue face, and make the sun-glasses look real cheap, the kind ZZ Top sang about."* O'Mara almost broke into laughter at the sight. She parked behind his Aston Martin. Saul walked down the steps.

"Good you could make it, hope the traffic wasn't too bad," Saul offered his hand.

"It's good to see you again, Saul, and thank you for the time. Some things I need to say and since I was here on other matters, meeting face to face was a good option."

"Please come in."

She was reminded of the steps that led up to the bank in Paris as they climbed up to the bronze doors. They opened before Saul touched the handles. A butler stood to one side as they entered the foyer, which was more like a great hall that cut through the heart of the building. As they strolled deeper into the house, O'Mara passed dark rooms flanking the passage on both sides.

"I made a lot of money over the past fifteen years," Saul said. "I put a good chunk of it into this house; it has a recorded history like the ownership of a fine painting. A young successful actor started this place in the early thirties; four more actors owned it through the forties and fifties and had it rebuilt, then a producer of horror movies finished the house and the gardens in the sixties. I spent a lot refurbishing and modernizing it. It's just after four; how about a cocktail?"

Saul led O'Mara through the remainder of the house during the tour; they finished at a terrace that overlooked the pool. The downtown Los Angeles towers could be seen through a gap in the trees, the air was crystal clear.

"Seldom see downtown, usually there's just enough crap in the air to hide the towers. You're lucky, Martini?"

"Scotch."

"Single or blend?"

"Single, since you're buying."

"Macallan 25?"

"Only had that once, pretty special."

"Wouldn't know, only drink Russian vodkas. Doc says it's better for my liver, as if the thing weren't pickled enough. Ice?" Saul asked, shaking a martini.

"Neat, thank you."

They took chairs near the overlook's railing; the butler walked onto the terrace and waited for a signal from Goldfarb. He whispered in Saul's ear, Saul nodded, the butler left.

"I have to take this call; I'm very sorry, a little thing at the studio, be right back."

Sharon nodded, and took a sip. The liquor, like the lobster salad, was beyond description. The scotch had a tangible feel in her mouth; it clung to the tongue and when air passed over the surface, flavors exploded. The damp musty hills of Scotland, oranges, dried fruits, caramels. As it evaporated from the glass, she could smell peat fires. *"At 600 bucks a bottle it better be good,"* she thought.

Saul came back to the terrace, his face all puffed and red. "The sons-a-bitches want to shut down my movie, as if they've ever had an original idea. Sure I am over budget a bit, but, in the end, they'll make a bundle. Fuck 'em, I'll be done in two weeks and then I'll show 'em." Saul gulped his vodka, and poured another, this time over ice. "Now, Ms. O'Mara, where the fuck are my paintings?"

"Very nice scotch," she said. "I don't know where Mr. Dumont's paintings are. But I will shortly. And I suggest, Mr. Goldfarb, that if you want to see those paintings, we remain on more civil ground. I know the stories you've been spreading and those people now know the truth, such as it is. And, I assure you, they believe me more than you."

"Who are you to tell me what to say?"

"Someone who can wreck your credibility, but, from what

I see, you do a good job of that yourself." She poured another two fingers of gold into the crystal tumbler. "I need you to
play ball if you want to see those paintings. It'll be hard, I know,
you're more a singles' player than a doubles', you never went in
for team sports, probably because of your attitude. Well, I can't
change you, won't even try, but I do need you to keep quiet."

"You can't tell me when to talk or not to talk."

"That's not what *I'm* saying; I need you to say nothing about
the paintings or the theft for two weeks. Turn down interviews,
don't make calls, nothing. Understand?"

"Why? What's in it for me?"

"Always about you, isn't it? To be blunt, I have a job to do
and that's to return the paintings to the Goldfarb family, not
specifically to you or any other single member of your family,
the whole family. Personally, I think they'd be wasted on you,
but that's my opinion. So, Mr. Goldfarb, can I accept your promise to keep your trap shut for the next two weeks?"

"Who the hell do you think you are, telling me what to do
or say? I had you checked out, I know your record, and you'd
probably make a good movie story. You have the balls to come
here and tell me to be quiet, have to admire that, but no one tells
me to be quiet." His words were a bit slurred; the two drinks had
not been the only two of the afternoon.

O'Mara sat the glass on the table, and walked up to the little
man; the sun flashing off his jewelry almost blinded her. She
stood five inches taller than the top of his bald sunburnt head.
"I have complete authority to do what's necessary to return the
paintings and if that means a protracted legal battle between you
and your siblings, I don't care."

"What do you mean?"

"Simply put, I can give the paintings to the great-great
grandchildren of the original owner, which will cut you out of
anything. They will be put in a trust for your nieces and neph-
ews; you will never see a penny or reap one column of copy. You
will be left out and then, knowing you, you will sue your own
brother and sisters to get what you want. Wreck a family, save

an ego."

"You wouldn't."

"Mr. Saul Goldfarb, I would, and gladly. I'd do it for the theater, I'd do it for the movie rights, and I'd do it just for sport. So, do I have your word, your bond? Do one honorable Goddamn thing in your life, you little asshole."

Saul poured more vodka on the ice still in his glass and walked to the rail. "You are a real fucking bitch."

"I've been called worse and in languages you don't understand."

"Two weeks?"

"Two weeks, and not a peep; I will know if you squeak. One sound, one word, and you will have set up the trust fund for the kids, your word."

O'Mara could tell, even though the man was an ass, that when he gave his word, he would stick to it. "You have my word; not a comment for two weeks."

"Excellent, thank you. If you don't mind, I have a plane to catch. And the scotch was excellent."

"That rot-gut, I never could stand the stuff;, take the bottle if you like."

He took the bottle off the bar and handed it to her. She knew from the heft of the bottle that three fingers of neat scotch were all that were missing.

On the way to the airport, she stopped at a FedEx shipping center, sealed up the bottle, packed it and had it sent to her home, she wasn't going to let some overweight airport TSA cop make her dump the bottle of pure amber gold.

Chapter 9

A dusting of snow covered the lawn. The rows of Malbec grapes stood like black ink lines etched against the white Argentine winter; Otto Speyer traced the lines up to the mountains. *"Will this be my last winter? How many more has God granted me before I join my comrades, some dead so long ago? There's much to do; will I live to see it begin?"*

He had pondered these questions a thousand times, but they were so close now. For the first time since the war, he believed that they would form the new Reich. He knew they would return the German people to leadership again, even if from a foreign land. It will be a start, they will lead from here and the world will follow, it must. The world, like the Germany of eighty years ago, is desperately searching for a new leader. By building a new nation in Argentina, they would influence the world. Speyer knew that people needed a leader, the Führer proved that. They would have it now, his time had passed, but through Margrite he knew there was a future, an heir, a leader.

"I'm going back to California," Margrite said to her grandfather. "I'll get the plate and return home. We have everything in place and once we know the location, our German comrades are ready. I will return here with the other coordinate and finalize the location. I will take it personally to Germany. We will start again, Grandfather."

"I have waited for this day for a long time," Otto Speyer said. "Your father would be very proud."

"I still miss him, but I will honor his memory by making this happen."

The bruising was almost gone; a touch of makeup brightened the remaining grayness. Margrite had felt caged for the two weeks since Paris; she could do nothing while she recuperated. She sent her bodyguard, Derek, back to Napa to insure that the paintings were in good order and secured in the winery warehouse. She would follow the day after tomorrow. Even with his limp, he was more mobile than her.

Margrite prided herself on her technical abilities. Through her international contacts and the Internet, she followed everything relating to the wine business, politics and art. A constant series of articles and data flowed across the screens in her office; she was notified when they responded to her key words. When the San Francisco *Chronicle's* story about the pizza shop shooting included a key word, she was pleased to see that some vengeance had occurred. But there were no follow-up stories, nothing about his condition. She would have Derek do some "research" before she arrived.

The instability in Argentina was continuing, some due to the natural incompetence of its leadership and some due to funds and contributions being placed in certain hands at certain times. For over twenty years, Margrite had been involved in the workings of this well-organized and well-disciplined shadow government in Argentina. Those that knew about the money and political power it wielded feared its wrath and appreciated its benevolence. Those that were naïve were left on the sidelines and, in some cases, literally left on the side of the road. She had led the resurgence after the loss of so many of the original leaders and soldiers, mostly due to age. Her father, Johann Speyer, had died thirty years earlier in an accident while fly-fishing in Chile. In her heart, she knew this was not a mishap and when Margrite was twenty-four, she watched as the man who admitted, after considerable effort and forceful persuasion, to drowning him was executed. She knew it would not bring him back but there were men and woman who wouldn't let World War Two die, the dreams of the new Reich must never die.

"And now there is new threat, this woman who embarrassed me on the streets of Paris," Margrite thought. *"This red-haired bitch now controls the fate of our people and our beliefs. She will not stand against me."*

Twice a year these fugitive families met; all had been helped, by Otto Skorzeny, to flee their homeland, soon after the war, with papers and money, some fled with their families, most escaped alone and penniless. The meeting, the next morning, in Mendoza had been called by Otto Speyer. Initially, these meetings had helped the refugees to get back on their feet and then it helped to fund their businesses, then local political control, and now, through banks and allied industries, worldwide influence had occurred over time. It was agreed to, at the first meetings, that the Führer, the flag, and Germany would never be mentioned; there were too many from the outside that would focus their vengeance on those symbols. It would hinder their goal, their future. They were a close fraternal society with strong European roots, Swiss, Austrian, Alsatian and other parts of Europe that had, over the years, felt the political boundary of Germany move back and forth over their lands. For all of them, there was a very close kinship to their cultural fatherland.

Senior officers, well above the rank of Otto Speyer, managed the initial meetings. Speyer admired some of these men; others, he thought, were strutting buffoons; if they had been caught and brought to Nuremburg, they would have danced on the end of an Allied rope. But they survived and were good sources of funds for the organization. In time, for many, their personal excesses killed them off. But many others were cunning, thoughtful men, excellent leaders and survivors. They were able to move about the western world, to Brazil, Uruguay, North Africa, and many would find a welcome home in Spain. Generalissimo Franco offered jobs and opportunities; connections were made to militants fighting the Zionists in Israel. There was support given to leaders such as Omar Quadafi and Yassar Arafat. Otto Skorzeny, the officer that gave Otto Speyer his assignment to move the box to Berchtesgaden, had attended many of the meetings before he died in 1975.

Otto Speyer was the last of his era, a generation that was responsible for the deaths of tens of millions and the enslavement of millions more. By the actions of these men, the history of the world had changed. Now he stood before one hundred of the children and grandchildren of his comrades. They were waiting for news, news that had grown into a sixty-year old legend. Margrite sat in the chair to his right.

"My fellow Germans and comrades, thank you for coming. I see we have more empty chairs, friends that have left us, friends that will not be forgotten, a moment of silence please." Speyer's eyes passed over the gathering, he knew every man and woman there, he knew their parents and their grandparents; many were his godchildren. Some were named Otto in his honor; he also knew that some would die for the cause.

"You all know the story of the golden plate; it is common knowledge. You also know that it was stolen by the Americans and lost for these past sixty-five years, but comrades, today, I can tell you it has been found."

Speyer watched the faces turn from stoic to surprise, then to smiles. Many turned to each other and whispered. Applause began at the back corner of the room and spread through the audience.

"Yes, we have found it," Speyer said, raising his hands, quieting the crowd. "In the next few days, operations will begin to retrieve the plate and it will be made whole with the other half we carried from Germany. When combined, this information will open the doors to our future, a future we have imagined and hoped for. I am grateful that my granddaughter and your leader, Margrite, was responsible for the discovery, and it will be by her efforts that it will be recovered."

Margrite smiled and acknowledged the applause. She didn't stand; she still limped and didn't want the families to be more aware of her injuries than they already were. The story of her chase after the plate in Paris was well known. It had been slightly altered from a bicycle accident to a personal confrontation with an Israeli Mossad agent and two others that had trapped her in an alley. Only through her fighting abilities and her injured bodyguard's help were they able to escape; the news that two of the Jews were killed added drama to the escape.

"We know where it is," Otto Speyer continued. "Margrite and her men will leave tomorrow; we expect the plate will be here, in our new homeland, within the month. We have waited a long time for this day; let us give thanks that we have lived to see it happen."

Speyer knew more than any of the others in the room what finding the plate would mean, salvation and forgiveness. For almost seventy years, he had borne the pain and shame of losing the box, now it would be lifted. He could stand tall again, the Führer's personal artifacts would be shown as the important relics they were and the billions in gold would change the world.

That day, when Skorzeny gave him the one half of the *"Goldbarren,"* the golden plate in the Hotel Ritz in Madrid, had remained fixed as one of the greatest days of his life. Speyer, visiting wineries in Spain, contacted his old friend.

"Herr Skorzeny, shall we have dinner at our favorite restaurant, my treat," Otto Speyer said.

"Otto, my boy," Speyer smiled; Skorzeny called him boy even though he was 56. "This old body of mine is falling apart; I can hardly leave my room. Meet me upstairs, a boy will show you where. I'll have food prepared, good German food, and we can talk. I have something very important to tell you."

Speyer was saddened to see the man, disease was eating him alive, the pain was excruciating, Skorzeny barely touched his dinner. They talked of old times, as men do when they are near the end, of successes and what could have been, never failure.

"The loss of the case and the Führer's personal effects was an unfortunate act of war, but Otto," Skorzeny said as he sipped a glass of Riesling, "I know you will find it, someday. There was also something else in the case that's as important as the Führer's personal items; there is a gold bar, a thin plate with incredibly valuable information incised into its face. It is this that must be found and made whole."

"Whole?" Speyer asked.

"Yes, whole, there were two plates," Skorzeny said with a smile. "Each is a brother to the other; each has half the number sequence to an incredible treasure we moved into a safe place during the war. Treasure unknown to the Reich in Berlin, mostly gold, found, shall we say, as our armies moved through Europe. Most of it is gold and silver that was never sent to Berlin, where it would have been lost during the war. Money that we knew would be helpful after the war to carry on our cause. It's still there, Otto, still there, locked deep in a limestone cave; it has never been discovered."

Speyer watched as a wave of pain passed through the man; he waited for Skorzeny to regain his composure.

"In the summer of 1943," Skorzeny said, "a small but determined group of officers in our order met to discuss the war's progress. We decided that, in time, we would lose. But the goals of the Führer and Germany were very high on our minds then. The future must be protected. As our forces moved through Europe, great wealth passed through our hands. This came from banks, private vaults, and the camps. We agreed to aggregate these opportunities, so we built caches where they would be preserved and protected. We didn't trust the bureaucrats in Berlin, especially the army." A cough racked the frame of the man; he quickly drank a shot glass of schnapps, the color momentarily returned to his face.

"One man in our group knew about a complex of limestone caves and mines near the village of Olpe, in Westphalia. They were caves he explored as a child. I went to those caves and then, over a period of months, with the help from labor at a nearby camp, a tunnel was constructed hundreds of feet below ground. An entrance secured by a steel door was built and excellent efforts were made to camouflage the entry. Even I could not find it without help or directions. Leaving more than a small guard would have only raised curiosity."

"What was placed in the vault?" Speyer asked.

"Gold and silver, nothing perishable, such as art, manuscripts, or even paper money. We knew the German marc would be worthless if we lost," Skorzeny said.

"Was there an accounting?"

"There was, the last information I was given is that over 500 tons of gold were recovered and placed there," the dying man said.

"A great help to our future," Speyer said, shocked at the magnitude. That amount of gold could do a lot for the cause in Argentina and the world.

"Indeed. And I will not see that future. I have done what I could during the last thirty years, but my efforts are now cut short by a lack of time and this fucking disease." Another tremor passed over the man; Speyer took the old SS-Obersturmbann-führer's hand and held it tight.

"Thank you, Otto; even though I'm only ten years older than you, I have always thought of you as a son, more than just a comrade. You have always been there for us. And I must ask you now to be strong and look to the future."

"Yes, Herr Skorzeny, I will. Why haven't we recovered this treasure?"

"War creates havoc wherever it goes," Skorzeny continued. "The location of the cache, the future of Germany, must remain a secret; all the men in our group agreed. This was in late 1944, around the time of our mid-winter advance against the enemy in the Ardennes. We decided to leave instructions on two gold bars, thin and rectangular like large printing plates. But it was also decided to put only half of the information on each, thus without one, the other is useless."

"How was this done?" Speyer asked.

"The location was fixed by latitude and longitude, down to the smallest measurable number. Thus, each plate has four numbers. When combined, they pinpoint the only spot on Earth where the entry to the vault can be accessed."

"With one number couldn't the entry be found?"

"Only by divine luck, the latitude line is over 550 kilometers long in Germany alone; it would be very difficult and you would have to know what to look for. None of that information is on either plate." Skorzeny reached into his jacket and extracted a red silk cloth, folded in the shape of a large envelope. It held something wrapped with care. "Otto, please take this and guard it with your life; it is the future of our people."

Otto Speyer laid the red sachet on the table. He looked at his mentor, who nodded. Speyer slowly lifted each corner of the silk cloth, until the golden surface was exposed. Four numbers sat left to right inside a frame at the edge. The divine symbol of their lost nation was engraved on the right side. The Teutonic SS had been simply carved in the lower right corner. Nothing else was carved or imprinted on either side; Speyer saw his eyes reflected in the polished surface.

"A simple and effective tool, don't you think?"

"Yes, sir, and the other gold plate was in the Führer's box?"

"Yes."

"Now I am even more dishonored by my loss of the box."

"Don't be, but it is critical to find the other plate."

"Yes sir, I understand. Couldn't someone else have found the vault?"

"It's possible, but our ears in Germany have heard nothing and that much wealth would have been leaked somehow," Skorzeny said.

"The workers, your team that built the vault, couldn't one of the builders recreate a map and location?"

"The workers were liquidated; they were all scum collected during our advance east. In December, during the final advance of our army, all of our team leaders and managers who built the tunnels were traveling east, escaping the push of the enemy through France and Luxembourg. They were all riding in the same railroad car when an air attack destroyed the train and killed everyone; there is no one alive who knows where the entry to the vault is."

"But you do," Speyer said.

"Yes, Otto, but only within three or four miles of the exact location. I was driven there at night, my orders, for security reasons. I can give you the general area but even now, if this shit of a body could function, I could not find it. Our only hope is the other plate." Skorzeny poured Speyer another schnapps.

"To the Fatherland! Heil Hitler"

"To Germany and its people."

Otto Speyer snapped to his feet and threw his hand up in salute; it had been years since he had heard his forsaken country's call to obedience and he reacted instinctively. Skorzeny began to cough and his body shuddered, an aid steadied him, some pills were offered and swallowed, in a few minutes the seizure passed. Speyer looked into Skorzeny's eyes and saw a tear slowly course down his cheek, it held for a moment on the edge of the scar slashed across his left cheek. Skorzeny, with his left hand, wiped away the tear and reached for the gold plate and passed it to Speyer.

"Make them whole Otto, make them whole."

Speyer held the small leather case and extracted the bar in the early light of the late Argentine winter. The surface revealed nothing, only four numbers; his heart ached as he ran his finger over the bar's mirrored finish and traced the hard angles of the swastika. He looked at the mountains again; Margrite will not fail, she cannot fail.

9b

Sharon, Evelyn and Gina sat around the small dining table in Sharon's Walnut Creek kitchen; Kevin was nestled in the guest room, asleep.

"Well that didn't go too bad, at least the back seat of your Jaguar gave that lanky body of his room to spread out," Evelyn said.

"I've never heard someone bitch so much, he's like a little baby," Gina added.

"Here's to our six foot-six inch baby hero," Sharon said, raising her cup of coffee. "Well that's done, now on to more important things, dinner?"

"Can't, Sharon dear, thing back in the city," Evelyn said. "Meeting with some jewelers about the clasps for a new line of bags, sorry."

"And you're back to work," Sharon said looking at Gina.

"Sadly, yes, but the Giants are on tonight, will be a good crowd, the staff's good but the till needs watching so you know where to find me," Gina Cavelli said with a smile.

Ten minutes later, Sharon sat at her computer; Basil took up station in the hall where he could watch both her and Kevin's door. She was looking for more information about the Trittenheim winery in Napa. She was sure that the paintings had been moved to the most secure location the Speyer's could control; it had to be the winery. Her searches for San Francisco Trittenheim distributors and warehouses turned up nothing. She Google Earthed the address of the winery, to the east of Yountville; the image zoomed in on a cluster of buildings snug against the hills that enclosed the Napa Valley. Rows of vineyards wrapped the compound. One road in and out, a large house to the front, the buildings to the back formed a square in the middle. Steep slopes extended up from the parking lot and the processing area, as if the complex were built into a half-shaped bowl. A large parking area for tourists flanked the south side of the complex. The vineyards almost ran to the face of the buildings on the open side of the winery.

Sharon said to Basil, "It's wide open, little cover, it won't be easy." Basil nodded affirmatively and sat his wide jowls on the hardwood floor, then, feeling a vibration through the floorboards, he bolted to his feet and took a defensive stance. He had a clear shot to the door. The doorbell rang.

Sharon had trained her partner never to bark at the door; he fought every instinct of his DNA, defending the cave was the prime directive. He would follow her directions when she signaled, but it would be done quietly.

Sharon keyed in the code for the security camera at the door; multiple images appeared on the screen. She smiled, seeing his tussled black hair, remembering the first time she had met the sergeant.

* * * *

Baghdad, Iraq Six years earlier

"Sergeant Robert Gillis, sir," he said with a crisp salute.

"At ease Gillis," O'Mara said. She reviewed his transfer papers. "This is your third tour Gillis, why the hell you want to keep coming back here to this God-forsaken land of sand, shit, and Shiites. Hell, most of the Iraqi's I know don't even want to be here, why do you? And for God's sake Gillis, relax."

"Yes sir and they usually call me Bobby," Gillis said visibly moving to rest, hands behind his back. "My boys would be lost without me, sir. I trained 'em and they work well together, I'd miss 'em, so here I am."

"California boy, Bakersfield. On a hot day, it must make you feel at home."

"Bakersfield is heaven compared to this, sir," Bobby said. "I have the family ranch of almonds and grapes and some brothers and sisters who take care of it for my granddaddy, lost my dad in Panama when I was a kid, my family's been soldiers since the Civil War, and most survived; my dad was our only loss. It's in our blood fighting assholes, sir."

For the next six months, Sharon worked on and off with Gillis and his men and women, guard duty, skirmishes, checkpoints, and the attempt to find the reporter, they covered a lot of territory around Baghdad. They bonded as only soldiers can; when Sharon left for home, there was one hell-of-a party.

* * * *

Basil stood to one side as Sharon opened the door, Bobby Gillis, tall and straight, still sporting a dark tan, a farmer's tan, almost saluted when he saw Sharon.

"None of that, Bobby, we're a team now, equals, other than the fact you're prettier. Now get in here before my neighbors think I'm running a whore-house with all the good-looking men and women coming and going today." She saw his red pickup parked at the curb.

Bobby ducked inside, a large dark army green canvas bag over his shoulder. Basil sniffed his legs, "He's one of the good guys, Basil. Sit."

The dog did as he was told and watched Bobby set the bag

on the floor; he waited patiently for his next command, his eyes never left the sergeant.

"Great dog, looks strong and healthy, trained?"

"Not sure who's training who," Sharon said. "He does what I ask without question and some days I'm sure I'm doing exactly what he wants me to do. It's a good relationship."

"Had working dogs all my life, they were a part of the ranch, but they were never close, good to see that he's as much a partner as a pet."

"Don't use the word pet around him; he'll take chunk out of you for the insult. He's saved my life a couple times, doesn't steal the covers, and seldom snores. If he was a man, I'd marry him, but for now we just live together. Into the living room, coffee? Fresh."

"Thanks, black."

For the next hour, Sharon brought Bobby up to date about what was happening in LA and San Francisco.

"I suggest a recon is in order," Bobby said.

"Agreed, unfortunately my face is known, probably wouldn't last ten minutes," Sharon added.

"They don't know this here country boy, and since I know a bit about the business, I may notice a few things that the average tourist might not, such as what belongs and what doesn't."

"That works, between the aerial and ground recon, we can put a good picture together and then we make a plan. When can you go?"

"The truck is gassed up; I'm checked in at the Marriot up the street, can go this afternoon. Only takes an hour to get up there, should be back by six. The tours probably stop at 5:00 p.m., if they're having them today."

"What tours?" a voice asked from the arched opening of the entry hall to the living room.

"Kevin, you shouldn't be out of bed," Sharon said as the detective hobbled into the room.

"A fellow can only lie about so long, boredom was setting in; nature called and Sharon you really do need to get a longer bed in there. I assume this fellow is Robert Gillis."

Bobby jumped to his feet, "Yes sir, heard a lot about you, sorry about the leg."

"Me too, she's put me on injured reserve," Kevin said, pointing to Sharon, "and you're pinch-hitting, not a big fan of that but I couldn't run ten feet before falling down."

"You sit," Sharon said to Kevin. "And that's enough about the bed. You spend enough nights here so you should buy the damn thing if you want it longer. I said sit!" Basil harrumphed.

Kevin collapsed into the big chair in the corner, his long legs stuck out from under the robe, his right leg was bandaged from the knee up; the wrapping disappeared under the hem.

"Your color looks better," Sharon said.

"And I feel better too and my strength's coming back. Now what are you two cooking up and do you want a biased opinion?"

"Bobby is going to check out the Trittenheim winery in Napa this afternoon, get the lay of the land, maybe even get an idea where the paintings are stashed, assuming they're there. Once that's done, we'll work up a plan to get them back. Without the paintings they'll have to resort to other means to get the information."

"Me, I'm just a country boy with his truck on a short holiday," Bobby added with a bit more theatrical twang than needed.

"Bobby, if I showed up with that much country, they'd throw me out on my red-neck head, I suggest dialing it down a bit," Kevin said.

"Not a problem, in the army you meet all sorts of fellows and the accents kind of stick with you. I'll stay with my Bakersfield twang, no harm there."

"Bobby, it's hard on the ears but it'll work," Sharon said.

The three of them worked through a plan that had Bobby arrive and join the wine tasting groups that wandered about the wineries this time of year, the harvest was just getting underway throughout the valley; it was the best time to see a winery in action. Large trucks with trailers were loaded with fresh grapes and moving up and down Highway 29, the backbone of the Napa Valley. Queues of trucks lined up inside the wineries to dump the grapes into huge hoppers that would de-stem and then transfer the grapes to strange contraptions that would slowly inflate, crushing the grapes, the free juice would then transfer to stainless steel tanks where it would be fermented. The new systems no longer crushed the grapes in mechanical devices that pulled the bitterness and tannins from the skins, here the grapes, and especially the white grapes, such as the chardonnays and the sauvignon blancs, were tenderly hugged and squeezed to give up their glorious liqueur.

They agreed it would be easier to mix in with the chaos in the receiving yard; all hands would be focused there. It was a well-calculated chance that the warehouse areas and storage rooms would be deserted. Even Nazi wineries have the same issues concerning employees and how many are really needed. Sharon would follow Bobby; they would stay in touch by phone. Bobby held up the latest model he had purchased at Safeway.

"Serviceable, but no music," Bobby said. "I'll manage."

Sharon turned to Kevin, "I'll keep you in the loop, but don't let the girls know what's happening. Last thing I need is to have them get all concerned. This will work, and then we'll figure out how to snatch the paintings."

9c

The ride from Walnut Creek to the Napa Valley is a straight shot north. Even mid-week the traffic was heavy; the growth in the Bay Area was pushing north. New bridges over the Sacramento River made the commute easier; Vallejo, Napa and even Sonoma were feeling the pressure of those wanting to live in wine country and work in Oakland or San Francisco. Sharon never lost Gillis's truck as they weaved back and forth within the freeway lanes, when they passed through Napa; she dropped back and gave him space. When she reached Yountville, she turned into a parking lot next to a large warehouse complex that had been converted into a shopping center. Her Jaguar, to its embarrassment, became just one more tourist's car among the rentals. Sharon clicked on the Pandora music app on her phone and waited for Coltrane. Her ear buds had a voice mike; if anyone called, she would be ready. She settled into the leather seat and waited, the air conditioning blew quietly over her tan legs and her khaki shorts. The tee shirt under her checkered shirt simply said "Go Army."

Bobby Gillis drove east through the small village, a few new homes were mixed in with older traditional styles as well as some structures that would have been field hand quarters fifty years earlier but were now half-million dollar summer homes. Bobby could only shake his head. Economically, his hometown was easily twenty years behind the Bay Area. But to its credit, it hadn't expanded as fast, so the blow up of the housing bubble wasn't as painful, but the region still had large numbers of unemployed. Illegals from Mexico and countries farther south came for the agricultural jobs, but stayed when they had no job or alternatives. Many could not go home. Now the Feds were cutting water to the region, resulting in the shutting down of even more acreage, higher unemployment, and more people living unintentionally off the grid. They were becoming a real problem, Bobby worried about his grandfather being alone in the house, "Don't worry, Bobby," the old man said, "I can't see but these ears hear just fine and this here shotgun covers a pretty wide area."

When he passed over the Napa River, he could see it was almost dry. This late in the summer, it was more like a series of puddles than a flowing river, but he also knew the whole area would flood six feet deep if enough storms rolled over the Valley in winter. *"I love farming,"* he thought, *"if only the weather wasn't such a son-of-a-bitch."*

After crossing the river, small oak covered hills seemed to grow from the vineyards. He counted five, the mountains climbed behind them, their flanks covered in orderly rows of grapes. To Bobby, these hills looked like islands in a sea of green water. The largest island held stucco buildings with terra cotta roofs nested among the evergreen oak trees. The double trac-tor-trailer rig directly in front of him slowed, flashed its right turn signal, and cautiously turned onto the lane that headed up toward the island. Thick stonewalls sat on each side of the paved road; a ten-foot high black T in an old German typeface was mounted on the left side, the wall on the right said Trittenheim Winery. A smaller sign said "WELCOME" and tours from 10:00 to 5:00, an "OPEN" sign hung on hooks below the welcome sign. Elaborate iron gates were open on both sides; these were hy-draulically equipped with large arms connected to black boxes that covered the motors.

Bobby watched the truck clear the gate, a white Chevy, fac-ing him, appeared through the dust cloud thrown up by the truck, its turn signal indicated that it was going to follow the truck, Bobby waved the tourists in; he followed them up the lane. *"The more the merrier,"* he thought.

The small parking lot was half-full. He guessed that there would be maybe thirty visitors, based on the car count, a small group sat under the shade of an oak tree having a late lunch, a bottle of wine sat in an ice bucket. Others milled about, one man leaned against a fence, smoking. The rig was lined up behind another pair of trailers equipped with large bins that could be rotated to allow the grapes to be dumped into the de-stemmer. Bobby noticed the sign that said winery tours and followed the middle-aged couple that had climbed out of the white rental car. Bobby watched the man stagger a bit, *"Obviously not the first win-ery of the day,"* he thought with a smile.

Inside, a small group had gathered. A striking young wom-an, very blond and very European, was addressing the crowd. Bobby thought it might be Margrite but when she turned to-ward him he was disappointed. It wasn't the Nazi, but at some other time or place he would have walked up and boldly asked for a date. She caught his eye and smiled, *"And she's a flirt,"* he thought. *"The mission, Bobby, stick to the mission."*

"My name is Elena, welcome." The twenty or so guests returned a murmur of acknowledgement. "I'll walk you through the process we have here at Trittenheim; you are lucky that grapes are being delivered today. These are early grapes from the Carneros appellation along the cooler areas next to San Pablo Bay to the south of us. These are Rieslings, the primary grape used at the home winery for our Trittenheim label in Germany. We make a very good dry Riesling here in Napa but there is nothing like the original produced along the Mosel, that wine is available in the shop after the tour, along with our own produced here, it's fun to compare them. If you have questions, just speak up; I will be glad to answer them."

Bobby tailed the crowd as it wandered along a catwalk over the de-stemmer; great piles of grapes were augured up into the stainless machinery. Between the trucks and the machinery, the noise drowned out anything Elena had to say about the wine-making process. Diagrams used for self-touring were mounted along the walls behind them. *"What our little operation could do if we had the money,"* he thought. *"But it's easier just to sell them to the bulk producers, but I can dream. Hell, it's only money."*

The group entered into the winery itself; the aromas are unique to the wine industry. The fresh chilled crispness of wine and yeast permeated the air. Huge twenty-foot tall wooden vats lined the wall; stainless steel tanks lined the other side. Red wines in the wood, white wines in the stainless. As the group followed Elena up the aisle between the tanks, Bobby casually turned to a door nestled between two stainless tanks, it was unlocked. He walked through it and shut it quietly behind him, a long corridor headed toward another area of the warehouse, stainless pipes hung from the ceiling, only one door at the end. He also saw no cameras. *"Could be a man trap?"* he thought. *"But no lock on the door and no camera, may be just a climate control break between rooms."*

He reached the door and slowly opened it, it teed into two corridors, left and right. Glass windows flanked one side, the rooms looked like high tech laboratories, beakers, tubes and glassware covered the tables; two people, a man and a woman, were hunched over one of the tables, holding test tubes. "Checking acidity and sugar," Bobby thought. He turned in the opposite direction and headed away from the labs; rounding the corner, he almost walked head-on into a man standing in the hall, the guard's blond head was looking in the opposite direction, he was talking into a mike attached to his shoulder, Bobby couldn't hear exactly what was being said, but he knew it was German.

9d

Bobby looked under the lapel of the sport coat; it bulged on the right side, and he saw the leather strap and tell-tail sign of a pistol's grip. *"Shit,"* was all he could think of. The man turned.

"What the hell are you doing here?" the guard asked in flawless English, there was even a touch of a Southern drawl to the accent.

"Looking for the bathroom, thought it was somewhere round here, saw a sign," Bobby quickly answered.

"No bathroom around here, you shouldn't leave the group sir, these areas are off-limits to visitors. Please, if you just pass through that door on the right, the second one, you will catch up with them. The restroom is near the shops."

"Thank you," Bobby said. "This is a real nice facility you have here, real nice. I grow some grapes down south, but this is real nice. Do you know how much wine you make here, must be thousands of cases, thousands."

"Wouldn't know sir, I'm just visiting from our facilities in South America. Now sir, if you would please join the others."

"Thank you, you've been real friendly, thanks. The first door you said?"

"No, the second door. Now please, sir."

"Gotcha and thanks again."

Bobby headed toward the second door, well aware that the man had never left the front of the door he was guarding. If a man was ever at station, no matter how friendly, he was it. There was something worth guarding behind the door, he was sure of that. As he opened the door, he heard the guard say, in German,

"Fand ihn, er wird wieder auf die Gruppe."

"You bet I'm going back to the group, Fritz," Bobby thought. "But I'll be back."

Bobby pulled into the parking lot and parked in the row across from Sharon's Jaguar. He casually crossed the parking lot and tapped on the roof, heard the doors unlock and quickly slid into the passenger's seat.

"That was fun and it's a great set-up they have. If I had a few bucks like that, I could make some great cabernet."

"And?"

"Found it, only one guard. I'm guessing that's where they are if they're at the winery. But too many steel doors between the outside and the room, too many places we can get stuck, going to be tough. Didn't see any cameras, but they knew I had left the tour. Fritz was ready for me when I showed up and he spoke German to their security. Has to be a control room somewhere, probably behind the door he was guarding, bet the paintings are there too."

"Fritz?"

"That's what I call him, spoke real good English,"

"Better than yours, I think."

"Anyway, spoke English, no accent, but his German was even better, said he was from South America. Why he offered that, I'm not sure, a slip-up I think."

Bobby made notes on the enlarged aerial photo Sharon had brought. Parking and roads were obvious, less obvious were the door locations and walks, some obscured by tree cover. The aerial photograph also showed air-conditioning and ventilation units on the roof. It was also obvious there was only one way in and out, unless you cut through the vineyards and took unpaved farm roads.

"Early dinner?" Sharon asked.

"Famished, this spy stuff makes me hungry. Any chance we can get a burger around here?"

"Best burger in the valley is just up the road at Mustards, I'll drive."

Mustards Grill is one of those places in touristy areas that you drive past and wonder about later. Great food, extensive wine list, a pork chop to die for, and some of the best onion rings this side of Saturn.

Sharon, to the disappointment of the waiter, drank club soda; Bobby ordered an Anchor Steam beer. An hour later, as the two pulled out of the parking lot, a black Mercedes pulled into the open spot directly in front of the entry; Bobby naturally was the first to notice the two blonds getting out of the rear seats.

"Now that's a good-looking pair of blonds!" Bobby said.

"That's no way to talk when you're with a girl, Bobby Gillis."

"The one on the left works at the winery, she was leading the tour. And that's Fritz getting out of the driver's side."

Sharon waited until the second blond turned to look at the fountain in the center of the restaurant's turn-around, "Shit."

"What?"

"That's Margrite Speyer, she's the head Nazi of the whole operation," Sharon said as she quickly accelerated the car onto Highway 29, through Yountville, and then home.

Chapter 10

10a

Los Angeles Times, Sunday Edition
Toulouse-Lautrec Painting Stolen by the Nazis
By Trent Smyth

During World War Two, the Nazis systematically looted some of the most important collections of privately held art in the world. As the Nazis marched east across Poland and into Russia, and west through Luxembourg, the Netherlands, Belgium, and into France, they employed both terrorist tactics as well as legal paperwork to loot tens of thousands of Europe's greatest paintings and artwork. Many were sold by escaping Jews and many more were confiscated, called abandoned by the Nazis, from their vacant and empty homes. This is the story of four of those pieces.

During the Belle Epoch of the 1890s, a young Jewish man from Haguenau, Saul Goldfarb, lived in Paris. At this time, Haguenau was in the German controlled Alsace-Lorraine annexed after the Franco-Prussian War. The Germans were to play a sad but important role in the Goldfarb family for the next hundred years.

Saul, an art student and scion of a wealthy family, befriended many in the Impressionist group of painters. Still in his exuberant youth, Saul would paint and draw at the Moulin Rouge and became a close friend of Henri Marie Raymond de Toulouse-Lautrec-Monfa, now known as Henri de Toulouse-Lautrec. Saul was a friend, confident, and also a patron to many of these struggling artists. He was also close to Camille Pissarro, a Jew, like himself. When they needed money, he would buy their paintings; when they needed a man to drink with, he was their companion.

Just months before Lautrec died in 1904 from alcoholism and syphilis at 36, Saul was given or may have purchased a large canvas that Lautrec had completed before his illness incapacitated him. It was never displayed or seen publicly. Saul carried the painting, along with others he had acquired, back to the family home in Haguenau, married Nina Weiss in 1904 and settled into the comfortable world of his father's clothing store. In 1905, their only son, Lev, was born. Haguenau changed hands and countries after World War One, and even through the economic difficulties of the 1920s, the Goldfarbs prospered.

In 1939, with the Nazis preparing to advance on France, Lev Goldfarb and his family escaped to Switzerland with only what they could carry, the collection of art remained in the house. Official Nazi documents, acquired by this reporter, indicate that the paintings were declared abandoned and confiscated by the Reich, three years later they turned up in Herman Goering's private collection. As the waves of the advancing Allied army pushed through France and into Germany, lost among the deaths and destruction were the Goldfarb paintings. They have been missing for almost 65 years.

Saul Goldfarb passed away in 1936. Lev Goldfarbs' only child, Jacob, married in 1960 and had five children. The Jacob Goldfarb family continued to live in Switzerland until the mid-1970s when, after Lev's untimely death in 1977, they moved to Los Angeles.

Earlier this year, the Goldfarbs were surprised by a phone call. It seems that the paintings, all four, had been kept in a private collection since the end of World War Two. Protected and restored, the caller said that these paintings would be returned to the family, no strings attached. Surprised, but cautious, the Goldfarbs met with the agent for the current holder of the pieces, and were shocked at the story and the proof shown in a pre-war photo found in a book on historic Haguenau homes. This photo as reproduced below, with the publisher's approval, clearly shows a large painting in the Lautrec style. The family was thrilled to have these paintings returned to them.

But all was not well. Someone else wanted the paintings. On the day they were to be returned to the family in San Francisco, they were hijacked by persons unknown. In an operation with almost military precision, motorcycles swept into the loading dock of the hotel and, at gunpoint, the riders seized the paintings, one man was pistol-whipped during the robbery. Nothing has been heard from the hijackers, no ransom demand, nothing.

"We never saw the paintings," Saul Goldfarb, the movie producer and son of Jacob Goldfarb, said in an interview. "To be honest, I don't know whether they even exist, or whether this is all a scam of some kind."

"Do you know who the benefactor is?"

"Yes, I have been told that it is the billionaire, Alain Dumont."

Mr. Dumont was badly injured earlier the same day as the hijacking by assailants who broke into his San Francisco home; one of the attackers was killed, shot by the 93 year old Dumont. The paintings are still missing, the man who was killed carried no identification and the police continue to investigate.

Many of the world's great works of art carry histories and stories with them; in the art world they're called provinces. Some have theirs rooted as booty from war, for others, it's their growing price at auction, and for others, fear and attendant death. Who would want these paintings so much that they would kill for them? Are there still people out there from World War Two that will do anything to get these works of art back? Are the Nazis back and if so why do they want these paintings?

10b

"Well, with Margrite Speyer being here, it complicates things," Sharon said to Bobby and Kevin, an open bottle of Cabernet sat on the low table in the center of the room. "With her here, the winery will have more security and be on its toes. Not good."

"I am also guessing that there will be an attempt to up the ante," Kevin said. "She wants the plate and, after Paris, she's going to come after it. You don't exactly have a low profile around here; she will find out where you live."

"*Moi*," Sharon said. "I may not be listed in the yellow pages but any good sleuthing will certainly turn up this address. That's why I added the additional security since the Chinese thing. My simple cottage has sensors and cameras everywhere, the windows are harder to break. They would have to drive through the front door to surprise me. And besides, I've got Basil."

"Jesus, what have I gotten myself into, lieutenant," Bobby said. "This country boy comes to the big city to learn a little about art and now I'm caught up in international newsmaking crimes, espionage and the return of the Nazis to power. I knew I should have just stayed on the farm."

"She'll do that to you, Bobby, O'Mara will suck you in before you know what's up, and then it's down that dark hallway to doom," Kevin added.

"You keep quiet," Sharon said pointing at Bryan; he tipped his wine glass to her and smiled. "We need to move fast, stay ahead of them. This operation will need a diversion, something to draw them out; Bobby, remember that op in Samara, where we smoked out the insurgents?"

"Yes, the wind was blowing just right and we lit up the tires. The smoke was so thick we almost couldn't see 'em as they ran out the far side, rounded up maybe twenty, mostly young kids."

"Maybe a similar diversion here, work on it. I'm going to see Alain in the morning and get his take on the situation. This needs to happen fast, maybe tomorrow tonight," Sharon said.

O'Mara found Dumont sitting in the same chair she left him in during her last visit; his color and attitude had improved tremendously.

"So you think you've found my Toulouse?" Alain asked.

"Yes," Sharon answered. "We'll know more after tonight; with good planning, we may even have them back in the house by tomorrow."

"Excellent, they'll let me leave today; seems I'm starting to annoy them, even though this is my hospital," he said with a wry smile. "It appears that nothing is getting done with me here and some of the other patients are complaining about getting less attention. So the director has asked me to go home."

"Good, you will be safer in your house; it has everything necessary that this hospital has."

"Yes. Evelyn has found me a nurse with a good military background, retired, Walter Reed I think. I won't be caught off-guard like last time. When the doorbell rang that morning, I actually thought it was you returning for something you had forgotten, didn't even check the monitor before opening the door. I just got too comfortable, my dear, with you around."

"Don't let it happen again," Sharon said, taking Alain's hand in hers. "I'll take care of you."

"That's just silly, my dear. I can take care of myself, but you have to be my arms and legs. We need to neutralize the advantage they think they have. Please get the paintings. That will force them to renegotiate; without the art, they have very little. I need to return those paintings to the Goldfarbs."

"Why this great desire to return these bits of oil paint and canvas?" Sharon asked. "While I love art, I have yet to see one painting I'd die or kill for."

"Sharon, my dear, in my youth I was, you might say, on the edge of the law. I was in it for myself. I wasn't educated, but I had a desire in my gut to succeed, I bent with the wind. My history with the gold and the art shows that. I am comfortable with the theft of the gold, but the artworks are expressions of love and creativity by the painters, and the appreciation for this effort by the patron, Saul Goldfarb. I would have liked to have known the man."

"The current Saul Goldfarb isn't exactly a work of art."

"That's not the great-grandfather's fault; in Saul case, he's a bastard, a self-made man."

"True, but does he deserve the reward?"

"No, probably not, but the family does own the artwork. I'm trying to return the art to them out of respect for Saul Goldfarb and his love of the painters of the nineteenth century."

"Do the right thing even when no one is watching, right?"

"Exactly, I'm a very selfish man; I'm doing this for myself," Dumont said, looking out the window into the courtyard. A small black boy in a wheelchair rolled by, an electronic game in his hands. "The *Times* printed your Mr. Smyth's article in the paper this morning."

"You don't miss anything, do you, Alain?"

"I try not to dear, but now our Argentine friends have some-one looking up their skirts. They have remained in the shadows for half a century, now a little light on them may cause them to make a mistake."

"My thinking as well, they will try to contact me today or tomorrow offering new negotiations. Right now, I don't think they know that we know who they are. The story might just spook them enough. We need to move before they call."

10c

Bobby Gillis and Sharon dressed in their finest all black, break into a winery, garb. The preparation helped to get them into the spirit of the job, as well as improve their invisibility. Sharon tucked her red hair up under a ski cap. She checked and rechecked the headset and microphone; it was good for a half-mile.

"I'll work my way through the vineyards and around, be-hind the parking lot," Sharon said. "My first point will be some-where in this grove of trees above the shipping area. You will control the access point and the entry road."

"Roger," Bobby answered.

"I know nothing about this Sharon," Kevin said, as he helped to check their weapons and electronics. "My captain would throw my ass in jail if he ever found out I was helping you commit a felony burglary and an arson. No, I don't think he would understand at all, even for all the right reasons. There, you two are set."

Two large canvas bags were stowed in the lockers mounted on the side panels of Bobby's truck; he had pulled up the driveway and parked close to the house. Sharon's Jaguar could be seen parked in the one-car detached garage ten feet ahead of the pickup.

"For luck," Kevin said, as he kissed Sharon. "Stay safe, I don't want Basil as a roommate."

"What, no kiss for me?" Bobby asked.

"When you bring her back safe, I will give you big kiss, so for now you'll just have to wait."

Bobby kept a safe and even pace as they headed north. When they arrived in Yountville, a little after midnight, the streets were deserted. If a town could be put to bed, Yountville was one of the best examples. For well-heeled foodies this sleepy village holds one of the greatest and most expensive restaurants in Northern California disguised as a stockade-style eighteenth century house. It, along with the rest of the village, is completely surrounded by some of the best vineyards in the western hemisphere. Forty years earlier, it was a dusty farm village for farm workers. Bobby's red pickup stood out on the dim streets.

They drove through the narrow streets, turned east, and followed a winding road toward the Trittenheim winery about a mile from the village center. Bobby slowed to a stop a quarter mile from the winery gate. Sharon got out, pulled one of the bags from the locker, rubbed black carbon on her face, reset her gear and secured her weapons.

"Break a leg," Bobby said.

"I'll try not to," Sharon answered, disappearing between the rows of grapes.

As she pushed her way through the canopy of vines, the rows glowed eerily from her night vision goggles. Sharon, even after wearing the goggles almost every night for years, couldn't shake the feeling that she was running through a bizarre leafy tunnel.

"We have to get them to move the paintings; there's no way we can break-in and take them. We'd need an army and the paintings might not even be there," she'd said to Bobby and Kevin before they loaded up. "If they think the building's on fire, maybe we can force them to get the paintings out of the building; then we can intercept Speyer and the paintings as they leave."

"Just like Samara," Bobby had said.

"Yes, but hopefully without all the AK-47s and RPGs."

"Yes, hopefully," Bobby added.

Sharon felt the side of the canvas bag, reassuring herself that the two makeshift incendiaries were nicely snuggled into their side pockets. Bobby had brought two sticks of dynamite from his ranch; they split one into two pieces and fused them. The aerial photos, even though they were two years old, showed a parking area immediately behind the laboratory and security center. Bobby confirmed that three trucks were parked there when he went through the winery. She hoped they would still be there. A soft breeze brushed her cheek, *Good, the breeze is in my favor, smoke will blow into the buildings."*

"If you light those trucks, the fire department will be there in twenty minutes, if not sooner," Kevin said as they went over the pre-planning.

"I'm counting on the fact that they don't want a bunch of firemen wandering about the buildings asking questions; I'm hoping they'll get the paintings out as fast as possible. Bobby, you blockade the road at the turn. After I light up the trucks, I'll hightail it to the bend, you hold the right flank; I'll come in from the vineyard side."

Planning is easy; execution is a whole other thing. Sharon was surprised when she reached the high ground above the unloading area cut into the side of the hill; six workers were washing down the equipment and bins near the crusher.

"Shit."

"What?"

"Still cleaning up from the crush this afternoon, I'm thinking they still have an hour to go."

"Shit."

"I said that already," Sharon answered on her headphone.

"I'll slide into the vineyard about fifty yards up the road, hide from any passing trucks. I suggest we sit it out 'till they're done," Bobby said.

"I've got 12:45 on my watch. Perhaps they'll be done by 1:30, let's consider starting the party at 2:30."

"Roger."

O'Mara found the base of an oak about fifty feet up the hill from the cleaners and settled her butt and back into the curve of the trunk. A mixture of German and Spanish echoed up the hill to her position. She heard a Mexican song roll into the trees, one she hadn't heard since her last trip to Cabo San Lucas. It was a sad lament over a lost love; she hummed along with the singer. The steel door to the labs opened, two blonds walked onto the damp paving, light flaring from the open door reflected off the stainless steel tanks.

"I'll be damned, it's little Margrite Speyer, the Tour de France champion," Sharon thought. *"And her leg is bandaged, that's even better."*

"Margrite Speyer's here," Sharon said to Bobby. "She's with that blond tour guide we saw yesterday. From the look of things, she's closing everything down. She's talking with the fellows who are cleaning up; they seem relieved and are heading toward the cars parked off the concrete. I see four cars, watch for them."

"They're clear," Bobby said ten minutes later. "You think the rest will stay?"

"Looks like it; I see two Germanic males, one looks like the fellow from the bank in Paris. I see only four, including the girls."

"Trucks?'

"Right where you spotted them, good cover up to the back side, all gas, not diesel," Sharon answered. "There's a small Mercedes step van parked near the lab door. I scanned for cameras, saw only two this side, more hidden probably. I'll work my way up and around to the high ground above the trucks. I'll tape the dynamite to the tanks and wick them to the fuel, when we're ready, I'll light 'em. I'll be at least sixty feet away when they go off."

"Should be enough, hold a second," Bobby said. "Another truck is turning into the lane, a small pickup, nothing special."

A minute later, Sharon answered, "He picked up the blond tour guide, must be a boyfriend or something. Good, that just leaves three, I hope."

Two minutes later, "Clear, they turned toward Silverado Highway.

"Forty minutes."

"Roger."

At the thirty minute mark, Sharon worked her way laterally across the slope of the hill, the goggles lit up everything, but peripheral vision was terrible, she used her ears as much as her eyes. "I'm moving down to the trucks."

"Roger."

She slid down the slope careful not to lose her footing; at the edge of the pavement, she was completely hidden from the building by the trucks; they were parked nose to ass end. She quickly duct-taped the single stick of dynamite to the sides of the fuel tanks hung behind the passenger side doors. At each tank, she opened the gas caps and gently eased a wick of heavy cotton cloth through the opening. They began to soak up the gas right away.

"You okay?" Bobby whispered.

"Good, all set. You ready?"

"Ready."

"Let the games begin," Sharon said as she fired off each wick with her butane lighter. She quickly slid into the trees.

The wick quickly burned up the three feet of cotton fuse to the half stick of dynamite. The explosion crushed the fuel tank, the gasoline ignited. The fire quickly reached the cab of the trucks; black acrid smoke immediately billowed over the lab buildings. From where O'Mara was standing, the heat was intense.

Ten seconds later, the lab door slammed open. The tall German took one look and quickly returned to the lab. No one else appeared.

"Bobby, I'm moving to the road, nothing to do here except wait."

"Roger."

Sharon continued to work the slope high above the buildings. Two more explosions followed her as the fuel tanks on the opposite side of the trucks exploded. The lights and shadows cast by the fire lit up the ground; her goggles were worthless. She slid down the slope to the road. Bobby had already reached the bend; he had angled his truck across the lane. The steep slope up the hill on one side closed that side to escape. The wires and vines on the opposite side would tangle up anything that turned and tried to escape in that direction.

O'Mara slipped her headphone off and stowed it in the bag; before she put the bag in the locker, she pulled out the M16 she had carried through the vineyards. She pushed the safety off the Beretta snugly nestled in its holster strapped to her hip.

Bobby clicked off the safety on his M16, "These may not be fully auto Sharon, but they still scare the hell out of people."

The fire still lit up the sky over the low crest of the hill, but was dying down slowly. Two headlight beams flashed on the lane; it got brighter as they rounded the bend. Sharon and Bobby flanked the road; Sharon found a small tree to stand behind. Bobby disappeared into the grapevines. The white van accelerated through the turn and headed directly toward the pickup; at one hundred feet, it slammed on its breaks. Dust, kicked up from the tires, engulfed the van; it careened along the road, almost losing control. It stopped; the dust began to settle around the trucks. The van sat like a trapped beast, Sharon could hear its engine panting. Suddenly flashes erupted from the door windows of the van, no sound. *"Silencers,"* Sharon thought, she could hear the bullets hitting high above her. Bobby fired four rounds back into the engine block, steam exploded from under the frame. Sharon followed suit on her side; four slugs tore into the tires, one exploded, the other, slowly deflated, at some point the right headlight blinked out.

"Out, now!' Sharon yelled toward the van, "Now, or we'll sweep the truck. Now!" At that point Bobby switched on the over-cab high beams of his truck and lit up the Mercedes like it was opening night on Broadway. Two people in the cab of the van shielded their eyes from the glare.

"Guns, now, throw them! Out, hands up!" Sharon yelled.

Their pistols, with the long steel silencers still attached, arced out the windows. The doors on each side slowly opened, Margrite and Olaf stepped to the ground cautiously, partially hidden behind the doors.

"Move away from the doors," Sharon ordered, recognizing the Mercedes driver as the same from Paris.

They hesitated.

"Now!" Sharon yelled.

In the glare of the truck's light, Bobby caught the slight bobbing of the van. "Sharon, someone's still inside. Watch your side."

As if a cue had been ordered, a figure suddenly appeared on Sharon's side of the van. Not prepared for the intense light, the man raised his pistol and shot wildly in the direction of the lights.

O'Mara screamed, "One more shot and you're dead. Drop it. Tell him, Speyer, you want that man dead?"

At the sound of her name, Margrite Speyer's face changed from surprise to hatred. "Drop the gun, Derek." After a beat, he did.

Sharon recognized the man as the one Kevin had held his Colt on in Paris and did a one and a half on a Parisian street.

"I thought a Paris reunion might be in order, missed you guys, hand's up," Sharon said. "You two, walk around to the front, slowly. Herr Derek, join them and be quick." The three stood in front of the van's grill. "Everyone get on the ground, now." They slowly dropped to the rough gravel.

"Truss 'em," Sharon said to Bobby.

Bobby moved to the three prone figures and with practiced moves, slid plastic ties around their wrists, hands behind their backs. He took three more and bound their ankles. He felt for and found the small pistols both men had strapped to their ankles.

"Don't think you'll need these," Bobby said, stuffing the 38s in the back pocket of his vest.

"Watch them, I'll check the truck," Sharon said.

She rounded the back of the van and pulled her flashlight; with the glare through the windshield she found that she didn't need it. Propped against the interior side, four boxes leaned at an angle. Two elastic bungee cords stretched from floor cleats to side panel hooks. She slung the M16 over her shoulder and slid out the two smallest boxes. *"They even left them in the same boxes; that's helpful,"* she thought.

O'Mara walked to Kevin's truck and set the cartons on the floor of the truck's box. She moved the third, and then, with Bobby's help, moved the Toulouse to the rear of the truck. She secured the boxes with bungee cords and threw a tarp over them.

"We have to go, Sharon, now," Bobby said. "Fire department and probably cops on the way." As if to reinforce his point, the quiet was disturbed by a faint siren coming from the direction of Yountville.

"Well Margrite, it was good seeing you again and I really hope it's the last time, but that's up to you. I'll let you know about the gold plate, but I doubt we can make arrangements."

"Sharon, now," Bobby insisted.

"And by the way, say 'heil' to your grandfather," Sharon said as she climbed into the cab, the landscape went black as Bobby shut down the lights. They drove quickly down the lane;

Bobby could see red flashing lights through the vineyard rows as they turned right onto the main road and headed toward the Silverado Trail. A half-mile later, they passed two sheriff prowlers, lights flashing, heading right where they had been a minute ago.

"Don't cut it so close next time Lieutenant, I really don't want to spend the rest of my youth in some county jail," Bobby said.

"Me neither, they're going to be surprised when they hit the lane," Sharon said. "My guess is that Speyer will already have concocted a story about local gangs and hijackers. She will stay away from the paintings and their business's true mission. Being a pillar of the community will probably gain her a little slack. Watch your speed, the adrenaline's working."

Bobby checked his speed and slowed to fifty miles an hour. "Thanks, not paying attention. Just like old times, Lieutenant, like the old days."

"Watch the road," Sharon said, feeling the adrenaline rush leaving her. She took a deep breath, slowly exhaled.

"You okay?" Bobby asked.

"Just great," Sharon said, turning her head toward Bobby, a car passed them lighting up the cab; near the shoulder of his right arm blood had soaked through his shirtsleeve.

"Damn it, have you been shot?"

"It's nothing, old Olaf got lucky with his wild shooting; it's just a nick. I sure as hell know the difference."

"Yes and I know how adrenaline covers pain; I need to look at that. When we reach town, pull into a fast food parking lot."

Five minutes later, they reached the Napa city limits. Traffic was building in the still dark early morning; they picked a fast food lot with plenty of light. The restaurant was not open. Sharon took her flashlight and ran the beam over Bobby's upper arm.

"Damn lucky, the shirt's more damaged than you arm."

"There's a kit behind the seat."

Sharon opened the door and reached behind her seat, the

white first aid kit had everything she needed. She quickly wrapped his arm with five layers of gauze directly over the shirt and then taped over the gauze.

"The bleeding has stopped, this should hold until we're home. I'm driving, no arguments." She saw that Bobby's face was tightening as the adrenaline wore off; he was starting to feel the pain.

"Roger, I know the drill."

He slid into her seat. Sharon walked around the box of the truck, adjusted a strap over the tarp, and climbed into the cab. She slipped the Bluetooth earpiece into her ear, pulled her phone, clicked off mute and dialed Kevin Bryan. He picked up after one ring.

"Where the hell have you been; it's been four hours since your last call. What's happening Sharon, say something!" Even Bobby could hear Kevin over the road noise as they slipped onto Highway 29 and headed south.

"Good morning and how are you?"

"Going out of my fucking mind, what happened? You were supposed to call two hours ago."

"A little delay, nothing too bad, there were workers cleaning up, we had to wait," Sharon said.

"And the paintings?"

"In the back, we should be home in an hour, maybe less."

"You okay?" Kevin asked.

"I'm fine, but Bobby was nicked in the right arm, nothing much, lucky."

"Are you going to stop at the hospital?"

"No, it's just a scratch, as I said, lucky. See you in sixty."

Sharon clicked off the headset, and looked at Bobby, his eyes were closed, his head nodded. *"Sleep sergeant, get your rest, this is far from over,"* she thought, as her eyes turned back to the road ahead.

Chapter 11

11a

Sharon pulled into the driveway and parked behind her Jaguar. Kevin, leaning on a crutch, stood in the open door. Basil stared intently from one side; when he saw his mistress he bolted out the door. She knelt and gave him a big hug. Bobby rounded the end of the truck and walked toward the door.

"Let's get these things inside before the neighbors wake up," Sharon said.

In less than two minutes, the boxes of paintings were propped against the wall of the living room. Kevin handed them both a cup of coffee.

"Fresh, not ten minutes old. You made good time," Kevin said.

"Traffic was light, even across the Benicia Bridge. Bobby caught a few winks; me, I'm wide-awake. I need to make a call," Sharon said

"Dumont?" Kevin asked.

"Yes, he said to call when it's over, no matter what time. My guess, he's been up most of the night. Give me five minutes."

She headed to her office, Basil followed.

"Let's look at that shoulder; I know there's a shirt around here that should fit," Kevin offered as he directed Bobby to the bathroom. Ten minutes later they all met in the kitchen.

"It wasn't too bad, it's more of a gash than a scratch; I put antiseptic and a pad over the cut. You're very lucky, an inch or two lower and the shoulder would have been busted; lower than that, a lung punctured, damn lucky," Kevin said.

"The son-of-a-bitch doing the shooting was the lucky one. Didn't know what the hell he was shooting at, just shot everywhere," Bobby answered.

"Well their luck ran out," Sharon said. "Alain thinks we should get the paintings back to his house. We can strategize from there. Want to see what all this fuss is about?"

The two men looked at each other, only Bobby had seen the Toulouse-Lautrec, and that was a grainy photo sixty-five years old. Together they both said, "Yes."

Sharon found a large flat head screwdriver she had stored in a kitchen drawer along with a hammer, they returned to the living room. She checked around the edges, "Seems they have been opened and then put back together. Not surprised."

After some tapping and prying, she pulled off the plywood panel that covered the Toulouse-Lautrec; a thin layer of paper still wrapped the painting.

"Just as I left it," she said. "To be honest, I was afraid that when I pulled the cover off I would find nothing, or they had removed the paintings and left a picture of dogs playing cards." At the word dog, Basil lifted his head from his strategic position in front of the door.

"Well, gentlemen," she said peeling away the paper.

In the early light cast through the living room window, the gasp from both men brought a smile to Sharon's face. The painting commanded the room, as bright and gay as the day she wrapped it at the start of their adventure. The painting's colors grew more vibrant as the sunlight streamed through the window. The dancers filled the upper part of the canvas, the patrons filed the foreground, you could almost hear the music and the laughter; the sound of an accordion and the aroma of cigar smoke filled the air.

"Damn," Bobby said, "the photo certainly didn't do this justice."

"Bobby, not sure a photo could ever do this justice," Kevin added. "The colors, the balance, the composition captures an era, the Belle Époque, Paris in the 1890s. It says it all."

"My God, you did study in school," Sharon said with a smile.

"Well there was the Moulin Rouge and Folies Bergère and all

those scantily clad women dancing about keeping up the interest of a high school kid studying French, I always did what mom wanted me to do," Kevin said.

"I'm amazed that Speyer took them on face value, curious, if you ask me," Sharon said.

"She's so focused on the gold plate that these wonders were irrelevant, just chips to barter with. Too bad," Bobby added, "they are glorious."

They opened the other three boxes and again the boys were awestruck. The art that now filled the living room of Sharon's small cottage in Walnut Creek instantly made it one of the most important, albeit temporary, art collections in the United States. That fact was not lost to Sharon.

"We need to get these out of here. For years I've wanted just a small painting, something nice to hang over the fireplace, maybe California Plein Air, East Coast or something, but for now, for an hour or so, I have the greatest private collection of Impressionist paintings in the world propped up against my living room walls. Just a second," Sharon said and disappeared.

The boys looked at each other, then the paintings, then Basil. He was asleep. Sharon reappeared with her camera.

"You two, stand there next to the art, I have got to get a picture," Sharon said. "At least in my old age I will remember this day and smile."

They each took turns grinning and posing. The men stood next to the paintings in a dozen shots, then all three together with the timer clicking away, and then Sharon alone with each piece. She even took one of Basil sprawled out in front of the Lautrec.

Another pot of coffee was made and Sharon cooked up a quick breakfast of sausage and eggs; they ate in the living room.

"Well boys, the fun is over," Sharon said finishing her fifth cup of coffee. "Kevin, you're still not mobile enough, sorry. Besides, as I said last night, you're grounded, if your captain finds out what went on here there would be hell to pay. Bobby, we'll load these in the Jaguar. The Toulouse should just fit; the others will sit nicely in the trunk."

"And as usual, I get KP, great," Kevin said.

"Oh, poor boy," Sharon said.

"That's a great thought, poor boy my ass," Kevin said. "I can make a few calls, haul these into the city to an auction house I know, cash them in and head for some secluded island in the Pacific, do the Gauguin thing."

"And all he got for that was dying from syphilis and being broke," Sharon said. "Same thing happened to the artist who painted that one." Sharon pointed to the Lautrec

"Good God, what a great bunch these Belle Époque artists were. Many were drunkards, some had syphilis, many with numerous mistresses, or a poor family life, and/or in decadent health. Too bad they couldn't have lived another hundred years, they'd all be multi-millionaires now," Bobby added with a laugh. "You just have to die ugly to become famous."

"Sergeant, just shut the fuck up," Sharon said with a grin.

Sharon's phone, sitting on the coffee table, began to ring, playing the Marseilles. The screen said 'Alain Dumont'. "Yes Alain, we are just leaving. Yes . . . yes . . . are you sure? Yes, I understand, I'll be right there, less than an hour. She'll be fine, I know she will, you just rest, I will be right there."

She looked at Bobby and Kevin, "They've kidnapped Claudette, snatched her this afternoon, Paris time, as she returned to work from lunch. They've heard nothing since."

11b

The Bay Bridge was jammed. The drive into San Francisco during the morning rush hour took over an hour. Sharon lost sight of Bobby in the Maze, a collection of freeways that intersect just before the tollbooths; they reconnected by phone while in the stop and go traffic on the bridge. They rejoined as she headed west across the City on Broadway. She pulled up the short drive at the front of Dumont's mansion and stopped at the elaborate gate. Bobby made a U-turn and parked across the street.

"This is one helluva pile of brick and glass, and he lives alone?" Bobby asked.

"Yes, he's one of the loneliest men I know, even with all the friends he has," Sharon said.

Sharon punched the front door bell; a multi-layered tone could be heard through the glass. In less than five seconds, a large black man stood in the doorway, his size and weight suggested something from central casting and the next superhero movie.

"I'm Sharon O'Mara, this is Bobby Gillis, Mr. Dumont is expecting us," she said.

"This way, Mr. Dumont is in the library. I am very pleased to finally meet you, Ms. O'Mara. I'm Peter Brass, Mr. Dumont's new medical and security assistant. Ms. Luca recommended me through the company I work for."

"Good to meet you. How is Mr. Dumont?" Sharon asked.

"Very good, all things considered; his blood pressure is up, I'm not sure why. Even after being here a week, I have learned that he does keep some things private, very private. His wounds are healing well even for someone his age. Seems to be trying to prove something to somebody," Brass said, as they entered the library.

Bobby was stunned by the interior of the house. "Sharon, I'm not in Bakersfield anymore," he said as he looked into the various rooms they passed. The large window in the back of the library framed a fog shrouded Alcatraz Island, a knot of early morning charter fishing boats drifted to the east side of the island. The sky above was clear, promising a good day for somebody.

Sharon saw the boats and her first thought was, *Halibut fishing.*

"Sharon, Sharon, my dear, good morning. I was beginning to worry, but even I know the traffic stinks. Please come, sit here," Alain Dumont said. He looked past Sharon to Bobby. "And you must be Bobby Gillis, Jimmy's grandson. God damn, you look a lot like him, from what I can remember, same cocky stance, pure

Gillis."

Sharon sat in the chair opposite Alain, the same chair she sat in the first day they met. "What happened?"

"Early this morning, at 5:30, I received a call from Claudette's assistant in Paris. She said that as Claudette was returning to the office from lunch and directly in front of the company's security station, a black Mercedes stopped in the street, two men ran up, grabbed her, threw a black sack over her head, pushed her into the car and sped off. Since then, there has been nothing. I just got off the phone with Paris two minutes ago."

"My guess is that you'll be the first person they contact, not her office. You're the one they want," Sharon said.

"I know you're right, but it pisses me off that I've dragged her into all this; she doesn't deserve it," Dumont said. "None of you do."

Dumont looked at Sharon for a long moment then turned to Bobby, "How's your grandfather?"

"He's well, considering he's eighty-nine, blind, and lives in one room of a great big ranch house he owns. His world is small, but his heart, as always, is big," Bobby said. "When he found out that you, or should I say Robert Dupont, were still alive, I think he gained back a few years he'd lost, seems livelier, happier."

"Good, I'm glad that he's had a good life, I can see that his legacy is doing him proud. Are there other Gillises?"

"My grandfather had three children, and I have eleven cousins. And now, there's a passel of grandkids and great-grandchildren; he's never short of company."

"Excellent, we only live on through our children and their children," Alain looked at Sharon.

"Alain, we need to be prepared," Sharon said, returning the conversation back to Claudette. "The kidnapping happened while we were retrieving the paintings; there's no way that the Nazis in Paris would have known. I'm sure it caught them by surprise. Claudette is something distinct, separate, not retaliation. This was bold, very public, and well planned."

"I agree," Dumont said. "It's that son-of-a-bitch Nazi in Argentina; he has his dirty fingers everywhere. When Claudette started to investigate their Argentine connections, a flag or two might have popped up, put her on his radar. It's my fault."

"No one's fault, this has been brewing for a long time. They saw a chance and took it; they are fanatic about achieving their goals," Sharon said.

"Damn, Nazis and fanaticism; never would have put the two together," Bobby said with a twist to his face. "I always thought they were about making trains run on time, marching and stuff."

Sharon looked at Bobby and saw that his grin remained, floating in the air like a Cheshire cat's. She turned back to Dumont.

"With the paintings gone," Sharon paused. "Damn, forgot about them. Bobby would you and Mr. Brass take the paintings from the car and bring them in. You can move them to the vault."

"Roger," Bobby said, then turned to Dumont's aide, scanning the man from head to toe. The man was big, real big, pro-athlete big. "Are you the Peter Brass that played half-back for USC maybe fifteen years ago?"

"The very same," Brass said.

"And now you're a nurse?"

"Even worse than that, after college I decided that the NFL wasn't for me, drafted by the Packers but it was too cold for this southern California boy, so I joined the navy, became a Seal, and fought in both Iraq and Afghanistan. Left four years ago, got involved with medical services, started working for a small company as a private contractor, and, as the French say, voila."

"Passed up a lot of opportunities," Sharon said.

"They weren't what my mom raised me to be. Pro football, high security, black ops, all quite boring, and besides, I'm a bit of a coward. Would like to live to old age, maybe write a book and retire to a warm beach somewhere."

"Knew I would like you, Peter, I think this the beginning of a beautiful friendship," Bobby said as they walked down the hall toward the Jaguar.

Sharon stood at the window and watched the fog. This morning it sat low across the bay, the halibut boats had moved with the change in tides. The fog's cap, as if it was alive, roiled and twisted in the wind pushed through the Golden Gate. "Where is this leading, Alain?" she asked.

"To a conclusion we have under our control, I hope. I have given my word to the Goldfarbs; with the paintings recovered, we can now proceed. The gold plate is secured in the French bank, waiting for the right moment. My actions, such as they are, are now focused on getting Claudette back safely."

A large globe of the Earth sat next to her, suspended in a bronze cradle on a stone pedestal. She traced her finger across the white Arctic sheet at the top of the globe. A distinct red line crossed the white ice cap and extended south through the Bering Sea, nicking Alaska, the line also extended north over the top of the globe toward Europe. She nudged the surface with her finger, the line coursed through the North Atlantic, Norway, the North Sea, landed on the coast of Germany just west of Hamburg, plunged south over Switzerland and Italy and disappeared in the arc of the globe as it passed over the Mediterranean Sea and continued into Africa at Algeria. She suddenly turned toward Alain, "That's it, isn't it?"

Alain Dumont sat in his wheelchair smiling. "Yes."

"Why didn't you tell me when we returned from Paris?"

"I don't know what you mean?" Dumont said.

"Alain, I'm sure you do. Since I started working with you, you have kept many things secret, things that I should have known. It started with the art and the bit you left out about Hitler's box, until the morning you were shot."

"Do we need to talk about this, now? I see the boys are moving the paintings to the elevator. Let's go see them."

"No, I need to know. There are more than secrets at stake here, Alain; my friend's life is at stake. The people in Argentina have shown that they'll stop at nothing to retrieve the other plate; I don't want friends of mine killed over this. Those four numbers describe a longitude, don't they?"

Alain paused then said, "Yes, I believe so. 7, 53, 37, and 72."

"How did you find out?" Sharon asked, as she followed the line to the South Pole.

"I didn't have the foggiest clue what those numbers were. For years I thought that it was a serial number to something, then a patent number, then an account number at some bank; for thirty years, those four numbers were never far from my mind. They almost drove me crazy. Then, one day, maybe twenty years ago, about the time I was remodeling this house, I decided a globe of the Earth would be a handsome edition to this room. That globe is pre-World War Two; you can see that the European nations are different. Some don't even exist now."

Sharon looked closely at the face of Europe in 1938, all the countries were there but their borders were different. Hitler loved maps, she remembered.

"It was delivered and set up right where it is now. One afternoon, the sun cut through the Golden Gate and lit up the globe. I thought, 'Just like the sun lighting up the real world.' The crisp edge of the shadow cut through Europe like a late evening in Germany. Suddenly I could almost see the numbers etched along the line. I knew that was what it had to be. I painstakingly drafted that line completely around the globe; it cuts a significant swath north to south across western Germany."

"Did you find anything?"

"I investigated strange events that might have happened along that line since the war, not much. I also realized then that the other void in its display box, the one you found in Paris, probably carried its brother at one time, sister longitude and brother latitude. Without the other numbers, it's just a line around the world. For all I know, where they cross might not even be in Germany."

Sharon watched the line transect many countries. "Could the line be west of Greenwich?"

"It's possible, but knowing the SS and the Germans, I would hold out for Germany or Switzerland. The other locations are too far away; they wanted control."

"I agree," Sharon said and watched the last two boxes disappear through the elevator doors. "She's more than just a president of a software company."

"Who?"

"Claudette, she means a lot more to you than just an executive for one of your companies," Sharon said.

Alain paused again, "This *is* a day for revelations, isn't it, Sharon my dear. An old man's secrets can only hide for so long."

"I understand secrets, especially personal ones, but I need to know all I can to help her. I want as few surprises as possible."

Alain looked at the photograph, still sitting on his desk, of the young woman he had loved in Paris so long ago, a tear escaped. He adjusted the oxygen prongs and took a deep breath. "When I told you that Dominique died from tuberculosis, that was so sadly correct. We had three wonderful years together, three fruitful years as well. We had a child, a beautiful girl we named Angelique. After Dominique died, I was almost destroyed by loneliness; Angelique helped to soften the pain. But my businesses were growing; it was hard for me to be the father I should have been. I thought she needed the best schools so I sent her away. She never forgave me; she became wild and independent, a lot like her mother."

Bobby and Peter had reentered the room; they stood to one side, listening, they said nothing.

"Before Angelique was twenty, she became pregnant. She returned home, I was living here in San Francisco. She was not sure who the father was. My heart ached. Claudette was born in 1970. Angelique left again after the baby was born, Claudette stayed with me. I only heard from my daughter twice during the next ten years. In 1988, on a cold damp winter day, I was told she had died in France from a seizure, alone and penniless. Sharon, my dear, this old heart of mine has been cut and slashed so many times; I wonder how I've lived so long. It's probably God's penance for my soul. Claudette, thank God, seems to be the mellower and smarter than all of us. She's never had mood swings like her mother and her grandmother. Yes, Claudette Leclair is my granddaughter."

"She knows?"

"Yes, but we keep it very quiet for many reasons, personal, safety, business, and even more. Other than a little seed money, she has always stood on her own without my help. But money does nothing without ideas and that dear granddaughter of mine has so many ideas, my head spins with excitement when we are together. I think she alone has made me live ten years longer than this body should have."

"The Argentines must never know she's your granddaughter, they would bring on more pressure than I think even you could bear," Sharon said to Alain.

"More than I carry now, I don't think it could be possible. Find her please, bring her home to me," Alain said, visibly slumping in his wheelchair.

11c

"You are a fool," Otto Speyer said to his granddaughter on Skype. "Of all the foolish things, trying to escape with the paintings. It's quite obvious they tricked you into removing the paintings; they staged the fire and then caught you. What were you thinking?"

"The paintings needed to be protected; they were all we had to force them to trade for the plate," Margrite said, visibly shaken by her grandfather's hard words. "What do you know? We had to move them. I'll get them back. I know where they are; I'll get them."

Speyer watched his granddaughter on the screen, her face red and her eyes dark. "What did the police say? I suppose you told them a story to make them believe it was something else."

Margrite regained her composure and slowly explained what happened. "When the first fire truck arrived, they found us trussed up and lying on the ground. A sheriff's car pulled up immediately after them. I told the police that a gang from Mexico tried to break into the winery, they set the fire, maybe looking for money. When we chased after them, they ambushed us on the lane. When they found nothing in the van, they tied us up and left."

"Did they believe you?"

"I think so."

"Are you sure you weren't compromised?"

"I'm sure of it."

"I hope so. Then what happened?"

"We went back to the winery. The fire was out when we arrived. Both trucks were destroyed but the fire hadn't spread to the buildings. We were lucky. We spent an hour with the police answering more questions and then they left. A fire truck stayed until morning. By the time it left, our morning crew had arrived. We cleared the burned vehicles and washed down the drive."

"They will try to send someone to investigate."

"They did, the man was very disappointed that we cleaned up the yard, said things about the law and evidence and procedures. I told him we have eight trucks of grapes arriving later in the morning ready to be crushed. The grapes cannot wait. He took pictures, then left. Probably not for the last time, but we will be ready with a much better story."

"Be very careful, this must be over as soon as possible," Otto Speyer said.

"I will get the paintings back," Margrite said.

"Don't worry about those Jewish trinkets," Otto said. "I have come up with a better plan and it's underway."

"What did you do?"

"Substantially improved our position and our chances of success."

"What did you do?" Margrite yelled.

"Found something even more important to Dumont and, by proxy, to your favorite redhead as well. I had Claudette Leclair kidnapped and removed from Paris. Our people are bringing her to us, even as we speak."

"Who's Leclair? Why her?"

"Claudette Leclair is the president of one of Dumont's investments," Speyer said. "You met her at the bank in Paris; she was with the two from California. It's my understanding, according to our comrades in Europe that she is very, very close to Dumont. Our contacts in Buenos Aires also say that she has been investigating us and asking questions. I put a stop to it."

"Someone saw you take her; they'll know she's been taken."

"Maybe, in fact, I hope so. But I believe that Dumont will not risk the police or their FBI; he will want this taken care of personally. I intend to deal with him myself, as only two soldiers can."

"He wasn't a soldier; he was an opportunist, a trader, a capitalist. He was not a soldier."

"Everything about the man says soldier. We have looked through the French records; there was no one fitting his description. The man didn't exist before the war, only after. I believe he was someone else, someone who stole the paintings and the box, maybe an ex-GI, maybe a criminal. He has what I want and I'm going to get it."

"I'll get it; I will get the plate."

"No, you take care of the crush and the winery. I'll deal with this personally."

"You can't, you're too . . ."

"Old? It's the youth that can't control the problem. I will be up there late this afternoon. Our plane from Paris is en route; I am meeting it in Miami, then we will fly on to Oakland. There my men will hide her."

"I will take care of it."

"No. I don't want you anywhere near this," Speyer demanded. "You will stay in Napa. I will fix your mistakes, get the plate, and secure our future.

"You can't do that, I control this. I'll meet the plane; trade the woman for the plate. I will do it."

"No, you are out of this. I will call you when I arrive at the Oakland private jet field later today. I don't want you there when I land; do you understand me?"

Margrite, stunned by his outburst and denigration, could only stare at the man. Otto Speyer broke the connection. Her computer screen went black.

Chapter 12

Brass pushed Alain to the elevator, the two men descended into the vault. Sharon and Bobby stood to one side when they entered. The paintings, still couched in their open cases, leaned against the far wall; their faces addressed the room once again.

"And how are my children?" Alain said to Sharon when Brass stopped the chair.

"They are unharmed and in excellent condition. I think they like being home," Sharon said. "I understand that the young lady in the Renoir didn't like the Germans. She was very glad to be rid of them."

"And so am I, yet I'm afraid that we have not heard the last of them. As the world saw seventy-five years ago, they can be a very insistent nasty bunch."

"To say the least," Bobby added.

"Yes, Bobby, to say the least," Alain said. "I know it's still early, but God damn it, I've been up most of the night and I need a drink."

"You know what your doctor said," Brass said, knowing the answer.

"When that son-of-a-bitch gets to be my age, he can tell me what to do, so fuck him. I'll have a Maker's Mark on the rocks; Sharon will have a Black Label on the rocks, Bobby, a beer? No? Then pour the soldier a Maker's as well. You, Peter, my dear boy, are driving. We'll celebrate later."

"Yes sir," Brass said, he smiled at Sharon and walked to the bar and began his duties. A few minutes later, the drinks arrived on a silver tray, a tall glass of sparking soda stood in contrast to the amber liquids and ice.

"To us, the four musketeers," Dumont said raising his glass.

"To us," they all answered in unison.

"And to Claudette and her recovery, I'll get her back, Alain," Sharon said.

"Yes, I know you will, but I have a premonition that she is coming to us," Alain said draining his tumbler.

Sharon's phone buzzed in her back pocket, a text message flashed. It said to go to a specific site on YouTube, watch the video.

"Alain, is this computer connected to the Internet?" Sharon asked, pointing to the latest Apple computer sitting on a low table.

"Yes, of course. Why?"

"I've been texted to a specific address on YouTube; let's find out what they want. I think your premonition was right."

Sharon activated the account, typed in the URL, and waited.

The usual YouTube home page appeared, a window opened. The header said, in German, *Sie haben 24 Stunden.*

"You have 24 hours," Peter Brass said from behind Sharon.

"Yes, I see that," she answered as the image loaded and ran.

The camera showed a dark room. At about the ten-second mark, an overhead light threw a spotlight on a person sitting in a chair, the person was Claudette Leclair. She was bound to a metal chair with duct tape. Her mouth was not covered. She looked directly at the camera. A voice said in French, *"Dites-leur que vous êtes bien."*

"Non," Claudette said. *"Va te faire foutre."*

"That's my girl, she's alright," Alain said with flair. "The French can swear when they need to."

The voice switched to English, with a slight German accent, "As you can see, Claudette Leclair is well and unharmed, except for the restraints. She has not been drugged or injured. For my part, I wish she had been drugged, she has been, to my dismay and displeasure, disagreeable and uncooperative, but I have my orders."

"Well done, Claudette," Sharon said.

"She will be released in exchange for the item we want.

This is a simple request, the item for Ms. Leclair. I don't want to harm her, but I have my orders. At 10:00 p.m. tonight, Pacific Time, you will receive a call with additional instructions. Please, I am not a killer, I do not wish to harm this woman, but again, I do have my orders." The camera zoomed in on Claudette until nothing but her eyes filled the screen, when she blinked, the video went black.

"Theatrical, to say the least," Bobby said.

"Alain, I think they're bringing her to you to make the exchange," Sharon said. "The time delay would allow them to prepare and fly her here. The old man cannot make the exchange without her. They're coming here."

"Makes sense, that's what I would do," Alain said.

"So the Speyer family's coming to San Francisco," Bobby said. "Have some crab, see the bridge, visit Fisherman's Wharf, gee just your regular Nazi tourists from Argentina. And what do you have that they want so bad that they'll kidnap a young woman and then fly her here with the possibility of customs and Homeland security sticking their noses into their little party? Sharon?"

Alain placed his hand on Sharon's arm and steadied himself, "Young man, when your grandfather and I liberated millions in gold for ourselves, as well as some art and a troublesome wooden box, we never believed or even thought that something like this would ever happen. We were three happy soldiers, thrilled to have outlived almost everyone we fought with. Sadly, Graham didn't make it, but I was very happy to learn, now so many years later, that your grandfather did survive. All I can surmise from this is that we found something that pointed to something of even greater value. Your grandfather and I found half a clue to the answer; the German's still have the other half. With the two pieces, brother and sister, if you will, the answer will reveal itself, simply and easily."

"Why haven't they found it before now?" Peter Brass asked.

"Too many questions would have been raised if hundreds of people started trouping over the German countryside," Alain said with a fervor that even surprised Sharon. "Secrets may be kept, but a full-scale treasure hunt would be hard to hide. No, they lost the key years ago and have only recently regained the ability to find it. Now they want the information hidden in that wine box that your grandfather and I found. A box of such strange memorabilia that even the most avid collector of Hitler artifacts would question their authenticity."

"You believe they're real?" Bobby asked.

"Very real and very important, if the ramblings of an insane megalomaniac can be believed. It's my belief that the two pieces, the box and the numbers, create a simple answer to a large question. What happened to the wealth of Europe stolen by the Schutzstaffel, the German Waffen-SS?" Alain moved his hand from Sharon's arm, his arm was shaking.

"Alain?"

"I'm fine dear," Alain said. "Sharon, when you showed me the photos of the old man, Speyer, I said I had seen the man before. I just couldn't remember when. I do now. That man, Otto Speyer, was the German SS officer that I challenged. Even standing in pig shit, he arrogantly ignored me. I never remembered his name, but sure as there is a heaven, that's the same man. We must get my granddaughter back and not give him the numbers; he must never have the numbers. With that wealth, the world might once again tremble from their power."

Peter made everyone comfortable; he even made a very acceptable lunch of deli-sandwiches. At 2:00, Sharon and Peter made Alain take a nap; he was asleep in less than five minutes.

"For someone his age, I am amazed at how easily he can fall sleep and sleep well," Peter Brass said. "Since his return from the hospital, these naps have helped rejuvenate him. I wish I could sleep that well."

"You and me both," Sharon said, looking at her boss. "He's had one helluva ride, and now all this. Would take down a far lesser man." Her phone buzzed.

"Oh wonderful, just what I need," she said, looking at the number. She took a deep breath, "Good afternoon, Saul, what can I do for you? . . . Yes, I did enjoy the scotch . . . no, I didn't drink it all. Saul, I'm very busy right now, what do you want? . . . The article in the *Times*, I don't know how that reporter got the information . . . yes, he called. We talked a few minutes on the phone. . . . yes, surprisingly well informed, he had done his research, . . . the paintings? We're still looking for them." She took another deep breath and smiled at the paintings laid out before her, leaning against the wall. "No, we have not heard anything . . . I will let you and your family know what I know when I know it."

Bobby scrunched his forehead and raised his right fist, thumb up. She smiled.

"I've got to go . . . Tell your family not to worry, I have everything under control." She clicked off the phone.

This time Peter rolled his eyes to the frescoed ceiling, an angel put its hands over its ears, lies, lies, lies.

"I assume that's one of the Los Angeles Goldfarbs?" Bobby asked.

"You know the old law of averages about smarts and beauty, a family has only so much to pass around with its genes," Sharon answered. "Sometimes, someone misses out. In the Goldfarb family, Saul Goldfarb won the genetic lottery. No brains, no beauty, just an inordinate amount of chutzpah. He's lived his whole life by bullying, bravado and luck. But Alain doesn't play favorites; it's his brothers and sisters that will have to control him when this is all over. I really wish them luck."

"Mr. Dumont is still going to give them the paintings?" Bobby asked.

"Yes, it's been his intention from the very beginning. Is that a problem?" Sharon said looking at Bobby.

"No, none, but my grandfather would probably want to know, so now I can tell him. For him, it's was the gold and the four paintings that he remembers. That's all he has and will ever have of them, just a memory, owning them for at least one afternoon. He smiles about it when he tells the story."

"Kind of like us this morning, weren't we rich then," Sharon said.

"As rich as Midas," Bobby said.

Sharon's phone buzzed again. "Kevin, yes, everything is fine, or at least it is here, they took Claudette, we saw her on YouTube." She continued to bring Kevin up to speed on the morning's events. "Tell Evelyn, if she calls, that I'll try to reach her later." She clicked off.

12b

Evelyn did reach Sharon and told her she wanted to see Alain.

"Six o'clock will be fine," Sharon said.

Brass returned to the library, "He's awake. I helped him get dressed; he is excited about this evening. I told him not to get too worked up, it may take time. 'No, it won't', he answered, 'It will happen tonight, I know it.' I'll bring him down in a few minutes."

"Peter, there's this great restaurant on Chestnut Street, I'll spring for dinner if you don't mind take-out," Sharon said.

"I don't mind at all, let's plan for six-thirty, after cocktails, it will give Ms. Lucca a bit of time to settle in. Bobby, could you pick up dinner?" Brass asked.

"No problem, what am I picking up?"

"Mexican," Sharon said.

"I come to one of the greatest places to eat in the Western hemisphere and my first dinner is take-out Mexican, I am so disappointed in myself. I thought this crew would eat better, steak with buerre blanc peppercorn sauce, mashed potatoes, crème brulee for desert."

"Bobby, it's free," Sharon said.

"Love it, Mexican is my favorite. Nothing better, make sure they put lots of chips and salsa in the bag, got beer?"

"We have plenty, Bobby," Peter said.

"One cocktail is all you're having, no beer. I don't know where this night is going but I want you sharp, understand?" Sharon said, "And that means you as well, Peter."

"No worries here ma'am, I don't drink." Bobby looked at Peter like he had just said he was a priest.

"Just great, new friend, big as a house, probably has the IQ of a genius, and doesn't drink. Sharon, the world is coming to an end. I feel it in my bones."

"I agree, Bobby, the world is coming to an end, let's just make sure it's not tonight."

Evelyn Lucca arrived at exactly 6:00; she had come directly from her shop, STIA, on Union Square. The shop was owned by her family; they sold the most expensive handbags in the world. Sharon once worked for Evelyn as a clerk for one day, made a $400 dollar commission, discovered a nest of Chinese thugs in the warehouse who were smuggling guns, then rescued two Chinese girls kidnapped for the sex trade, and with a flourish, took out a Mexican cartel of drug traffickers. And all she got was a per-diem check and two fake handbags. Evelyn Lucca also became a close friend and a now and then drinking buddy.

"How's Alain doing?" she asked, pulling off her coat; the early evening fog had started to blow down Broadway; her face was damp.

"He's well, but there are strange events to tell," Sharon said. Over cocktails, (Sharon and Bobby had only one) she told Evelyn about the recovery of the paintings, their escape, Alain's early morning call, and the message and video from the Argentines.

"Bastards," Evelyn said. "So they'll contact us at 10:00 p.m., then what?"

"Not sure, it's Alain's play," Sharon said. "We left the plate in Paris; the Nazis don't know what's on it. They may believe there is a series of numbers on it, maybe more information, or maybe even a map."

"You have the same questions regarding the plate they hold," Evelyn said. "Don't you?"

"Yes, neither of us knows what's on the other plate, we can only speculate," Sharon said.

Alain interrupted as Brass pushed him into the room, "Phooey, the other is the sister to ours, four numbers is all it has on it, that's what I believe and have believed for twenty years. With both coordinates, the location of the SS cache will be revealed. This I believe." He started to cough, Peter handed him a glass of water. "Thank you, Peter. My God, Evelyn, where did you find this man? He is fantastic and speaks German as well, with almost no accent. And he makes an excellent drink!" Alain said, raising his tumbler to the group. "To us, may this evening be a fruitful and safe one."

"To us," was the unanimous call.

There was enough Mexican food to feed a small army; the chips filled a bowl to overflowing. Enchilladas, tacos, chimichangas, rice and more refried things than Sharon wanted to remember. For all his protestations, Bobby was in heaven. He and Peter compared Mexican restaurants they had eaten at; eventually they agreed that one place on Wilshire Boulevard in Los Angeles was the best. Neither could remember the name.

At 10:00, Sharon's phone chimed with a text. "Post this address on your Skype account, we will talk with you at 10:15."

"Alain, do you have Skype?"

Evelyn laughed, "He put up the initial seed money for the enterprise. He has his fingers in everything."

Sharon looked at Alain, he smiled. "On that computer, log on, and wait."

He gave her the password, the Skype screen opened. They waited.

12c

At precisely 10:15, Claudette's face appeared on the screen, a grey piece of tape covered her mouth.

"My guess is they couldn't keep her quiet," Evelyn said.

An older man's voice was heard over the image. "She is unharmed, but unlike her French homeland of seventy years ago, she still puts up a fight; she is restrained but unharmed."

"She takes after her grandmother, Herr Speyer," Alain said, "who told me she was personally responsible for the death of ten German soldiers in France. She was especially fond of removing

SS officers from the streets of Paris."

There was a pause, "I wondered where this one got her *wut*, rage. I am, like you, an old man, the war is half a century gone, but our beliefs are not dissimilar. We respect creativity, honor, discipline, our heritage. Yes, Mr. Dumont, we have a lot in common."

"Herr Speyer, the only thing we have in common is that we are both breathing," Alain said. "Outside of that, everything you believe in is an abomination; it spoils the very earth of Germany. Yes, I have what you seek and I will trade the four numbers for my granddaughter."

"Granddaughter?" Speyer said.

"Yes, she is my granddaughter and my only living relative. For her to die over these trinkets and baubles would be the worst thing I would have ever done in my poor life. She is, to me, equal to all the gold in the world, all the sunlight that falls on the Earth, and all the songs that have ever been sung. No harm will come to her, your bond as a soldier?"

Speyer paused, "No harm, my bond. How shall we do this?"

"The safest place I have is my house; I'm an invalid. I'm recovering from the bullet your granddaughter shot into my side. I cannot leave. By the way, I have not heard from her since we recovered my paintings, is she alright? We did leave her quite unharmed."

"She is no longer involved, I have taken control of this situation," Speyer said.

"That's surprising. I was told that she was quite competent when it came to strong-arm stuff and Parisian bike rides, according to my technical assistant." Dumont looked at Sharon and smiled. She smiled back.

"Yes, that woman has certainly gotten under Margrite's skin; I would suggest to Ms. O'Mara, and I assume she is there with you, that she be very careful. As you can see, we Germans have long memories."

"I would also suggest you remember what happened to your

Reich, a memory that the world will never forget," Alain said.

"From the sound of people like Mahmoud Ahmadinejad, the world is beginning to forget."

"He will be but a footnote, a stain in the history of Iran. The world will remember . . ."

"Yes, the Jews. Israel."

"This isn't the time, Herr Speyer, to discuss world politics," Alain said, interrupting Speyer. "Bring my granddaughter to me this evening in two hours. I will give you the numbers then. Come with whomever you like, armed if you must, I am well protected. I think, that even after all this time, we can meet and resolve this like gentlemen. I assume the scar on your face was received in a chivalrous duel, I know you to be an honorable man, again, your bond."

"Two hours? Impossible."

"I believe that you are here in San Francisco and you have my granddaughter with you. My sources say that your aircraft landed in Oakland earlier this evening. I believe that two hours is adequate. After sixty-five years, it will be nice to get this off my back. I'm tired and want to go to bed, two hours. Your word."

Again a pause, a hand slowly removed the tape from Claudette's mouth, for once she didn't talk. She looked at the camera and blew her grandfather a kiss, *"En deux heures, mon cher grand-père."*

"My bond, Mr. Dumont."

"Two hours, my love," Alain said. The screen went black.

Alain Dumont continued to look at the screen and then touched it with his finger, sighed and then collapsed. Peter looked at the readout on the back of the chair quickly, and then turned up the flow of oxygen.

"In his excitement, he forgot to breath, it happens sometimes. He fainted. All the signs and blips and beeps are just fine." He placed a cold cloth over Alain's forehead. Slowly the man regained his composure and color and smiled at Evelyn.

"Gave you a scare, didn't I. Thought you'd have to fight off the Nazis without me." Alain took a deep breath of oxygen rich air. "And since they're too arrogant to realize that Claudette has seen the numbers and Sharon would probably shoot them before giving up the other coordinate, I figured I'd just give it to them. Then let's see what happens; sometimes you want something for so long that the quest is the reason to go on, not the treasure or the reward."

"How did you know about the plane?" Sharon asked.

"Peter," Alain said.

"While we were upstairs, Alain had me call the Oakland airport; they confirmed that one plane had landed, quickly passed through customs, no problems. One flight direct from Miami; the plane was owned by Trittenheim."

"I assumed that Speyer met the plane from Paris in Miami after he had flown up from Argentina," Alain said.

"Secrets, Alain. Remember what I said."

"Yes, my dear, secrets," Alain answered with a smile.

Sharon watched as Bobby continued to munch on the remains of dinner; she had to admit that the salsa and guacamole were excellent, in fact, too good. She knew that when this was over, the gym and the road would be her companions for a month. She could feel the few pounds she'd gained tugging at her hips. She stepped out onto the small terrace that was connected to the library and lit a Marlboro. Another cigarette's smoke washed by in the fog.

"After all this time, I never knew you smoked, Evelyn," Sharon said.

"I really don't, but from my misspent youth and my boarding school days and considering the brothers I have, smoking just happens. I regress when I'm nervous. And I'm sure as hell nervous now, in fact scared to almost shaking. I'm scared for Claudette and for Alain and for all of us. Why are you so calm?"

"Calm? You should see my insides; I'm quaking. I like being in control, I feel one step, maybe even two removed from all this, like the strings are pulled by someone else. Me, I'm a string puller, as you know. We have the goddamn Nazis coming for a pow-wow and I haven't a clue how this will end up. So we're going to improvise."

"Improvise?"

"Speyer will come with guns and muscle, maybe one man inside, certainly others outside. My guess is two, maybe three cars." The door to the library opened, Bobby walked onto the terrace.

"What are you two cooking up? Need some help?" Bobby asked.

"We need eyes on the street and you're what I've got sergeant. I need you with a radio, there are two in my bag in your truck; it's still in the locker. Wear the mike. I'll be inside, tell me when they arrive. They won't make a big deal, not on this street. The cars will be in radio contact with Speyer and move out after they drop off Claudette and the old man. Watch for them; I don't like surprises."

"Roger, can do." Bobby left to pull their gear and weapons.

"And me?" Evelyn asked.

"I want you to take care of Alain, if anything happens, and I mean anything. Get him in the elevator as fast as possible. Shut the door; we'll be okay. I'll need Peter with his skills and experience if this goes sideways; I'll talk with him after we go back in. This will turn out just fine, so don't be nervous."

"With all you told Bobby, how can I *not* be nervous," Evelyn said with a laugh, "anyway, there's worse places to die."

"Now you're making me nervous," Sharon said as she crushed out her cigarette.

12d

At precisely 12:30 a.m., Sharon heard Bobby's voice in her earpiece.

"Three black Mercedes, very nice and shiny. All three are stopped in front. Three guys in the first car and three in the last car; they've taken serious positions around the center car; I see automatics in every hand. They're watching every corner. Hold a second, center car's door's opening and one man out, not grandpa - too young. Now, a woman, Sharon, why didn't you tell me Claudette was gorgeous."

"Shut up and watch, Speyer?"

"Now the old man is exiting slowly, not bad for someone his age. They're heading to the door. Ten seconds to the bell."

Sharon heard the chime; things seemed so civilized, with the Huns literally at the gate. Peter walked to the door; the bulge in the back of his coat from Sharon's backup Beretta barely showed. He checked the monitor in the hall, "Good evening, Herr Speyer, I assume?"

"Yes."

"Please come in," Peter said. The gate's locks were released, Peter opened the door and was met by the demure Claudette, next, a tall arrogant-looking blond fellow followed, then the slightly stooped but very athletic-looking Otto Speyer.

Claudette pushed her way past Peter and headed directly down the hall to the living room; seeing her grandfather, she kissed and hugged him. Tears coursed down both of their cheeks.

"You're safe now, you're safe," Alain said, stroking her black hair.

Claudette stood and saw Sharon and Evelyn; she gave them both a hug.

"Where's Kevin?" Claudette asked.

"Home, recovering from a run-in with a gang shooting, he's fine. He'd love to see you again. Later, I'm sure."

Otto Speyer walked into the room, "You have done very well for yourself, Alain Dumont, and your investments with our gold have turned out well. Once I found out who had the numbers, our resources developed an excellent profile. I am amazed what a man can do with his life if he puts his mind to it: inventor, investor, entrepreneur, philanthropist, art collector, high-tech capitalist; it reminds me of myself. It's astonishing what a war can do to set the mind straight."

"As I said, we have little in common," Alain said.

"Tonight it all comes around and we can start anew," Speyer continued. "I watched their mistakes. I know what needs to be done. We have comrades and friends across the globe in almost every civilized nation. I have returned your granddaughter; now give me the numbers."

"How uncivil of me, Herr Speyer, a drink to celebrate my granddaughter's return; you must have a glass of wine, it's what we old vintners must do," Alain said, pointing to the bottle of wine Peter had retrieved earlier in the evening. "This is an unworldly Petrus, 1944. It must have been a shock to the retreating German's, while they ran through the vineyards being chased by the Americans in 1944, that the French could still take the time to pick and crush the grapes to make this excellent wine. Care for a glass?"

"Yes, Mr. Dumont, a glass. I still have a few bottles from a case of that same wine," Speyer said taking the goblet. "When I want to see how our wines are doing, I taste a little of this. It makes me wonder if I will ever become a winemaker. I understand you have a vineyard in the Loire."

"Yes, a few hectares, sancerres and pinot noirs, just a few thousand cases, not like Trittenheim. You're a force in the industry. Mine is just a hobby."

"Would I know the label?"

"Possibly, I called it Dominique, after Claudette's grandmother."

Evelyn poured wine for everyone; Sharon was shocked by how absolutely fabulous the wine was. And she was also amazed at how civil these two men were to each other. She sat the glass down for later. "Bobby, what's happening," she said from down the hallway, out of earshot of the discussion in the living room. For all she knew, it seemed like ancient friends were getting together to talk of the old days. She didn't like it; it was too calm. "Bobby?"

"Sorry, changing locations, couldn't talk. The cars have moved out, but they have passed me once already. My guess is that they won't stop until they have to pick up Speyer. They'll keep circling the block."

"They may be settled in for few minutes; they're having a

glass of wine."

"Drinking wine and I'm out here in the cold fog, can't see fifty feet. The street lights kind of glow through it all, eerie. Wait a second, I see someone walking down the street, strange at this hour."

"You stay put. Don't engage."

"Roger, it's a woman; I see blond hair under her hoody, she's heading toward . . ." All Sharon could hear was a thud and a sound like static.

"Bobby, come back!" she said. More static, then a rustling sound.

"My dear O'Mara, he's out, if you make more of a fuss I will kill him; I must get even for last night."

Sharon recognized Margrite's voice, "If he's dead . . ."

"You'll what, kill me. That's a laugh. I understand there's a party going on and I was not invited. Well, I'm crashing it."

At that, like Margrite voicing the password to the land of chaos, the front door exploded inward, glass and debris flew through the hall like crystal shrapnel from a grenade. Sharon, standing off to one side, protected from the direct force of the blast by a sharp turn in the hallway, was thrown against the wall. She recovered quickly, pulled her Beretta, and waited. A canister flew through the blasted doorway and rolled into the hallway, a flash-bang exploded, knocking out what sense she had left. She collapsed to her knees.

Three men stormed into the hallway, one pointed his pistol at Sharon; she stood slowly shaking her head. He pointed at her gun and then to the floor, she dropped the Beretta. He waved with his weapon toward the living room. The room was a mess. Peter tended to a cut on Alain's forehead, ignoring the cuts on his own arms. Otto Speyer had wounds on his hands and arms and walked with a noticeable limp. Evelyn sat in a chair, deathly white, breathing heavily; a piece of glass was noticeably lodged in her leg.

"*Fuck,*" was all that Sharon could think of, "*goddamn fucking shit.*"

Following the men, Margrite Speyer marched into the room, "Well, that was loud! Everybody okay?" Speyer, in a tight black top and black jeans, scanned the room, the Glock in her right hand flared from the overhead lighting. "Sorry about the cuts, Grandfather, but that's what happens when you turn on your only granddaughter; she gets testy. Well, I see I have two-thirds of our Paris adventure here. Ms. O'Mara, Derek would like to have a conversation with you later. Seems he'll need surgery to fix his knee; he holds you responsible."

"Not my fault he can't ride a bike. He looked a bit silly anyway, besides, he rode like a girl," Sharon said.

Derek started to walk toward Sharon, "Not now, later. Sharon, he has talked about nothing else since his return from Paris; he has so many things he wants to do to you, even I'm curious. And where is that tall angular fellow? I liked him, really did. I understand that some of your American criminals shot him, that's too bad. I wanted him for myself."

"You need to expand your circle of friends," Sharon said.

"Well, old man," Margrite said, turning toward her grandfather. "After all these years, how does it feel to finally know the other coordinate? All the troubles and death just to find four little numbers, if you'd be so kind, please tell them to me."

Otto Speyer turned to Alain, "Give me the numbers."

"Do you mean that you have been here all this time and only drank wine?" Margrite barked, seeing the bottle of Petrus on the floor, thousands of dollars of red gold staining the carpet. "You still don't know, Grandfather? I'll put a stop to that right now. Claudette, please stand up."

Claudette ignored the request.

"NOW!" Margrite demanded. "NOW!" She pointed the gun at Alain.

Claudette slowly stood. Sharon saw she was uninjured; she was lucky.

"Now, Mr. Dumont, you have three seconds to tell me the numbers, starting now. One... two...three." At three, she shot Claudette in the upper leg. Claudette screamed and fell to the floor. Brass moved quickly to help her.

"Do not move. Stand right there or you'll be next. Mr. Dumont, I want the numbers."

Alain looked at his granddaughter; blood covered one side of his face from the gash on his forehead. He slowly mumbled something.

"What, I didn't hear you, old man, louder. Or should I aim at her head?" She adjusted her aim.

"Stop this, Margrite, stop this right now!" Otto Speyer yelled. His bodyguard moved toward Derek. Derek lifted his Glock calmly and shot the man in the chest. The impact of the bullet pushed the man over the chair sitting behind him, he sprawled across the floor. Otto Speyer stood looking at his man, than at Margrite. "What the hell are you doing?"

"Doing Grandfather? I'm taking control. I'll find the gold, it's mine. It will not be used for some twisted dream of yours or of those ancient thugs you hang around with. No. I'll put it to better use, my uses."

"You can't have the gold; it's to be used for the future of our people, for the return of the Reich. It's your future too," Otto Speyer said. "Our people."

"Not if I find it first. Now, Mr. Dumont, the numbers!"

Alain looked at Sharon and saw it was hopeless; four guns covered the room, only Peter's was still tucked in his pants' waist. If he moved, Derek would kill him.

"7, 53, 37, and 72. I believe it's east, now get the hell out of here," Alain said.

"7 degrees, 53 minutes, and 37.72 seconds east. Now that wasn't too bad," Margrite said, waving her pistol at the group. "If you'd have been just a second faster, I wouldn't have had to shoot Ms. Leclair. It's all your fault, Mr. Dumont, you started all this."

With that remark, Otto Speyer lunged at his granddaughter using every muscle that remained in his frail body. He tumbled into her, knocking her to the floor, with the old man on top. Derek reached down to help, but lurched back at the sound of

Margrite's pistol exploding. The room was deathly still for two seconds before Margrite pushed her grandfather off her chest. Blood covered her blouse. Otto Speyer lay gasping on the floor, blood pumping from the hole in his chest.

Margrite Speyer straightened herself, looked at her grandfather one last time, turned and fled down the hallway and out the door. The three men took positions around the room; it was obvious their orders were to leave no one alive. Derek looked at the others and they raised their weapons. The German turned toward Sharon and smiled. His pistol was at her eye level.

She looked down the barrel of the Glock, toward the blond-headed face and smiled back. Derek looked at her quizzically, squinting at Sharon. A half second later, he spun around from the impact of a bullet to the side of his head. A bit of Nazi brain matter sprayed her face. In rapid succession, three more shots were heard; in the small room it was deafening. One second later, all three Nazis lay on the Persian rug; it would definitely need cleaning.

Bobby Gillis walked into the room, followed by a limping Kevin Bryan. Sharon smiled at her men, "You okay?"

"He found me walking the street; I was really out of it," Bobby said, hooking his thumb over his shoulder. "I recognized Margrite walking up the street and I was out a second later. When I came around, I wasn't sure where I was, then this tall guy limps up to me, gives me a shake and it all comes back to me. We started running, or at least hobbling and limping, to the house; I see Margrite bolt out the door and get into one of the Mercedes. They must have been with her, not the old man. They took off; one's still parked on the street, that driver's dead."

Sharon bent down to Otto Speyer; this was one war wound he wouldn't survive. "Can I get you something?"

"No, I'm ready to see my comrades; they have been waiting a long time. I'm sorry I didn't recover the box; it's haunted me since that day in Merkers. I know now that the treasure is somewhere in Westphalia; please stop her. If we can't have it, at least keep it from her, she doesn't deserve it."

"I'm not sure anyone does, the treasure belongs to the ages and the dead," Alain Dumont said as he leaned over from his wheelchair and looked into the cold steel blues eyes of Speyer, the scar on his cheek almost glowed white. "It is the lost wealth of the SS, isn't it?"

"Yes," Speyer said, a trickle of blood trailed down from the corner of his lips. "You must stop her, Alain," Speyer looked at Dumont and paused, his eyes fluttered, "it's you, the same insolent soldier I met in Merkers. It's you."

"Yes, Herr Speyer, it is me."

"I have wondered about that, now, two old soldiers meet again." Speyer's lungs were collapsing, he coughed blood. "Listen carefully; the numbers I have kept in my heart are 51 degrees, 6 minutes, and 19.06 seconds. You have to stop her." Speyer reached up, took Alain's hand and held it until he died.

Epilogue

In the early days of the Twentieth Century, near the village of Attendorn, Germany, mine workers exposed one of Europe's most interesting and spectacular limestone caves. It foretold the possibility of other caves extending under this rolling German countryside. Throughout this region of Germany, as well as most of Europe, limestone sheets of varying thicknesses and at variable depths extend under the continent. In time, and with the dissolving effect of water and millions of years, caves and tunnels evolved, and, like the Atta Cave in Attendorn, these cavities were often discovered at strange and opportune times. The cave complex at Atta is now a must-see tourist trap, pictures are not allowed; you have to buy them from the cave owner.

North of the village of Olpe, a few kilometers south of Attendorn, in the mid-1930s during a camping trip of the Hitler Youth, a young man noticed bats flying in and out of an almost invisible fissure rent in the side of a hill. He squeezed into the crack and followed the narrow tunnel until it opened into a wonderful cave full of stalactites and stalagmites. Instead of telling everyone, he kept the discovery to himself.

Seven years later, this young man, a dedicated member of Himmler's *Waffen-Schutzstaffel*, the *Waffen-SS*, held the rank of SS-Sturmbannführer. It was his sworn secret duty to help hide the wealth accumulated by the SS as it marched through Europe. It was his suggestion to secretly use his cavern and its system of caves in the Westphalian limestone as a vault to hold this enormous growing wealth. Using forced labor from a nearby concentration camp, the cave was widened and secured with huge steel doors, its armor as thick as the hull of a battleship. The entire labor force was later liquidated. The entrance was obscured and hidden by a chalet style house built over the entrance. To the locals, it was nothing more than a summer vacation home in the hills used by the army, no questions were asked. In the late winter of 1944, as the Allies were preparing for the final push into Germany, the SS group was ordered east, deeper into Germany. Their skills were needed elsewhere; the treasure had to be abandoned. The train they were riding in was attacked by one lone P-38. After two strafing runs, the young twenty-two year old Iowan pilot from the 370th Fighter Group released a 500 pound bomb, from 250 feet, through the roof of the train car the SS Group was riding. One second later, the last Germans who knew about the cavern with its hundreds of tons of gold were vaporized; the young Hitler Youth camper was among the dead.

After the war and the return of a stable government in Germany, great efforts were made to increase electrical power and the availability of clean water to the region of Westphalia. The valley that contains the Ruhr River, north of Olpe, was selected as an excellent location for a dam and hydroelectric power station. In 1956, after approval by the local government, the work began. In 1965 the dam was completed and the Biggesee Lake formed above the town of Attendorn. The SS summer vacation home and the cavern was submerged under one hundred and fifty feet of water.

Margrite Speyer slowly walked across the top of the Biggesee Dam, Sharon O'Mara watched as Speyer continued to look at something in her hand. Sharon knew it had to be a GPS unit.

Sharon had flown alone into the Frankfurt Airport from San Francisco two days after the death of Otto Speyer. The 120 kilometer trip was very fast and very German along its excellent Bundesautobahn 45, the rented BMW allowed her to keep pace with the manic traffic, the speedometer held steady at 185 km/hr. She expected Margrite Speyer would arrive in town as fast as possible. Margrite, too intent on her mission, paid little attention to the people she passed on the street; Sharon spotted her while she enjoyed a wonderful lunch of sausages and sauerkraut. For the last hour, she had followed Speyer as the woman circled the reservoir in a black Mercedes, obviously gathering her bearings. The countryside was rich in fall colors and the sharp German evenings added to the impending change in the season. Margrite stopped walking halfway across the dam and held onto the railing at the overlook. A tour boat passed quietly over the glass-like water; the rich reds and yellows of the trees in their royal regalia reflected off the disturbed surface. The railing began to shake from Margrite's torturing grip.

"It's all gone, Speyer, lost under hundreds of feet of water and earth," Sharon said.

Margrite spun toward Sharon's voice, "You!"

"Yes, me. It's amazing what seventy years does to the land. This was once a pretty valley, a river flowed through it, probably a cottage or something on the hillside. Then progress. Kind of like a kick in the teeth; isn't it?"

Margrite reached into her black, almost SS-looking, leather jacket and pulled out a pistol.

"No need for that, I didn't come alone," Sharon hooked her thumb over her shoulder. Five men were advancing up the path toward them. Margrite looked for a means of escape; three more were heading toward them from the opposite direction. "Shall we put that away?"

Margrite rotated the pistol butt first and passed the gun to Sharon.

"There's 500 tons of gold somewhere under that lake, Ms. O'Mara. More gold and silver than the world has seen in one place in years, it's worth billions. And it's mine, by right. I'll share it with you. I'll give you whatever you want, just let me go."

"I love a dreamer," Sharon said. "Especially one as pretty as you, they'll love you in prison. You were always after the gold all for yourself, weren't you?"

"Ever since I was a little girl, the stories told over wine and campfires fired my imagination and desire for the gold. I knew I would find a way to get it, someday. All my schemes fell into place with my lucky meeting with Remy. Poor boy, he really was someone I could have spent my life with. He didn't die well. But I had my dream and he was not in it."

"You will have what's left of your miserable life to think about it," Sharon said, signaling the police.

When Sharon returned to San Francisco, she and Alain decided that the extreme efforts required to retrieve the gold would not be worth the social and political problems it would cause. Besides, 500 tons of gold would disappear in a month in the German government's maw; they would, of course, want it all. Sharon was sure there wouldn't even be a finder's fee. Very few people knew about the location of the gold, whether Margrite Speyer would tell anyone else remained to be seen; probably no one would believe her anyway. Someday, well into the future, after the dam is gone, the Ruhr River will again reclaim its valley. Someday maybe a lone boy, on a camping trip, will also find the cave and have a story to tell around the campfire about how he is the richest boy alive. Only time will tell.

* * * *

Fairmont Hotel
The Pavilion Room
San Francisco, California

Sharon's 'TO DO' list, after she returned from Germany, was two pages long; there was no particular order. But Evelyn and Claudette and Gina had other things that required her assistance and it took precedence. Her list would have to wait.

"You are a mess," Evelyn Luca said over a celebratory afternoon cocktail at Ginos. "Sometimes I'm embarrassed to be at the same gun fight with you, you must improve your look. Here's what we are going to do."

Gina leaned over the bar, smiled and raised a glass of vodka to the redhead. "Two words, road trip."

"No way," Sharon said, "too much to do, with the paintings and everything. And what the hell's wrong with my look? I just can't go gallivanting about with the three of you, besides, Evelyn, you can't go anywhere, you're stuck in that wheelchair for at least another week."

"Phooey, I'm ready to go. In fact, we are leaving tomorrow," Claudette said. "No arguments!"

The next day they left in Dumont's jet. They spent a long weekend in New York City. They made Sharon buy an amazing pile of clothes, from embarrassing underwear to silk jackets, from high heeled shoes to expensive handbags. Her bags included silks, leather, and bits of jewelry that might have been, at one time, in the salt mines of Merkers. About 5:00 Saturday afternoon, Sharon O'Mara actually began to enjoy shopping, but she bitched every chance she got, she would not be found out.

When her personal shopper at Bergdorfs asked if the fit of her new suit was acceptable, she wasn't sure about Sharon's answer, "It needs a bit more room to soften the look of my gun." Was it a joke? Gina told the woman, "No, she's serious." The woman was even more helpful after that.

They began to plan the return of the paintings to the Goldfarbs on the flight home. She called the Fairmont Hotel from somewhere over Chicago.

"Are you ready to host another reception, Mr. Blanco?" Sharon asked.

"Will it include another hijacking? I'm not sure that I, or the hotel, could take another adventure of that sort," the hotel manager said.

"I will try my best not to host another hijacking, one was more than enough. Can we get the Pavilion Room again, with the same setup? I think that the crowd will be much bigger this time around, this story, as they say, has legs."

"Yes, that will not be a problem. We never did return your deposit; I will apply it to the room. Will it be a simple affair like last time, non-alcoholic refreshments?"

"Mr. Blanco, I can assure you this party will definitely have alcohol and food, lots and lots of both."

"Excellent, excellent!" replied Mr. Blanco.

Her next call was to LA *Times* reporter Trent Smyth and, as promised, she told him the rest of the story. She only left out the tidbit about the location of the treasure in Germany.

"Do you have any idea where this treasure cave may be located?"

"There is some speculation, but it seems to have been lost to time and the death of the war's few survivors who were involved. Someday, way in the future, someone will find it. But it won't be us."

"I expect that might happen; it's happened before, caches of gold and silver, lost to time, and then found. My final article on stolen Jewish art needs about a thousand words, can you be of any help?" Smyth asked.

"Yes, in fact I may have exactly what you need; we're having another reception in San Francisco to turn over the art to the Goldfarbs. Like the last time, it will be at the Fairmont, you're invited."

"Will there be another hijacking?" Smyth asked expectantly.

"Not you, too? God, I hope not. I'm not sure whether the art or I could take another adventure like that of the last few months. It's next Sunday afternoon, see you then."

Zoe Goldfarb was next on her list.

"Are you all right?" Zoe asked. "I saw the reports on the news and the story in the *Times*; is it true that it was Nazis?"

"Yes, it was Nazis. But the paintings are secure and in excellent shape. The bad guys are in jail or dead. Mr. Dumont is doing well, and the rest of the people who were at his house when the attack happened are also better, mostly cuts from flying glass from an explosion. I got lucky and only have a bruise or two. Are you interested in a party?"

"A party? Look what happened last time," Zoe said. "Will there be another hijacking?"

"Good God, what's with this hijacking thing?" Sharon said.

"What did I say?" Zoe answered. "Saul has become an impatient wreck since the story in the *Times* about the art and the attack at Mr. Dumont's house. His only concern is about the art, never once has he asked if anyone was hurt. Typical."

"Are you sure he's your brother?"

"Sometimes, I wonder. Compared to the rest of us, he's a manipulative conniving bastard; but he is family, so we're stuck with him."

"Is he going to be a problem? I know people," Sharon offered with a laugh.

"I'm sure you do. No, we have worked out a very good self-serving agreement between us kids and Saul has agreed to sign it. Essentially, without going into the gory details, the paintings will be held in a family charitable trust; the paintings will be lent to museums and specialty shows for Impressionists. Fees and income received will go toward the maintenance of the artwork. Excess income will be used to acquire more paintings to expand the collection. An important focus on the acquisitions will be that the artwork be specifically recovered pieces stolen by the Nazis."

"I believe that Alain Dumont would be proud of your decision."

For the rest of the week, Sharon found time to get to the gym and begin to sweat off the nervous pounds she had gained; some of the clothes she bought actually began to fit even better. After three days, she could get two fingers down the front her jeans, "Good start," she said to Basil. From the way he greeted her when she returned from Germany, she knew it would a month before he forgave her for leaving him alone. "You don't know how alone you might be right now if momma hadn't turned at the corner of the hallway."

It was to Kevin Bryan that she owed another debt, her life. His arrivals in the nick-of-time were becoming tedious. It seems he was bored sitting around Sharon's cottage and was becoming impatient waiting for updates, which were far from as often as he wanted. His leg was in good shape except for some pain when he walked, but he girded himself for the effort, walked the few blocks to BART and took the train into San Francisco. There he taxied to Dumont's Broadway address, three black Mercedes passed by on Broadway as they pulled to a stop at Divisadero Street.

"Shit, why does it always have to be black Mercedes," he thought.

"Here's just fine, driver," he said as he slipped two twenties to the cabbie. The house was two blocks away. Checking the pistol in his shoulder harness, he pulled the poplin jacket tight around his shoulders; the fog blew in billowing clouds up the street from one street light to the next; he thought he smelled cordite or burnt gunpowder mixed in the damp air. The chill cut to the bone, he hurried up the street.

Half a block from the house, he found Bobby Gillis stumbling out of a clipped hedge that lined the street. Kevin shook the man to sensibility and listened to what had happened. They raced or hobbled, as was the case, to the house. The black cars were lined up the street nose to tail; they watched a blond run out Dumont's gate and jump into the first Mercedes; it raced uphill and turned left into the fog. Kevin and Bobby bolted through the gate and up the steps, the door was open, glass and splintered doorframe filled the long marbled hallway.

Covering each other, they slowly worked their way toward the living room; three men in black leather jackets, their backs to Bobby and Kevin, faced the people in the room. Kevin immediately recognized his buddy from Paris; what really caught his attention was the 9mm Glock pointed at Sharon's forehead. He moved into her view, she saw him and smiled. He fired. Bobby followed; all three leather jackets were down in two seconds.

Police, fire trucks and ambulances followed, the police cordoned off the street. The quiet neighborhood of upper Broadway hadn't seen this much excitement since the last time the Dumont house had been attacked. The neighbors were beginning to consider asking their very wealthy neighbor to move. His presence was becoming a nuisance and a safety issue. "Fuck 'em," was Alain Dumont's response to the CBS television crew after the impertinent question was asked. Alain Dumont's quote was edited out of the story. It was the lead on the 4:30 a.m. broadcast. "Broadway Billionaire Attacked, Again," was the tease. The story lasted until the 6:00 p.m. news, when it was replaced by an afternoon drive-by shooting in Oakland and the Athletics' losing streak during the final week of the season.

Sharon met Peter Brass and Alain in the lobby of the Fairmont hotel. Dumont waved at Peter, motioning him to stop, and watched Sharon walk across the lobby. The little black dress she was wearing attracted every male eye in the gilded room. One woman hit her husband in the back of the head.

"She's that woman from Paris," the man said as he admired the redhead crossing the lobby.

"No, she's not, and Michael quit staring, you're making a scene, just like you did at that stupid Paris bike stop and look what that dumb idea cost us." Michael continued to stare; he hadn't heard a word his wife had said.

When Sharon reached Dumont, he told her to stop and slowly turn around, she did as ordered. "You look absolutely wonderful my dear, wonderful," he smiled wistfully. "Just a small question if I may?"

"Please, Alain please."

He wiggled his finger for her to come closer to him, she came very close, Alain's view of her soft cleavage made his heart skip a beat. "Where, my dear, do you hide your gun?"

Sharon, for the first time, in a very long time, blushed. She then took charge of his chair and pushed Alain Dumont into the Pavilion Room of the Fairmont Hotel, precisely thirty minutes before the start of the festivities. The Goldfarbs, all the siblings, wives, husbands, and children, were dressing upstairs in the suites provided by Mr. Dumont. The paintings, well draped in red silk, were set on easels along the back of the stage placed there for the presentation. A large bar and a long table filled with food braced the one wall not paneled in windows. The view across San Francisco was 270 degrees, from south to east to north. Mr. Blanco greeted them as they entered. Peter Brass followed closely behind Alain and Sharon.

"Ms. O'Mara, I hope all is in order, and I'm thrilled to see that the paintings arrived safely," Mr. Blanco said. "And, if I'm not speaking out of turn, may I say you look fabulous."

"No, you are not," she said with a self-satisfying smile. Mr. Blanco smiled back.

"Yes, the room looks great, and I'm relieved as well. No troubles this time, no hijacking," Sharon said. And there were no detours either, the paintings came directly from Dumont's house, three cars with armed guards followed and led the procession across the city, Kevin didn't see one black Mercedes en route.

"A glass of red wine, my dear, I'm parched," Alain said to Sharon.

"I'll get it, Mr. Dumont," Peter said and walked toward the bar.

"In a few hours this will be over," Alain said looking up at Sharon. "Sorry about all the bullshit you've had to go through. I really thought that it would be easy, just a few paintings and then I could relax and prepare myself to die."

"You won't die," Sharon said.

"Oh please my dear, of course I'm going to die. That's the price for admission."

"Admission?"

"Yes, admission. To live means that you will die, I'm not cynical about this, just realistic. There are no other options, period. But I think I did contribute a few things to the world; I left my mark, pissed on a tree or two, and left a legacy."

Sharon watched as Claudette Leclair walked into the room, Bobby Gillis held her arm. An older man walked on his other arm; he was bald, well-dressed in a western shirt, dress jeans and ostrich cowboy boots. He was also wearing dark glasses. They headed directly toward Alain and Sharon. Claudette was dressed as only a French woman could dress, *magnifiquement*.

"Grandfather," Claudette said. "I would like to reintroduce you to Jimmy Gillis;, he is Bobby's grandfather and I believe you knew him in Germany at one time."

Alain stood slowly, both hands braced on the arms of his wheelchair. Sharon tried to help; he waved her off. He took two steps and hugged his comrade, tears streamed down both men's cheeks, the youngsters stood off to the side. The warriors embraced again, whispers flew from ear to ear.

"What are you two conspiring?" Bobby asked.

"Nothing, my boy, nothing," Jimmy Gillis said. "It's been too long Robert, far too long."

"Robert?" Claudette asked. "Who's Robert?"

"Claudette, my love, I will tell you later, but this man, and only this man," Alain said pointing at Jimmy Gillis, gently placing his hand over the man's heart, "has the right to call me Robert Dupont. To the rest of this damn world, the man with that name is dead."

Claudette looked at her grandfather and held back the questions that jumped into her head, hundreds of questions.

"Bobby, please take this envelope for your grandfather, it's really for you and your family; it's something that's rightfully theirs, had not circumstances and the war intervened in our lives."

Bobby accepted the envelope.

"Please look inside it and tell your grandfather what's there," Alain said.

Bobby opened the envelope and took a deep breath; he turned to his grandfather and whispered in his ear. Jimmy Gillis smiled.

"Now Robert, what the hell am I going to do with twenty million dollars? What I really need is a full night's sleep, the ability to piss again, and a stiff glass of bourbon," Jimmy said with a laugh.

"My old friend, that's your portion of the treasure we found, with interest," Alain said. "I was never able to find Graham's family."

"It's not worth that much even at today's gold price," Jimmy said.

"Jimmy, I've learned a few things since we parted, and one of them is the wonder of compound interest. Use it to make sure those grandchildren and great-grandchildren of yours get the best goddamn education they can, help them buy land, find good mates to settle down with. It's never about us; it's always about the future. Dinner is at my house later; Bobby make sure your grandfather arrives safely."

"He will sir, he will, and thank you," Bobby answered and smiled at Sharon.

Alain sipped his wine as Sharon rolled him out onto the terrace, the fall air was warm, no fog coursed through the city's canyons. San Francisco Bay was clear, ferries bustled about.

"My dear, I want to thank you for all the help you and your friends gave to this operation, as I said, had I known all hell was going to break out, I might have done it differently, maybe just mailed them the paintings. Six people died, none needed to. But the head of the snake has been severed; maybe those people can get on with their lives and not try to forge a Nazi rebirth. Only time will tell."

"I hope so, but I wouldn't have missed it for the world. It's been an education, but then again, every day working for you is an adventure," Sharon said.

Kevin Bryan walked through the doors toward the two soldiers, a drink in each hand. "Thought you might need this; I understand that Saul Goldfarb is looking for you."

"Great. Mr. Dumont would you like to meet a horse's ass, a real one? I expect one is going to come through that door any minute," Sharon said, taking a liberal sip of Johnny Walker Red.

As if cued for a walk-on part in one of his movies, Saul Goldfarb strolled onto the deck with an air that said, "This is my party, welcome, welcome, kiss my ring." He spotted Sharon and headed directly toward them.

"Let me do the talking," Alain said with a laugh. He turned the chair and his back to Goldfarb and raised his voice. "Sharon, I don't give a damn, I've changed my mind. I don't want that son-of-a-bitch to have my paintings. You heard me, no arguments. I'm tired, that prick doesn't deserve them, after what we went through. I want them wrapped up, loaded into the armored truck and taken back to my house. I've got money and a building full of useless lawyers; I'll use every dime I have to fight Saul Goldfarb in court; I'll do it just for the hell of it."

Sharon watched Saul Goldfarb's face collapse, as Alain's words echoed around in his thick skull; she wondered if his head would explode.

"Oh, alright, Sharon, I guess they belong to the family, but if I ever meet that SOB, I'll give him a piece of my mind," Alain turned toward Saul, who was, as usual, over dressed for the event. "Waiter, would you bring me another red wine, the last stuff you served was swill, there's some of my pinot noir in there, get me a fresh glass. That's a good boy, run along, I'm thirsty." Alain turned to the Sharon and Kevin, his back once again to Saul, a huge grin on his leathery face.

Saul turned toward the Pavilion, not sure what just happened, and headed toward the bar to get Mr. Dumont a glass of pinot noir.

"You are a bastard," Sharon said to Alain.

"Like I said before, a self-made man, that's what I am."

Sharon and Kevin started to laugh, Alain put his hand up, "Just an old man using his age as leverage; I'll talk to him later and apologize. But once in a while it's fun to mete out a little justice for the underdog." Alain paused. "And Sharon my dear, there's a nip in the air and that dress does look wonderful on you."

Sharon took a brief look at herself in the window and, for the second time that day, she blushed.

"You are a letch, Mr. Dumont," Sharon said, kissing Alain on the cheek. "You must certainly are."

They returned to the room and Sharon introduced Alain to the rest of the Goldfarb family, Zoe was the most appreciative, and spoke for the whole family, including her great-grandfather, who started the reason for this party over one-hundred years earlier with the purchase of the paintings. Alain was pleased with the disposition and the plans the family had for the upcoming tour of American museums. The focus was on recovered art from World War Two. There would be almost one hundred and fifty pieces, paintings and sculptures. It would open at the Getty Museum in Los Angeles, then on to Chicago and eventually, New York and Washington.

When the paintings were unveiled (two of Zoe's children pulled the red silk straps), the audience was stunned. Sharon was sure the de Young Museum's director was crying. Cameras clicked and flashed, the paintings were once again lit like the explosions they once saw through the windows of their last Jewish home in Haguenau. Sharon saw Trent Smyth's head over the crowd; he was furiously speaking into his pen or something, his other hand held a camera. She walked toward him; he waved and cut the distance in half. To his shock, she gave him a big kiss. Her surprise made Trent blush.

"Sharon, contrary to what you might think," Trent said with a grin, "this old So-Cal boy only loves girls, the more, the merrier, and may I say, you are stunning.

"You may, even though I'm getting tired of all the comments," Sharon said.

"You shouldn't be, they mean it," Trent said then paused for a moment. "My article has opened incredible museum doors; I'm thinking there's a book in this somewhere. And Saul Goldfarb cornered me to help with the research for his next movie; he's doing it on stolen art and Argentine Nazis."

"Why didn't I think of that, brilliant, just brilliant! Nothing gets by Saul Goldfarb, nothing," Sharon said. Across the room she watched Saul walk up to Alain Dumont slowly. If he had a hat, he would be ringing it in his hands. Peter stood cross-armed behind Alain, like a great Nubian guard, he was easily a foot and a half taller than Saul; all that was missing was a scimitar. Alain said something, laughed, pointed at Saul, laughed again. Saul smiled and shook Alain's hand.

"Bet he's trying to get Mr. Dumont to invest in his next movie," Trent said.

"If he is, he's in for a rude awakening," Sharon answered. "I understand that Alain is the fifty-one percent owner of the independent studio that Saul works in, and Saul doesn't know it. This will be fun to watch over the next few months."

Kevin greeted Evelyn Lucca at the door; she was on crutches. They stopped by Alain; she gave her godfather a kiss on the cheek. He beamed.

Then they hobbled over to Sharon who had separated from Smyth.

"You two are a sight, each hobbling around, holding each other up. But you look wonderful," Sharon said to Evelyn. "The shop okay?"

"A girl has to work, I have a wheelchair at the shop," Evelyn said. "I don't know how Alain puts up with it, that thing drives me crazy, two more weeks the doctor says. I was not going to show up here in the damn thing. I'm certain I'm going to knock over a display or something and it's hard to find good help. Most just preen and prance; I could bust'em over the head once in a while. But business is good, I'm happy. Kevin, could I bribe you for a Pernod?"

"Bribery? Oh just try me." He limped toward the bar.

At 4:30, Gina walked into the room or, mostly, was towed into the room by Basil. He scanned the room, raised his nose, and spotted his mistress. There was no stopping him. Gina released the hound and he bounded in great leaps across the parquet floor, almost knocking Sharon to the deck. She gave him a huge hug. "Sit."

Basil tried very hard to sit, but his butt never felt the cold wood of the floor, it hovered an inch above the ground and his tail would have cleared the dishes off the table, if it could have reached it.

"I swear that dog knew we were coming here from the minute I picked him up. The back of the Suburban's a disaster. But we made it, seems happy now that he's with mom." Kevin and Evelyn headed back toward the bar, Gina followed; she couldn't take her eyes off the paintings as she crossed the room.

Mr. Blanco stood off to one side, as Sharon took a deep breath and looked across the room.

"Is everything satisfactory, Ms. O'Mara?" Mr. Blanco asked.

"Yes, Mr. Blanco, everything is satisfactory. Don't you just love happy endings?"

The End

A Note from the Author
The Flyer

I have tried to pare these stories into a manageable length that you can read in less than eight hours. At about 60–75,000 words, the idea is that you can read about half the book on a four-hour flight and the rest on the way home. I call them *Flyers*. But if you aren't flying, settle back, pour a good drink, and enjoy.

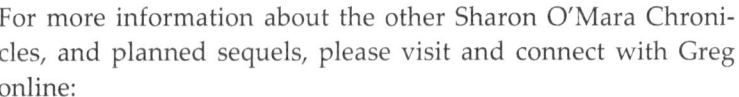

Gregory C. Randall was born in Traverse City, Michigan. He grew up in Chicago. Greg has never forgotten his roots. Mr. Randall makes his home in California.

Mr. Randall is the author of fiction and nonfiction works available through Amazon.com.

For more information about the other Sharon O'Mara Chronicles, and planned sequels, please visit and connect with Greg online:

www.gregorycrandall.info

See his blogs:
http://www.writing4death.blogspot.com

Other books by Mr. Randall:
Fiction
The Cherry Pickers

The Sharon O'Mara Chronicles
Land Swap For Death
Containers For Death
Toulouse For Death
12ᵗʰ Man For Death
Diamonds For Death
Limerick For Death

The Alex Polonia Thrillers
Venice Black
Saigon Red
St. Petersburg White

The Tony Alfano Thrillers
Chicago Swing
Chicago Jazz
Chicago Fix
Chicago Boogie Woogie

Max Adler OSS WWII
This Face of Evil
Pawns in an Ancient Game

Science Fiction and Slipstream
Sector 73
Seven Hours to Barstow

Nonfiction
America's Original GI Town, Park Forest, Illinois

Additional copies can be purchased through Amazon.coms.

www.ingramcontent.com/pod-product-compliance
Lightning Source LLC
Chambersburg PA
CBHW022040240626
47154CB00007B/2499